DARK
SEED

Lawrence Verigin

PROMONTORY
P R E S S

DARK SEED

Promontory Press
www.promontorypress.com

ISBN: 978-1-927559-17-8

First Edition: October 2013

Typeset at SpicaBookDesign in Sabon

Cover – Adrian Cunningham

Printed in Canada

0 9 8 7 6 5 4 3 2 1

This book is dedicated to:

Paul A. Verigin
My father
You were my mentor in life

❧

Don McQuinn
My writing mentor
Thank you for your guidance

DARK
SEED

Lawrence Verigin

PROLOGUE

The last of nineteen black Mercedes Benz sedans pushed through the gray dusk of winter. The engine strained up the winding, snow covered drive toward the Austrian castle. It was 1947: Seven dangerous years since the members had all gathered in one place.

Europe and Asia had begun the physical restoration of their cities and all over the world key people of their organizations had to be re-positioned. The time had come to review what had been accomplished and begin the next phase of molding the future.

As chimes began to toll, the group moved from the large study where they'd been mingling to the spacious meeting hall. The men were somber as they considered the gravity of the evening's main discussion: how to turn waste from the war into profit.

The hall's opulence mirrored the stature of the evening's occupants. The room glistened under chandeliers of gold and crystal. Sparkles of light danced softly on the polished granite floor. Silk and wool tapestries hung on dark oak walls, next to paintings long believed to have disappeared from the world.

The men took their places at the long rectangular mahogany table. They sipped from monogrammed crystal snifters and tumblers and drew on robust cigars. It didn't camouflage their anxious anticipation.

The chairman stood; Dr. Hendrick Schmidt, a tall, solid man in his middle years. Dressed in a dark three-piece wool suit he raised his glass. "Gentlemen, let us begin with a toast to our success." Even though German was his mother tongue, he spoke in fluent English, as was the custom at all the group's meetings.

They all raised their glasses and tapped the table with their free hands.

Dr. Schmidt waited until the room settled. "Let us take a moment to recognize each brother who has passed on since we last met." His gray-blue eyes scanned the room. With their families working together for generations, many really did feel like brothers.

The men acknowledged his sentiments with nods and lowered eyes.

The majority of the room's occupants were entrepreneurs; Dr. Schmidt, however, was also a renowned scientist. He had overseen the operations of this cartel of organizations for the last seven years and often wondered if the others recognized what a monumental task it was during this part of history.

"Now, let us get down to the business at hand. We have a report on specific chemicals left over from the war." Dr. Schmidt motioned to a man seated to his left. "Mr. Carter."

The distinguished, smartly suited man with dark-rimmed glasses rose from his chair, holding a handful of papers. "I'll get right to the point." Mr. Carter spoke with arrogant confidence in a southern American drawl. "DDT has proven to be an effective insecticide. Although there may be long term health effects when people are exposed to DDT, in diluted portions agricultural use will be a satisfactory way to consume the large supply that's been manufactured. As we speak, a team is developing strategies to market it to the public."

He lifted a snifter of cognac to his lips, while he gauged the response of his peers.

Other than a few nods, the men were silent.

Referring back to his papers, Mr. Carter continued, "We have also been working on uses for the post-war excess of nitrogen, phosphorus and potassium. We've found that when combined they can be used effectively as fertilizer. Initial research suggests that although they have no improved effect on nutritional value, these chemicals can improve the growth rates and physical appearance of many crops. We do not yet have sufficient data on the long-term effects of replenishing soil with only these three elements. However, there are large stores of all three chemicals and this would be an efficient use for them."

He then went on to summarize costs, manufacturing details, geographic logistics and which companies would be responsible for production.

When he was finished, Mr. Carter adjusted his glasses and glanced up. "You've all been briefed on these initial findings, so we must now vote on the continuation of both projects."

In front of each member was a stack of papers with a code at the top and a simple YEA or NAY written underneath. They circled their votes and placed the papers in a large bowl passed along the table.

The bowl was then given to the secretary for tabulation.

After all the ballots were cast, the chairman rose. "Our next order of business is an update on the future of controlled pharmaceutical experiments. With the human testing at Auschwitz stopped, the affiliate organization has taken all the steps needed to convert to animal testing. However, human research is preferable. Early indications suggest that Bolivia, Argentina or South Africa can accommodate their needs. We will keep you abreast of the progress."

A murmur swept through the audience. Dr. Schmidt took a drink of water and reviewed his next page of notes, waiting for the noise to abate.

When it was sufficiently quiet, he moved on to the next topic. "As always, our media contacts are doing an exceptional job. However, please remember it is important to continue to recruit new sources. Without the media we cannot communicate to the masses, implement our strategies and drive our future forward. We need the most influential people possible in these positions."

His words elicited nods of agreement.

"Mr. Lovemark." Dr. Schmidt gave the floor over to the man on his right.

Theodor Lovemark was a tall, thin gentleman in a three piece, dark gray wool suit. He wore spectacles and his hair

was slicked back. He motioned to the secretary, who prompt-
ly passed sheets of paper around the large table.

Mr. Lovemark spoke with a proper British accent. "In front
of everyone is the most recent gold sheet. Note the new list of
stocks that are scheduled to rise and the currencies to invest
in. The banking roll programs will resume in May." He gave
a thin smile. "The future looks very profitable for us all."

The meeting continued with another two hours of report-
ing, strategizing, voting, and planning.

Finally, the chairman turned over the last piece of paper.
"There is much work to be done. We have the necessary tools
to lead the world into a new age of progress." He paused and
made eye contact with every man in front of him in the lavish
hall. "The next phase is in place. We will assist the people and
in turn, profit in kind."

Cheers erupted.

Dr. Schmidt raised his hand. "Communication between us
will continue as before. When it is time to gather again, the
new chairman will contact you or your successor. I wish you
all a good evening and rich, fulfilling lives."

⁕

The last set of taillights disappeared into the snowy night.

Dr. Schmidt and the new chairman, Theodor Lovemark,
watched from the second floor study window. The glow from
the fireplace created dancing shadows at their backs.

Dr. Schmidt turned to look at the man beside him. "The
decisions made tonight will irreversibly impact the world for
generations to follow."

Mr. Lovemark raised his snifter of brandy. His slow, devil-
ish grin exaggerated the wrinkles on his face.

CHAPTER 1

SEPTEMBER 2000

I noticed how tightly I was hanging on to the receiver. "My piece wasn't meant to be an investigative story. It was just a short article about advances in how our food is grown."

"Yes, of course, Nick," Dr. Elles said, on the other end of the line. "I am not questioning the validity of your story or criticizing it in any way. I'd like to talk about the possibility of taking it further."

I couldn't place his accent. Eastern Europe, maybe. He sounded concise, like a scientist. I loosened my grip on the phone.

"Can we continue this discussion in person?" Dr. Elles said. "Would you have time to meet this morning? I will supply you with proof of my credibility."

I didn't have a deadline for my work today. Monday was my slowest day. Why not? "Okay, sure."

We agreed to meet in an hour at a popular coffee shop just off Pioneer Square.

"How will I recognize you?" I asked.

"I know what you look like. I will see you there."

How'd he know? That bothered me. Had we met before? He'd hung up before I could ask.

It was a typical Pacific Northwest September day; gray with the threat of rain, yet warm.

It was a ten minute walk from the newsroom, which gave me time to focus. I shouldn't have had that last scotch the night before.

There was a message from a Dr. Carl Elles on my voice mail when I had gotten to work. He wanted to talk to me about the potato article I'd written in the Lifestyles section of the weekend's paper.

When I called him back he questioned my quotes from a Naintosa spokeswoman and a farmer who used their seed. Great, the first time in a year I wrote something remotely close to a real article and there was a problem.

He said he worked at Naintosa for a number of years and personally developed many of their patents. He could supply me in-depth research on genetically engineered food. He asked if I was interested in writing more extensively on the subject. He sounded sincere.

The subject of genetically engineered food didn't really excite me, but it was worth having a chat.

I arrived at the coffee shop a few minutes early.

A steady stream of people were going in and out. The hardwood floor was well worn from all the traffic. I stood in line and surveyed the baked goods and desserts in the glass display case. The smell of freshly brewed coffee filled the air. The room was done all in dark wood, with a green counter and table tops.

I always got a kick listening to the variety and complexity of ways people ordered their blended drinks. I picked up my plain old cappuccino and found a seat by the window.

At precisely 10:00am a black Volvo S80 pulled up and parked right across the street. Somehow, I knew it was Dr. Elles.

As he entered the restaurant I nearly choked on my coffee. I'd seen him before. He was older, short gray hair, tall and slim, with a sincere looking face. That only added to the puzzling fact that he knew what I looked like. There was a definite reason for meeting this man.

He walked up to me. "Good morning Mr. Barnes." The way he said it, with his strong accent, sounded like we'd known each other for years.

"Good morning." I managed to smile as goose bumps popped up all over my skin.

"I see you've already purchased a beverage." He removed his raincoat, revealing an expensive navy blue suit. "I will only be a moment."

He was definitely the man I'd seen in a vision. A few weeks ago I was at a retreat in Taos. I was meditating in the shade of a large tree on a warm morning, when the image of a man appeared. It was Dr. Elles. The only difference was that he was wearing a lab coat, not a suit. The white lab coat turned deep red and then black. He had caring eyes and I sensed he wanted to tell me something. But as soon as he opened his mouth the vision disappeared. I hoped now I was going to find out what it was about.

I looked over at him. The lineup had grown since I'd bought my coffee, so Dr. Elles was only placing his order.

While I waited, I looked out the window. I saw what appeared to be a man in the passenger seat of a car focusing binoculars on the coffee shop. He quickly put them down, as if he saw me looking back. The car was a mid-sized, gray Chevy, parked four spots behind Dr. Elles' Volvo.

Dr. Elles sat down with his coffee. "You look concerned Mr. Barnes."

"Oh no, um, I was just looking out the window." Who was the guy watching? Dr. Elles? It couldn't possibly be me. "Please, call me Nick."

"All right Nick, please call me Carl."

"Okay, Carl. Can I ask you something?"

"That's why we're meeting." He smiled. The deep wrinkles at the outer edges of his eyes made him look wise.

"Where are you originally from? I can't pinpoint your accent."

"I've heard that before." He stirred two packets of sugar into his cup. "I'm originally from Johannesburg, South Africa. I attended Cambridge University in England. I've lived and worked in many European countries, as well as most recently the United States. So, my accent must be a mix."

"Wow, okay. How long have you been in America?"

"For the last twelve years I've worked for Naintosa at their laboratory in Boston. A few months ago I retired and moved here to be close to my daughter, Morgan."

"Okay." It sounded like the guy had led an interesting life. "How'd you know what I look like?"

"Morgan sent me a series of articles you wrote some time ago on political corruption and how it affected people locally. One of those articles had a picture of you talking to a Senator."

"Oh, yes." How could I forget the articles that screwed up my career? "Why were those of interest to you, Dr. Elles? I mean Carl."

"Let's just say corruption is a hobby of mine." He gave me a small smile. "I also like your writing style. You're understandable, not egotistical, and you are idealistic. You're still young and not set in your ways and opinions."

"Thank you, I guess." I wasn't sure about the idealistic part. Not anymore, anyway. And thirty wasn't so young.

He placed his cup on the table and looked me straight in the eyes. "When I read your article on genetically engineered potatoes, I thought you might be the one to help me."

"What do you mean, help you?" It was hard for me to keep my guard up. He seemed nice, but I had to stay objective. I sure wasn't going to tell him about my vision.

"First, what is your journalism background and where are you originally from?"

"My background's not all that exciting. I grew up just south of here, in Olympia, and received my degree from Washington State University. I've been at the *Seattle News* about four years."

"On the contrary, it is exactly what I'm looking for."

"For what?"

"I'm going to write a book. I need someone to shape my research into a form that everyone can understand. I want to tell people what is really happening with genetic engineering and what it really means to the future."

"Is it good or bad?"

"Bad, I'm afraid."

"Hmm." The piece I'd just written portrayed Naintosa as good. Did I not get my facts straight again? Who was telling the truth? I looked closely at Dr. Elles to see if I could gauge his sincerity. He looked honest, but I wasn't sure if I could trust my own read. "Sounds interesting, but I'd need to know more."

"Of course. Are you free for dinner tonight? We can discuss the details then."

I decided I wanted to hear him out. If he was telling the truth the book could make a difference. If at any point I felt he was lying I'd walk away. The fact that I'd seen this guy in a meditation months before I met him couldn't be ignored. Especially since I'd never had a vision so vivid before. "Okay, fine."

"Think about your fee. I anticipate it'll take approximately one year, working part time. I want to compensate you fairly." Then he frowned, "And please don't tell anyone. Let's keep this between us."

"I understand." That wasn't at all an unusual request in my business.

"Is 7:00pm at *Seasons* to your liking?"

"That's the restaurant at the *Nuevo*, right?"

◦

Leaving the coffee shop, I looked at the gray Chevy I'd noticed earlier. A glint of light came from the driver's side. The sun had peeked through the clouds and reflected off what looked like a camera lens. Did he just take my picture?

I kept walking and glanced over when I was directly across the street. The side windows were tinted, so I couldn't get a clear look at the occupants.

As I continued, I looked back a few times, but the car stayed where it was.

CHAPTER 2

That evening I'd found a parking spot a block away and walked to the Hotel Nuevo.

As I approached the entrance I saw the same gray Chevy across the street or at least the same model. I couldn't see anyone inside, so I walked over to it. I had to look through the front windshield, because the side windows had such a deep tint. The interior was clean; nothing on the seats. Only an empty bottle of water in the centre console cup holder. I went around back and discovered that it was a Lumina. Reaching into my black blazer pocket, I pulled out the pad I always had with me and wrote down the Washington State plate number.

Later I'd check with the DMV to find out who owned it.

Seasons was accented by large, colorful floral arrangements. Candlelight flickered against avocado green walls. A pianist with a soft touch played in the background, the music muting the murmur of conversation throughout the room.

The maitre d' escorted me over to Dr. Elles. The table was next to the window, with a beautiful view of Elliott Bay.

"Good evening, Nick." He stood and shook my hand.

"Nice place." I looked down at the silver place settings atop a pressed white linen tablecloth. "I've never been here before."

"The food is exceptional." He motioned for me to sit. "Would you like some wine?"

He poured me a glass from the bottle of cabernet sauvignon already at the table. I didn't recognize the name, but it looked expensive.

Our waiter arrived. I chose the dill salmon featured that evening and Dr. Elles went with the tenderloin in a chanterelle sauce.

While we waited for our meals we chatted about our pasts. His life had been a collage of interesting people and extraordinary places. My life was just the opposite; the most exotic places I'd been were the Dominican Republic and Mexico. I'd always wanted to visit Europe, but so far hadn't had the time or money. That didn't seem to bother him as he listened intently when I spoke.

"Has Mrs. Elles moved to Seattle with you?" I asked.

"Unfortunately, Morgan's mother passed away three years ago." For a brief moment his eyes focused on the distant wall. "In a car accident."

"Sorry to hear that." I took a sip of the rich and peppery wine, sorry I'd asked the question.

Dr. Elles was quiet for a moment, then cleared his throat. "She was also a scientist at Naintosa."

"Oh." I felt I should change the subject. "Tell me more about why you want to publish your experiments?"

His accent had softened. "I have created some very good things with my work. However, unintentionally, I have discovered some very bad things as well. Now, I must warn people about those bad things."

"Were they failed experiments?"

"Yes. However, Naintosa thinks they are successes. That's why I have to publish this book. I'm sixty-three years old and at a point in my life where I want to place everything in order."

Was this merely a personal axe to grind? I wondered if I was being gullible.

"Have you decided on your compensation?" Dr. Elles asked.

"No. I have to see your notes before I can totally wrap my head around the amount of work needed." And decide if I even wanted to take it on, I didn't say out loud. The vision wasn't enough, even though I'd had a few before and they had steered me in the right direction. I needed facts.

"You want to be sure that what I tell you is genuine?" His right eyebrow rose and he looked amused.

"No offense sir, but I have to feel comfortable that what you're telling me is true."

"Of course."

I sank my fork into the salad that the waiter had set down in front of me. "Do you know what information laundering is?"

"No." Dr. Elles leaned forward in his chair.

"It's similar to money laundering. Someone feeds false information to the media, it's reported on, and people believe it to be true. Then the person or group can quote the media, making their information appear to be valid when it's not."

Dr. Elles' eyes opened wide. "Interesting. I've never heard it articulated that way before. It makes total sense. Naintosa employs that strategy on a regular basis."

Shit. Was he referring to my potato article? I let it go. "It happened to me when I wrote the political corruption articles last year. The ones your daughter gave you." I wanted to squirm in my seat. I hadn't talked about it with anyone but my old editor and my best friend Sue, until now.

"I didn't know." Dr. Elles nodded. "I understand why you are cautious."

"That's why I need to see your research before I agree to work with you. I can't let that happen again."

"Yes, of course."

His open reaction to my obvious doubts and willingness to show me his research made it easier to trust him. The notes would be the deciding factor.

After dinner, he wrote down the address of the office he said he had just leased. We agreed to meet there the following evening.

CHAPTER 3

Something wasn't right.

I stepped into the dimly lit office. It took me a moment to realize what I was looking at. A pair of legs stretched out from behind the desk.

"Dr. Elles?"

I rushed over and knelt to feel his neck for a pulse. Nothing. His skin felt cool. "Shit!"

I looked him over. No blood, no marks. Did he have a heart attack...a massive stroke?

Holy fuck. Holy fuck. Holy fuck! I pushed back against the desk to stabilize myself.

At that moment I looked into his open, blank eyes. My knees buckled and I slid to the floor, my right leg only inches from his head.

I'd never seen a dead person in real life before.

Now what?

With what felt like great effort I pulled myself up and reached across the desktop for the cordless phone to dial 911.

I couldn't believe this was happening.

After a short wait, a professional female voice came on the line, "Police, fire or ambulance?"

"Uh, police. Or ambulance. I'm not sure. Both."

"Your location?"

I dug the piece of paper Dr. Elles gave me out of my pocket and read it to her.

"Thank you. Your name sir?"

"Nick Barnes."

"Can you spell your last name?" She spoke in a detached tone with no recognizable accent.

I did as she asked.

"Thank you. Please explain your situation."

I told her that I came to see Dr. Elles for a scheduled meeting and found him dead on the floor of his office.

I'd spoken too quickly. It took a gasp of air, followed by a few deep breaths to catch up.

"Have you checked for a pulse, Mr. Barnes?"

"He has no pulse." Trying to sound composed, I added, "He must've had a heart attack or a stroke or something."

"Do you know his age, sir?"

"Sixty three, he told me."

"Please hold."

I looked down at Dr. Elles, but avoided looking into his eyes. What happened? Why was this man lying dead on the floor of his office just as he was starting what could have been the most important work of his life?

Just my luck. That was my next thought. The first opportunity I'd had to maybe make a difference was gone before I even got started. But I couldn't think about myself, I had to focus on Dr. Elles.

Within a minute the operator was back. "Mr. Barnes, the police and paramedics are on their way. I need to ask you a few personal questions."

"Okay."

"Your home address?"

"Apartment two zero three, one one zero four, Cherry Street, here in Seattle."

"Telephone number?"

I gave her my home number and then without thinking blurted out, "I'm thirty years old, six feet tall, weigh one hundred eighty five pounds..."

"That's fine sir. That's all the information I need for now."

"Oh, sorry. I guess I'm in a little bit of shock."

"That's understandable. Please stay on the line while you wait for the authorities to arrive. Also, do not disturb the scene in any way."

As I waited, I perched myself half up on the desk with one foot still on the ground. I heard talking in the background and faint typing on a keyboard on the other end of the line.

I realized I was holding my breath and exhaled.

My journalist instincts were to look for clues and try to decipher what had happened here. However, I thought it best to leave that to the authorities, as per my instructions.

My eyes had adjusted to the dim light and I could see out through the double doorway into the entry area. There was a receptionist's desk with an empty file organizer sitting on it. Across the room was a glass topped coffee table pushed up against a brown leather couch.

I turned my attention back to Dr. Elles' office. It smelled musty, like a room that hadn't been used in a long time. It held an oak desk, two chairs, and the white phone I was using. Light from a single lamp cast a shadow on the walls.

Where were all the moving boxes and files? Where was the computer? Who doesn't have a computer in 2000?

The faint squeak of a door hinge came from the reception area.

"Someone's here," I said, into the phone. There was the mumble of the operator talking to someone else, "Ma'am?"

A tall, broad-shouldered man wearing a charcoal suit entered the office. As he walked toward me he flashed a badge. "Lieutenant Thompson, Special Unit." He tucked the badge into his inside pocket.

"Sir, can you repeat your last statement?" the operator asked.

"A police officer has arrived."

"They'll be able to help you now. You may hang up the phone."

"Thanks." I placed the receiver onto its charger.

The Lieutenant stood beside the body, looked down at it and then up at me. "Your name, sir?"

"You're with the special what?" He'd said his name and unit so fast, that the only thing that registered was that he was a Lieutenant.

He ignored my question. "Your name, please?"

"Oh, uh, Nick Barnes."

"And the deceased's name?"

"Dr. Carl Elles." I felt awkward sitting, so I thought it best to stand. I slid off the desk, but still held onto the edge for stability.

"How long have you known Dr. Elles?"

"Only a few days."

"What brought you here tonight?" His tone was firm and without emotion.

"I came to meet him. Can I ask…"

"Was it social or business?"

"Business, but…" His aggressiveness made me uncomfortable.

"Were you in business with the deceased?"

"No. I mean, not yet."

He had a deep scar just below his right eye, about two inches long and shaped like a frown. It looked fairly fresh, because it was still pink. I pictured him on the wrong side of a blade in a bar.

"I was planning on doing some business with him."

"What type of business would that be?"

"I'm a writer. Can you please repeat…"

"What type of writing were you going to do for Dr. Elles?"

"I was going to help him with his memoirs. Uh…"

"Had he given any details to you?"

"No, that's what this meeting was for."

The lights in the reception area went on.

Two paramedics wearing standard white uniforms with black trim entered the office wheeling a gurney.

The heavier paramedic eyed us. "Are you the guys who found the body?"

"I am." Seeing the gurney gave me a sad sense of finality for Dr. Elles.

The second, slimmer paramedic placed what looked like a black toolbox on the desk and opened it. The one who had asked the question squatted beside the corpse.

I looked around. Where was the Lieutenant? I took a few steps over to get a better view of the entrance. I couldn't see him anywhere.

The larger paramedic looked at me. "Do you have any idea what happened or anything about this man's medical history?"

I turned back towards the men. "No, that's the way I found him. I don't know him well enough to know his history."

The slimmer paramedic threw me a quick glance. "Can you wait on the other side of the room sir?"

"Oh, yeah sure."

When I got to the other side of the desk a police officer in uniform entered. He was middle aged and stocky. He walked past me, acknowledged the paramedics, and knelt down beside the body.

The desk was in the way, so I couldn't see exactly what he was doing and their conversation was murmured.

Within a few moments the officer got to his feet. "Officer Casey." He stepped toward me.

"Nick Barnes."

"So you're the one who found the deceased?"

"Yes, sir."

"Is there anything you can tell me about what happened here?" He removed a small pad and pen from his right breast shirt pocket.

"Nothing I haven't already told the other officer."

He glanced around the room with a quizzical expression. "What other officer?"

"He left just before you got here. He was Lieutenant someone, from the Special something." As I said that, I began to feel stupid and uncomfortable. "I'm sorry, but with all that's happened tonight I didn't catch everything he said."

"That's understandable."

"I think the paramedics saw him," I said. "Oh, he had a scar under one of his eyes."

Officer Casey looked over his shoulder. "Steve, Rick, you guys recognize the officer that was here when you arrived?"

"Nah." The heavy paramedic shook his head.

"Didn't get a good look," the slim one added.

Officer Casey's right eyebrow rose. "I'll find out who it was later." He turned back to me. "I need some information from you."

He took notes while asking me the same questions the Lieutenant and 911 operator had.

My answers seemed to satisfy him, at least. "Have a seat on the couch out there and I'll get back to you." He pointed with his pen to the reception area.

Two more police officers in suits, with their badges pinned over their breast pockets walked in. Officer Casey went over to them and they spoke quietly for a moment.

"Do all officers wear their badges where you can see them, when they're on scene?" I asked Officer Casey, when he returned.

"Why?"

"The Lieutenant flashed me his badge and then put it back in his pocket."

A look of interest rose in Officer Casey's eyes. "Give me a few minutes." He motioned to the detectives and they went into a huddle.

I walked out to the leather couch and sat down.

Within a moment Officer Casey came up to me with the other two men. "Mr. Barnes. This is Detective McHale and Detective Cortes."

"Hi." I got to my feet.

"Mr. Barnes, can you describe the Lieutenant who questioned you earlier and what he said to you?" asked the Latino guy I assumed was Cortes.

I gave them his physical description, including the scar and everything else I could recall. I added that he asked questions very fast, he didn't let me fully answer, he made me feel uncomfortable and he never even checked to make sure Dr. Elles was actually dead.

Cortes made some notes.

"Do you know the Lieutenant?" I asked.

"Not sure yet," he said.

Detective McHale was watching me intently. "Is there anything you can tell us about your meetings with Dr. Elles? Anything he said that might indicate he had health concerns?"

"No. He seemed fine."

Cortes asked, "What about the surroundings? Anything seem out of place?"

"Actually, yes," I said. "The two times I met with Dr. Elles, I'm almost certain we were being watched by two men in a gray Chevy."

McHale gave me a sharp look. "Why would you think that?"

I explained what I had seen at the coffee shop, including the binoculars and camera.

Cortes started writing on his pad again. "Can you give us more detail? Like model, license plate and description of the men?"

"It was a late model Lumina sedan, with tinted windows." I pulled my small, tattered pad from my back jean pocket, flipped to the right page and showed him the plate number. "I didn't get a chance to run the number to find out who owns it."

McHale raised an eyebrow.

"I'm a journalist." I shrugged.

McHale's eyebrow went back to its usual position.

"But I'm not a hundred percent positive that it was the same car I saw the first time. I got the number the second time I saw it outside the Hotel Nuevo. There was no one in the car, that time."

"We'll check it out," Cortes said.

McHale was still watching me closely. "We'll be in touch if we have any further questions."

The two detectives turned and went back into Dr. Elles' office. Cortes punched numbers on his cell phone as he walked.

"Do you know if Dr. Elles has any next of kin?" Officer Casey's pen was poised to his pad.

"Yes, he has a daughter, but I can't remember her name." I looked around the room, but there was nothing that looked as if it might contain personal information. Morgan. The name popped into my head. "His daughter's name is Morgan."

He wrote down the name. "That makes it easier."

"Can you tell me what happened to Dr. Elles?"

"Looks like a heart attack."

"That would explain it."

CHAPTER 4

"That's terrible, Nick." Sue propped her left hip up on my desk and pulled at the edge of her black skirt to cover most of her thigh. "Do you believe he was telling the truth?"

"I think so," I said. "But something wasn't right about the whole thing. You know, even other than Dr. Elles' death."

Sympathy glinted in Sue's blue eyes. "Wow." She shook her head and her brown hair brushed her shoulders.

I was tired. I'd been up most of last night, feeling sad about Dr. Elles' circumstances and being frustrated about my own.

"I have to go finish up a few things before the council meeting." Sue stood up straight and adjusted her foot in the black pump that'd been dangling. "We can talk about it more later."

"Uhuh, see you in a bit." I turned back to my computer.

I had to tidy up the entertainment listings, which was the most menial task in the editorial department. It was taking me a long time, because my mind kept wandering. I thought about the article I'd written; the one that Dr. Elles had referred to when he initially left the message on my voice mail.

As I stared blankly at my screen I recalled every detail I could remember.

It was ten days ago, on a Monday morning, when I heard, "Hey, Barnes."

I had recognized the voice immediately. Shit. "Hi, Dan."

He leaned on my desk with one hand. "What's on your plate right now?" He continued without waiting for a reply. "Here are a few background notes for a six hundred word story you're going to write for the weekend edition. It's nothing major." His lip curled. "I'm sure even you can handle it." He dropped a few pieces of paper on my desk and walked away.

Dan had replaced a man who was one of the all time greats in journalism. I sure missed Paul.

Dan started at the *News* after my information laundering incident, so he'd never seen me in real action. Most people's impression of Dan, mine included, was that he was a jerk. He had small man's syndrome, always arrogant and defensive. But this wasn't the time to dwell on his shortcomings. He was still my boss and I had to prove my abilities to him. If this story worked out I'd get juicier work again.

I placed my other tasks aside and started reading the notes he gave me. The story was going to be about potatoes grown in Idaho. But these weren't your average Idaho spuds; they were genetically altered. I knew very little about the subject. Most of my opinions about the environment and food came from Sue and she was against screwing with either one.

The information that was in front of me said that genetically engineered seeds helped farmers produce larger and better crops, while reducing strain on the environment. Genetic engineering protected the potatoes from certain insects and reduced the need for insecticides. All of this was accomplished by adding genes from living organisms into the DNA of plants to create new characteristics. That sounded interesting.

I made my first call to Naintosa, the company that genetically engineered the seeds.

"Good morning, Naintosa," a receptionist answered. "How may I help you?"

"Cindy Carmichael please."

"Just one moment, please. Whom should I say is calling."

I gave her my name and press credentials.

"Good morning, Cindy speaking."

"Hello Cindy, my name's Nick Barnes. I'm with the *Seattle News*. I'm doing a story about genetically altered potatoes and your name was given as the contact in your Media Relations department."

"Yes, I'm the right person. What questions can I answer for you today, Nick?" Her Boston accent was polite and charming.

"I just want to verify some information." I glanced at a paragraph I'd highlighted. "What makes your potatoes better than regular, unaltered ones?"

"Ours are resistant to potato leafroll virus. As a result, farmers have reduced insecticide use by eighty percent. They're also less susceptible to rotting and internal defects, which protects yields and improves quality."

"Interesting."

For the next five minutes she'd clarified the information I already had, then talked about the company. She seemed very sincere. "Naintosa isn't a huge conglomerate of scientists, but rather it's a group of people who really care. We want to take food production to the next level of evolution. We want to help feed the world."

I always saw Media Relations people just as spin-doctors, but Cindy sounded pretty genuine.

Next I had called a commercial farmer who was growing a thousand acres of potatoes near Boise. He didn't sound like a man that had just come in from the fields, all dirty and weathered from hard work. He was professional and concise. I wondered if this guy ever actually got his hands dirty. He sure sounded like a businessman. Heck, he was probably wearing a tie for all I knew.

"I allowed Naintosa to run tests on my crops in exchange for use of their genetically engineered seed potatoes and some subsidies. It's only the second year we've done this, so it's too soon to see the long-term results."

"How do you find Naintosa as a company?" I had asked.

"Naintosa isn't a huge conglomerate of scientists, but a group of people who really care. They want to take food production to the next level of evolution."

"That's what the Media Relations person at Naintosa said." Word for word actually.

"Well, they mean it, over there."

The article had come together easily and I was satisfied

with it. Dan was too. It wasn't a hard hitting investigative piece, but a little step to help me get back on track. Or so I thought at the time.

I kept staring at my computer screen. If Dr. Elles was right, I'd screwed up again. Or, I'd been used.

CHAPTER 5

I didn't know how many more times I could handle the sheer nausea of having to sit through another Seattle City Council meeting. Around me were other reporters, equally enthusiastic about having to spend two hours of their Wednesday night taking notes on zoning, garbage pick-up, dog shit ordinances and tonight's main topic – barbequing in the parks. Some were slumped in their chairs, others staring off into space and one guy was absentmindedly picking his nose. And then there were the Council Watchers sitting behind us. They attended all the sessions, because they had nothing better to do.

The meeting dragged on...

"Nick. Nick, wake up," Sue hissed in a whisper, as she nudged me.

"Quit pushing me."

"You're snoring." She pretended to cuff me on the side of the head.

"Oh. Sorry, what'd I miss?" I stifled a yawn.

She glared down at my pad. "Pretty much everything."

I sat up and looked at the paper on my lap. There was a crude drawing of the Mayor, with the words "BLAH, BLAH, BLAH" coming out of his mouth. I'd sketched it in the corner of the page while we were waiting for the meeting to begin. The rest of the page was blank.

I shrugged at Sue. "I guess I'm gonna have to borrow your notes again."

She raised her eyebrows. "It'll cost you." Sue was petite, but didn't take crap from anyone. Even in her sleeveless tight white top and short black skirt she could take a round out of me.

"The usual?"

"Yep." She half grinned and the annoyance disappeared from her face.

I took notes for the last ten minutes and witnessed a great victory for city barbequers in the year 2000. We could all still cook our meat in the park.

When the meeting was over, Sue and I headed to our favorite 'post City Council' spot. As usual, I'd be buying.

As we crossed the quiet street, I noticed a car slowly turn onto the far end of the block and stop. It was dusk, so the light was poor, but I could still tell it was a gray Chevy sedan. Dr. Elles was gone. Were they following me now? Was I being paranoid? Or was it time to freak out?

I didn't say anything; just kept walking, but quickened my pace.

"What's the hurry?" Sue asked, falling behind.

"I'm thirsty."

McMynn's had been open for two years and looked modern and clean. Thick ferns and Scottish memorabilia were everywhere. Kilts and family crests were framed on the walls and numerous display cases contained bagpipes in various sizes and stages of wear.

I felt safe in the crowded room. We made our way to a table next to the bar.

I noticed the usual male stares and leers at Sue. One guy even poked his buddy in the side with his elbow to make sure he got a look. Sue seemed oblivious to it, but it bugged me. I automatically walked closer to her.

Sue focused in on me immediately after we sat down. "Shit Nick, you've gotta snap out of it and get back to being your old self."

"I've had an unusual couple of days. Give me a break." I picked up a cloth napkin and wove it through my fingers.

She pulled the napkin out of my hand. "I'm talking about the last year. Those guys were pros and you got used. A journalist getting taken in isn't uncommon. What's done is done.

I can understand that what's happened in the last week with Dr..."

"Elles."

At that moment a slim, young, strawberry-blonde waitress, wearing a sheer white blouse, black bra and short tartan skirt arrived to take our drink order. The usual for Sue was Pyramid Pale Ale and I ordered my new favorite, Aberlour single malt scotch.

McMynn's prided itself on its scotch selection. Soft blue light glistened from the base of the bar, reflecting through the ranks of fine amber nectars displayed on mirrored shelves.

The distraction hadn't thrown Sue off her train of thought. "You have to become more aggressive again. You know that your weakness has always been checking the validity of your facts."

"Research." I cringed. That was the only part of the job I never liked and admittedly was lazy about.

"Sources are always going to try take advantage of you. If you're more skeptical and thorough, you'll have a better chance at finding the truth."

"No one cares about the truth anymore." I ran my hand through my hair. Self doubt had become implanted in my mind.

"Ever since you got back from sitting on the mountain in Taos, three weeks ago, you've gotten worse." Sue crossed her arms under her breasts, pushing them up. She always unintentionally did that when she was frustrated. "That was over a thousand dollars up the cat's ass as far as I'm concerned."

"It was less than a thousand."

"It was one thousand and sixty six dollars, if I remember what you told me. It's not a ton of money, but wasted money none the less."

"For some it was all the money they had left." I took a stiff belt of the scotch that just arrived. The sensation of it flowing down my throat comforted me.

The TV over the bar suddenly drew Sue's attention. "Hold on a second. I heard something about that story earlier today." She turned her chair to face the screen.

The sound was barely audible from the noise in the crowded pub, but the closed captioning was on, so we half listened, half read.

The news anchor, a perfectly coiffed man trying hard to sound believable, said, "...now, let's get the details from Karen."

The camera cut to a stylish woman beside the anchor. "Thanks, Brad." Karen leaned forward slightly. "In health news today, pharmaceutical giant Pharmalin announced the development of a drug that will improve the nutrition of food." The screen to her left showed video of a big green industrial tractor plowing a field. "Studies have shown that the food we eat today doesn't contain the same level of nutrients it used to fifty years ago. Research suggests that since World War Two, the soil in many countries has been depleted by over-farming. Because of this, people need to eat more food just to receive the same amount of nutrition."

"What about vitamin supplements?" I asked the TV.

"Hold on." Sue raised her hand.

The screen beside the co-anchor now showed a still image of a sign in front of an industrial building. It read Pharmalin Pharmaceuticals. "Once approved by the FDA, a person would only need to take one pill with every meal. The drug is said to synthetically enhance the nutrition of the food by up to thirty seven percent. In other health news..."

Sue turned her chair back to face me. "That really pisses me off."

"Why? They're helping people become healthier." I shrugged. "What's wrong with that?"

"Because it's not real," Sue said. "They're just synthetically mimicking the food's nutrients. That doesn't mean the food actually has more nutritional value."

"Huh?"

"Why can't they focus on the real problem instead of just making another pill? Why can't they work on replenishing the soil's nutrients?"

"Isn't that what fertilizer's for?"

"Commercial fertilizer is what got us into this mess. It hasn't replenished all the minerals plants take out."

"Oh, I didn't know that." To be honest, I didn't really care. I had other problems to worry about.

Sue always had an interest in nutrition, which stemmed from her hippie parents. When she was a child they lived in a commune and grew their own food. She'd been a vegetarian all of her life; which is the reason people said she always looked so healthy and younger than twenty nine. I bet it helped that she worked out a lot and was five foot three.

Sue also had a natural ability to see the bigger picture in life, which lent itself to a more esoteric and metaphysical way of thinking.

"Everyone wants a quick fix." Her voice rose. "People have been programmed not to look at what got them unhealthy and remedy the problem. They're told to mask their symptoms so they don't have to think about it. Then the drug companies can sell more and more pills."

"I can see *your* passion hasn't disappeared," I said, half heartedly trying to keep up with what she was saying.

"Doesn't it bother you?"

I shrugged and leaned back against my chair. "Well a lot of people predicted the world would end this year. Maybe this is all just a part of it."

"That's exactly what I mean." She rolled her eyes and pointed a finger at me. "Before, just my reaction to this story would've provoked a strong opinion from you. Now you just try make stupid jokes." She held up her glass, saw it was empty and looked even more annoyed.

I guess I'd put it off as long as I could. We had to have the conversation. I sat up straight. "I feel like everything I've worked for has been for shit...education, work, career path. I've hit a wall."

Sue leaned in and placed her hands on the table. "Everything you've worked for has got you to this point. You've learned and paid for your mistakes. You gotta get back to your original plan. That way, when another opportunity comes up, like potentially the one with the Dr. Elles guy, you'll be ready for it."

"I guess." I stared at some old bagpipes on the wall to avoid looking at her.

"Nick, you're only thirty. You can't give up yet. You're smart, except for your current minor mental problem."

That made me smile and I looked back at her.

She was studying my face. A sly grin appeared. "You're still good looking. Maybe it's time for you to get a little action or another girlfriend. How long has it been again?"

"Whatever." I felt my skin warm. Yeah, getting laid might help loosen me up. It always had in the past. I just hadn't felt like *that kind* of female companionship lately.

"You know the only reason I bug you like this is because I care, don't you?" She reached over and touched my hand that cradled the scotch glass.

"You don't have to tell me that Sue, I know." I took the last sip of my Aberlour. "Do you want another drink?"

"Sure, I'll get them." She got up and went over to the bar.

I followed her with my eyes. She never gave up on me.

We met ten years ago in a composition class at Washington State University where we were both studying journalism. Sue was really cute, full of spunk, fresh and athletic. She could be a bit crude at times, but you always knew how she felt. After she shot down my numerous sexual advances we'd developed a great friendship.

After college, I got a job with a small community paper and Sue landed a position doing research at the *Seattle News*. After two years, she was promoted to the newsroom and helped me get a job there.

We were set. Two buddies working at a major daily paper. Nick Barnes and Sue Clark were on the *Seattle News* masthead. We were making enough to live on and were happy in what we thought was a noble profession.

There had always remained some sexual tension between us and I sometimes wondered if we'd end up together one day.

"What are you thinking about?" Sue asked, returning with fresh drinks.

"I was just reflecting about the early days at the *News*. We were so gung-ho, but so naïve."

"Oh yeah, the old glory days." She swallowed some of her fresh beer. "Forget about that, let's focus on Taos."

"Hmm." I figured she'd think what happened was stupid. That's why I hadn't told her anything about the trip.

"I know you don't like to talk about things until you've figured them out, Nick. But maybe I can help you put the pieces together."

I stirred my new scotch with my left index finger, and then popped the finger into my mouth. That action bought me a few seconds to formulate my thoughts. "Taos was supposed to rejuvenate me."

"That's why I said it was a waste of money."

"Yeah, part of the problem is that you're right. It's embarrassing to go spend a bunch of money on a course to help you get your act together and come back with an even worse attitude."

"I understand." Sue leaned closer, putting her elbows on the table. "So, what happened?"

"I tried to be positive, do the things the instructors suggested and I even tried to meditate a few times. But, it all seemed so...so not reality."

"Not reality?"

"People taking the course had such sad stories. Like this one farmer who lost the land his family owned for generations. He said they couldn't keep up with progress and got sucked up by a farming conglomerate."

"Yeah, you hear tons of those stories," Sue said. "It's interesting that a farmer would take a course like that."

"At first I thought so too. But it turned out that I was the one who didn't belong. They were all entrepreneurs."

"That failed?"

"Failed is too strong a word. *Beaten* would summarize it better. There was a small businessman who got leveled by a multinational, a store owner who had a big box open across the street, a computer wiz guy who'd had his work stolen. They were all stories of people's lives being destroyed by big, faceless, uncaring organizations."

Sue nodded. "The course should've been called, *how to go on after the big guys take over.*"

"At least then I wouldn't have taken the course. Everyone

was there to try to get their lives together, but instead their stories combined to show just how pointless it really is."

"Hmm, I understand how you feel, but..."

"We live in the so called land of opportunity, at the start of a new century, but it seems like we have less freedom and hope than ever before."

Sue's expression changed from sympathetic to stern. "It may seem bleak at times, but people can still go after their dreams and make a difference. That especially counts for *you* who can reach a large population with your writing."

"What's the use?" The scotch was taking effect and letting me be more honest. "No matter how many *get your shit together* and *positive thinking* courses I take, reality is reality. Look at what happened to Dr. Elles."

The attractive waitress placed our order of nachos on the table.

"When was the last time you meditated?" Sue asked.

"Like I said, I tried in Taos." I didn't feel like telling her that Dr. Elles came through in one. A sudden pang of guilt swept over me. The lab coat Dr. Elles was wearing in the vision went from white, to red, then black. That must've meant death...and I didn't warn him.

"You need to start regularly again." Sue pulled a nacho chip off the edge of the plate. "You know how meditating helps; how you feel after actually going into the gap."

"Huh? Yeah, you're right."

"I don't know what else to tell you." Sue was back to sympathetic, but firm. "File away what happened and do what it takes to get yourself moving forward again."

CHAPTER 6

I woke up early Thursday morning in a cold sweat. I'd dreamt that I lived in a suburb where all the houses were the same. The people dressed alike. Even the dogs and cats were identical. Looking down the street was like looking into the mirrors in a funhouse. The image repeated again and again into eternity. The fear of living a dull existence for the rest of my life was even getting into my dreams.

I propped my pillow up and leaned back against it.

I had to do something. But what?

Change. I had to change my patterns.

Sue was right, as usual. It was time to start meditating again. It would balance me out while I made other changes.

I got up and searched through my bookshelf until I found the one I needed. "Now let's see...where's that chapter about meditations that focus on the beauty in nature." I flipped pages. "Here it is."

I grabbed a t-shirt and sweat pants off the carpet and put them on. I needed to get started before I changed my mind.

With the book in hand I went down to the center courtyard of my apartment building. The garden was small, framed by rhododendron bushes and two hemlock trees. In the middle was an old rickety weathered wooden bench. Even though the little patch of garden was in the middle of a concrete city, it was my oasis.

I got comfortable on the bench and reviewed a few pages of the book. Putting it down, I focused on the beauty and energy of the smaller hemlock. The longer I stared, the more illuminated it became. The light between the branches was warm and soft.

I closed my eyes and concentrated on deep, calm breaths. A sudden image appeared: Dr. Elles sitting in his leather office chair, waiting for me. The shadow of a man grabbing him from behind, then standing over Dr. Elles' fallen body.

I quickly opened my eyes.

Was I making up a scenario? Did he die of a heart attack or did someone kill him somehow?

I couldn't meditate anymore, because the image was stuck in my mind.

On my way back up to my apartment, I considered trying to contact Dr. Elles' daughter. Morgan.

⁑

As soon as I arrived at my cubicle, I reached for the phone book I kept in the bottom left drawer of my desk. Hopefully she was in there; otherwise I'd have to try search for her on the Internet. There was one M. Elles listed in the book. "Worth a shot," I said, out loud.

"Hello," a quiet voice answered on the third ring.

"Hello, is Morgan there?"

"Speaking."

Great. "Hello Morgan, my name is Nick Barnes. I was an acquaintance of your father's."

There was a pause before she responded. Her voice trembled, "Yes, I helped him find you."

"You have my deepest condolences. Although I'd just met your father, he seemed like a very good man."

"Thank you, he was. Will you be coming to the funeral?"

"Uh...yes, of course." I instantly felt obligated to go. "When is it?"

"It's on Saturday at eleven, in the Lutheran Church on Fourth." She had a sweet sounding voice with no apparent accent like Dr. Elles'. "My father's friends are scattered all over the world and hard to reach, so I'm afraid there won't be many people there."

"I'll make sure to introduce myself."

"I'll see you in two days," she said.

CHAPTER 7

My mind wasn't into work.

After an hour of staring blankly at my computer screen, I decided to go for an early lunch.

It was a sunny Friday, so there were a fair number of people on the street. My feet automatically took me toward the small park near the office.

My thoughts bounced around as I walked. What was going to happen to Dr. Elles' life's work now? Would his story ever be told? What about my future? Was I going to become a bitter, hack journalist, with disheveled hair, wearing clothes that looked like I'd slept in them for days and have permanent whiskey breath?

When I eventually returned to work there was a note on my desk: *edit the Carter article by four*. It wasn't signed, but I knew it was from Dan, because of the sharp little letters.

I searched for the file and brought it up on my screen. It was a small follow-up article about a fourth generation cattle rancher and oil zillionaire from Houston. Jack Carter had recently caused a stir in the business world. He'd liquidated his assets for an undisclosed amount. The local angle was that he'd donated a huge sum to a wilderness preservation group in Seattle that promoted vegetarianism. A cattleman giving to vegetarians.

I'd read the original story written by a colleague a week ago. It had a biographical element to it. Jack Carter defied the stereotype of a man of privilege. He ruffled a lot of feathers as he went through life. He did his own thing; whatever he thought was right, clearly. That didn't always go over well with the oil and cattle establishments. What I'd read gave me respect for him. Sure would be interesting to interview him, but from the sounds of it, he didn't do that sort of thing. The last sentence read, *Mr. Carter could not be reached for comment.*

I tried to concentrate on editing, but when I came across the word *fact*, my mind wandered sideways. When you break it down, isn't everything just someone's opinion? Is there really such a thing as a *fact*? As journalists, were we really qualified to decide what was a fact and what was not? Usually we weren't even present when the event occurred. Even the people who witnessed the event might not have *really* seen exactly what happened. Or two people could see the same thing and describe it in totally different ways.

"Hello." Sue kneed the armrest of my chair. "Working hard I see."

I hadn't heard her walk up. "I'm editing an article."

Sue rolled her eyes with over exaggeration and smiled. "How much time do you need?"

"Couple of minutes."

"Okay, I'll go get my stuff."

I read the last two paragraphs, changed a few words, typed "edited N.B." at the top and saved the document.

Sue was back. "Ready?"

"Yeah, let's go." I dropped the pen I'd been chewing on.

* * *

We got to McMynn's and found a seat on the patio. Actually, it was a table on the wide sidewalk. They'd just roped off a section and placed green patio furniture on the cement.

"What can I get for you two?" asked the perky, slim, blond server, with her tight white top and the usual short tartan skirt.

We ordered a pitcher of beer and some dinner.

Sue got up. "I'll be right back. I gotta pee."

I looked around. No grey Chevys. Great. Was I becoming paranoid? Maybe they got tired of watching my underachieving existence.

While I waited, my mind wandered. What about destiny? I pondered the concept. If we were all destined to live a certain life, then we'd just go through the motions and whatever was supposed to happen would happen. Or did we actually create our destiny? I liked that idea best because it meant we had unlimited possibilities. In other words there was no destiny because if you could create it, it's not destined. Or I've heard people say you could change your destiny. That one to me was bullshit. If it's destined, how can you change it? I was going around in circles. If creating our own destiny was the way it worked, I wasn't doing a good job of it at the moment.

"Earth to Nick." Sue sat back down.

I sure was having some deep mind wanderings lately, I thought.

Behind Sue was our server. She set down two double Aberlour's with the pitcher of Pyramid Ale.

"Wow, both." I eyed the scotch.

"It's Friday and you had a rough week." Sue raised her glass of scotch. "Let's just relax."

"Good, I've been thinking too much." I took a sip of my scotch. The ice hadn't had enough time to dilute it, so the liquor burned going down. "Ah, that's nice."

"You know, I forgot to mention that I remember reading about Dr. Elles," Sue said. "He was responsible for a lot of the so called breakthroughs in genetic food research. I think some of the patents actually belonged to him."

"Yeah, he told me about that. Some of the earlier ones did; before he went to Naintosa."

Sue was quiet for a moment, before asking, "so what are you gonna do now?"

"I talked to his daughter and I'm going to the funeral tomorrow."

"Good."

CHAPTER 8

I was startled awake by my radio alarm. There are few things more traumatic than waking to heavy metal. I smashed the snooze button and lay back, holding my forehead. Ouch. My temples throbbed. I drank too much again.

After a shower, four aspirin, six blue green algae capsules, half a gallon of water and three fried eggs, I started feeling better. Not perfect, but the hangover was manageable.

I put on my only suit and headed for the funeral.

As I drove into the parking lot, I tried to remember when I was last in a church. It'd been a long time; years. I hoped I wouldn't disintegrate into ashes when I crossed the threshold.

The building was a modest A-frame; a tasteful chapel made of brown stained wood.

The interior was larger than it appeared from the outside. The ceiling swept down sharply on either side. The clean varnished pine pillars and rows of pews gleamed. The far wall was made entirely of stained glass, softly reflecting sunlight in. At the front, beside the altar, was Dr. Elles' casket.

The service was well underway, so I sat down quietly at the back.

A man with a strong eastern European accent was speaking to the few dozen people in attendance. His hair and close cut beard matched his black suit with white pin stripes. After he said some nice words about Dr. Elles, he stepped down and was replaced at the podium by the pastor.

I zoned out to what was happening at the front of the church.

What about the Lieutenant at Dr. Elles' office? There was something not right about him. He was too aggressive. And why did he just take off? The detectives and Officer Casey sure were interested in who he was and why he left so suddenly. I tried not to concoct a bunch of theories. I had enough craziness going through my mind as it was. I hoped the police got it all straightened out.

The service took another half hour to complete.

I stood when everyone else did and watched as eight men carried the coffin from the church to the hearse waiting in the driveway. The first two people in the procession were a slim young woman and the middle-aged man who had spoken. He had a consoling arm around her. The woman was dressed in a black jacket and skirt. Her long strawberry blonde hair framed a distraught face.

That must be Morgan, I thought. Even in her sorrow, she was quite stunning.

I followed the procession to the cemetery and stood in the back at the burial site.

The sky had turned gray and dark. The clouds looked ready to release at any time. The bland light contrasted with the luminous green of the grass and trees.

I felt sadness and compassion for Dr. Elles' daughter. I personally had never thought death was something to be sad about. I believed we were all infinite and our souls never died. We just moved on to our next adventure. The sadness came from the loss felt by the people left behind.

I glanced around at the attendees. There wasn't a lot of crying, but emotion was in everyone's eyes. Most of the people were Dr. Elles' age, a mix of male and female. No children or teenagers were present.

When the ceremony finished the small crowd began to disperse. It was the appropriate time to introduce myself.

"Ms. Elles?" I asked, as I approached her.

"Are you Nick?" she asked, with an uncontrolled sniffle.

"Yes." She had the most amazing dark blue eyes. I was mesmerized for a second. I'd never seen that shade of blue before.

Morgan cleared her throat as she struggled to gain composure. "This is Dr. Ivan Popov, a close friend of my father's." Her voice was low and soft.

Ivan stretched out his hand. There was a classiness about him. "It is a pleasure to meet you, Nick." Up close his accent definitely sounded Russian.

Morgan looked at me. "Do you have a few minutes to talk?"

I reached to shake Ivan's hand. "Sure."

A stout man, in a flat black double breasted suit walked up and kissed Morgan on the cheek. He was her height, about five foot seven. When he spoke he had a heavy British accent, "How are you holding up, my dear?"

She nodded and took a deep breath. "Would you like to walk with us as we talk to Nick?"

He shook my hand. "It's a pleasure to meet you, Nick. The name's William Clancy, but you can call me Bill." His hair was close cropped and what was left was all gray.

"Hello, Bill."

The four of us walked slowly along a path between rows of headstones.

"We understand Carl hired you to help him write a book about his life's research." You could tell that English wasn't Ivan's first language, but he'd developed it in an institution of higher learning. He pronounced every word articulately.

"Yes, he did," I replied. "Or almost did."

Bill touched my shoulder. "Have you read any of the research?"

"No I haven't. We were supposed to start, the night he passed away."

Morgan wiped her eyes with a handkerchief. "I talked to my father only a few hours before you found him."

"Did your father know he was sick?"

Ivan interrupted before Morgan could say anything, "He was not sick. He was in excellent health."

"The paramedics and police told me it was most likely a heart attack."

Ivan's tone was serious. "He did not have a heart condition. Nick, this is a much more dangerous situation than you are aware of. The people Carl intended to implicate would do anything to make sure the information did not get out."

"Hold on." Without thinking, I began to back away. "You're sure he was killed?"

Bill put his hand on my shoulder, stopping my retreat. "Carl obviously didn't have time to explain everything to you."

With a slight twist I shrugged off Bill's hand. "You've got that right."

Ivan gestured to a nearby bench. "Nick, can you give us a moment?"

I needed a few minutes myself. "Yeah, fine."

As I walked over to it, I saw the gray Chevy at the end of a row of parked cars some distance away. Why wouldn't they leave me the fuck alone?

The bench was angled so when I sat down I could see the car as well as the three of them. The overhanging branches from a large oak tree gave me a sense of shelter.

This situation wasn't what I'd expected. Sure, I had my suspicions that Dr. Elles was killed, but Ivan and Bill sounded sure of it. Was it true? It was good that the project never ended up happening. But why was I still being watched? I felt relieved and more nervous at the same time.

The three of them talked for a few minutes before joining me at the bench.

"I'm pretty positive I'm being followed."

Morgan gave me a startled look. "What do you mean?"

I motioned with my head in the direction of the car. "You see that gray Chevy over there? The first time I saw it was when I'd just met your father. I've seen it every day since."

Morgan frowned.

I was getting frustrated. "Do you guys know what it's about? Are any of you being tailed?"

Bill squinted, as he surveyed the car. "Not that we're aware of. Have they approached you or just observed from a distance?"

"Just observed. So what do I do?"

Ivan turned in the opposite direction; toward Dr. Elles' burial site. "We must be cautious. Make sure you are facing away from the vehicle when you speak."

"But it's over; a non-starter. Why don't they leave me

alone?" If the men in the car were listening or reading my lips, I wanted them to get that.

Morgan sat down beside me, while the two men angled their bodies to block the view from the Chevy.

Ivan spoke in a deliberate voice. "Would it be all right if we gave you some background before you decide whether or not to continue?"

I felt my body stiffen. "You still want me to work on the manuscript?"

"Yes we do," Bill said. "But we want you to know the risks involved."

"I know that one risk is that I get followed by hell knows who."

Bill said, "If you don't openly let on that you're working on the memoir, I'm sure they'll go away. If they haven't approached you already, I doubt they will."

They didn't seem to be *that* worried about the guys in the sedan. Was I overreacting? No. "Can we go to the other end of the cemetery to talk?" I got to my feet.

Morgan stood up too. "Let's go for a walk."

We slowly began to move away, Morgan and me in the middle, Ivan on the left, Bill on the right.

Ivan was frowning. "It is important for your safety and ours that you agree not to tell anyone about this conversation."

I thought about it for a second. He was right. "I promise I won't say anything." Even though I knew I'd tell Sue.

"So you understand, Bill and I were scientists at Naintosa, working with Carl and Claudia."

Morgan must've seen the confusion on my face. "Dr. Claudia Elles was my mother."

I remembered Dr. Elles telling me that he worked with his wife and she'd died in a car accident.

"Bill and I retired from Naintosa three years ago, shortly after Claudia died. We did not want to contribute to their business practices any longer. Carl stayed, because he had a burning desire to expose Naintosa."

Bill shook his head. "We weren't as courageous as Carl."

"No, we were not," Ivan said. "We realize that now and

are committed to help finish what Carl started. Morgan has agreed to devote all of her time to help you write the manuscript."

"After you had dinner with my father, he said he felt very comfortable with you. He was confident you were the right person for the job."

"I'm not sure," I said. "This might be too much for me."

Morgan's face flushed. "This was his life's work. He thought he was helping people with his research, not harming them."

Bill squinted and frowned. "We all did."

Ivan nodded and looked down.

"My father couldn't bear the thought of Naintosa taking his work and causing harm to people just for profit. We have to finish this before more people get hurt."

"By killing Carl," Bill broke in, "they're hoping everything he knew would die with him."

I had to ask, "But what if he just died of a plain old heart attack?" I had to make sure this all made sense to me before I made a decision.

"Two nights before he died, his office was broken into and the files he stored there were taken," Ivan said. "Naintosa suspected Carl had copied research documents and wanted to expose them. They didn't know how much he knew until they obtained the files."

I glanced back and saw that we'd created some distance from the car and the tree I'd sat under now blocked their view of us. "Okay, let's say the break-in theory is correct, how can someone make another person have a heart attack?"

Bill lifted his right index finger. "By injecting an untraceable drug called Cirachrome."

Morgan reached in her pocket for a tissue and wiped her eyes.

I remembered the vision I had in my meditation of a man coming up behind Dr. Elles. "Wasn't there an autopsy? Have the police been told?"

"The coroner's report said it was death by natural causes," Ivan said.

"That means they aren't sure what happened," Bill added.

Ivan looked grim. "And we do not want to attract undue attention right now."

Morgan sniffled. "The police can't help."

"What? Why?" This was crazy. I would much rather let the police investigate and then write the manuscript when it was all settled. "It doesn't make sense."

Bill looked sympathetic. "You'll understand in time."

"But if they broke in and took the files, Naintosa already knows what information he had. And don't the police know what was taken?" Was there something they weren't telling me? Or was I just not getting it?

"The documents taken from Carl's office were incomplete," Ivan said. "There was only enough to get you started."

Morgan spoke up, "He didn't tell the police about the files. As far as we know, they aren't doing anything more about the break-in. They think it was just kids or an addict trying to find money."

I tried to look at it from the police's perspective. "But, then he died in the same office a few days later. Wouldn't the police be suspicious?"

"If they are they haven't told us," Bill said.

This was way out of my comfort zone. "I need to think about it."

"Unfortunately," Ivan said, "time is becoming a factor."

"I still haven't seen any of his notes."

"Of course." Morgan took a business card out of a small case in her purse, wrote an address on the back of it and handed it to me. "We can all meet at 10:00am at my place."

CHAPTER 9

It had begun to drizzle as I walked to my Blazer.

I decided to drive around and to see if the gray car followed me. I couldn't see it, so I headed out of town toward Snoqualmie Pass. I craved a serene place.

I rehashed the conversation as I drove.

After close to an hour, I turned off the highway onto an old logging road. It led me to a spot I'd visited before.

A large rock overhang jutted out above an expansive green forest below. Not a soul around, just the beautiful calm of nature.

It was raining harder now and cloud cover hung so low, if I stretched out my arm I could almost touch it.

I pulled on the red waterproof shell I always kept in the back storage compartment and walked over to the rock.

A rhythm of rain hit the hood of my parka and little splashes bounced at angles everywhere. I listened to it as I looked out over the valley below.

I'd been burned and needed a project to redeem myself. I had to show that I could do good work again. I needed to prove it to myself more than anyone else.

I'd been offered to write about information that a company was willing to kill over. Supposedly. That meant physical danger. I wasn't good with that. But maybe it was time for me to change and step up. I had to admit that the adventure of it was exhilarating.

I sat on the rock and pondered. My ass was all wet, but I didn't care.

I still hadn't seen any of the research. There would be no

commitment from me until I had a look at it. I wished Dr. Elles had given me a few written facts right off the bat that proved his case.

Something else was missing. Something they wouldn't tell me at the cemetery.

I needed to stall them tomorrow and buy some time. Then do some research of my own. See what I could dig up on Naintosa, Dr. Carl Elles, Dr. Ivan Popov, Dr. William Clancy and Morgan Elles.

I watched the clouds begin to dissipate and the outline of the sun appear behind them.

In the end I'd have to go with my gut feeling. But I was so out of whack that I wasn't sure I'd recognize it.

CHAPTER 10

Usually we had an Indian summer, but not this year. It was drizzling. Soon we'd have to endure this weather for four straight months, only colder.

I arrived at the address Morgan had given me. It was a well-manicured townhouse complex.

The buildings appeared newly painted deep brown, with cedar shrubs neatly arranged around the perimeter. Small trees beginning to show their autumn colors were strategically placed. The complex stood on a quiet hillside with a picturesque view of Elliott Bay. A low fog over the water made the scene surreal.

You can't be poor and own one of these, I said to myself.

I walked along a path bordered by emerald green ferns and passed a small playground.

When I met Morgan yesterday, I didn't even consider that she might be married and have children. Had she been wearing a ring?

I rang the doorbell.

Within a few seconds Morgan opened the door. "Morning, Nick."

I looked at her brilliant blue eyes and stammered. "Uh, hi." I'd have to consciously avoid looking at them. They messed me up.

She motioned me inside. "Come in and make yourself at home."

We walked through a short hallway and down a few steps into the living room. One wall was a floor to ceiling window that showed me three sailboat masts gliding through the harbor mist below.

"Can I get you some coffee?" She strolled past me toward the kitchen.

"That would be great."

Her home was both casual and elegant, coordinated in warm beiges. On the fireplace mantle stood a number of framed pictures. Morgan was in most of them. No sign of a husband and children. At the center was a larger photograph of a teenage Morgan, Dr. Elles, and a blonde haired woman, taken in a tropical location. That must've been her mother. Morgan sure looked like her.

As Morgan walked into the room with a coffee tray, I realized that she was the embodiment of her home. Even in jeans and a t-shirt, she was casual and elegant. Her strawberry blonde hair was in a neat, tidy ponytail and the small amount of makeup she wore highlighted her features.

"Here you go." She passed the coffee and sat down next to me on the sofa. "Help yourself to cream and sugar. Ivan and Bill are going to be a few minutes late, so we can get to know each other."

"All right." I decided to be light hearted and make it sound like a dating video. "I'm thirty years old, six feet tall, I could stand to lose ten pounds, I'm a reporter for the *Seattle News*, single, live alone, I'm a Leo, like long walks in the park and am a nine handicap. My favorite color is green, like my eyes."

"My turn." She gave me an endearing smile and played along. "I'm twenty seven years old, work for Perkins Wheeler Public Relations, have a boyfriend named Joshua, live alone, my sign is Pisces and I also like long walks in the park. Hmm, what else?"

"What's your favorite color and handicap?"

"Oh, I also like kick boxing mixed in with my aerobics. My favorite color is teal, even though it's not in style right now. What do you mean by handicap?"

"How many strokes over par you average in golf...never mind."

We leaned back on the sofa at the same time.

"Don't forget to add that you have a good sense of humor," I said.

"As do you." Her smile revealed a small dimple on her left cheek. "What else do you want to know?"

I couldn't deny I was a little disappointed to hear she had a boyfriend. Why wouldn't she? Of course she would. She was out of my league, so why even worry about it?

I decided to ask a different question. "If you aren't married, why don't you have a loft downtown instead of living here? Not that this place isn't great."

"My dad bought it as an investment. I couldn't afford to buy a place on my own at the time. Maybe I will now."

"Makes sense." I paused for a moment. "What about the boyfriend, are you serious?" Shoot, I'd just blurted that out.

"Not too serious. We've only been dating for four months. He's a flight engineer for an airline, so he's away a lot." She fiddled with her coffee cup. "He's nine years older than I am and has two young kids from a previous marriage. But I really care for him, so I think I can learn to live with that."

She was upfront and honest, but I felt uncomfortable talking more about the boyfriend. In fact, only seconds ago I'd told myself not to worry about it. I heard Sue's voice in my mind, "jackass."

I decided to change the subject. "I remember you saying yesterday that you were going to work full time on this project. What about your job?"

There was a natural confidence about her. "I've asked for a six month leave of absence. I'll play it by ear from there. It depends on how far along we are. That's if you're going to help, of course." She raised her eyebrows and leaned toward me, anticipating my response.

Man, she had stunning eyes.

On cue, the doorbell rang.

She frowned as she got up.

Her departure gave me time to assess the situation. I could definitely work with her. But, if after my research on them I decided to go ahead, what about my job? I hadn't considered doing this project full time. My job was a big security blanket.

Morgan escorted the two scientists into the living room before returning to the kitchen.

"Good morning Nick," they said in unison.

We shook hands and then each took a place in chairs at opposite ends of the coffee table.

Morgan gave them each a cup of coffee and sat back down next to me on the sofa.

Bill got straight to the point. "So, have you decided to help us?"

"I have questions."

"Let us try answer your questions," Ivan said.

"Originally, Dr. Elles said it was going to be an after-hours project. I get the impression now you want me to work full time?"

"You could always take a leave of absence," Morgan said. "Like I am."

"That's true." I knew a guy who had done that at the *News* and he did get his old job back. But that was before Dan. "I could ask my boss."

Morgan looked over at the scientists, then back at me. "We should discuss compensation. I'd like to pay you five thousand a month plus expenses if you work full time."

Dollar signs went off in my head, but I tried to hide my enthusiasm. "Hmm, let me see." I got up and walked over to the patio doors. That was definitely more than I was making now. "I think that would work."

Bill clapped his hands together. "Fantastic. You'll do it then."

"The money is fine, but like I said, I need more time."

Ivan sighed. "What else is holding you back?"

"Would it be possible to look through the notes for a couple of days?"

They looked at each other.

Ivan stood up, reached into his inside jacket pocket and pulled out a document. He handed it to me, along with a pen. "We do not see a problem with that. As long as Morgan is present and the notes do not leave the premises. Here is a confidentiality agreement for you to sign."

"What for?" Dumb question.

"It states that you agree not to write articles about the

information you are about to learn or share it with anyone," Ivan said, in his articulate manner, "until it is public knowledge. In other words, until the book is published."

I briefly looked at the two-page document, and signed it.

Bill rose from his chair. "Welcome aboard."

Bill was kind of pushy, I thought, but didn't say anything. I was going to stick to my plan.

Ivan stowed the agreement in his inner pocket. "Morgan knows how to reach us when you need our assistance."

I shook their hands before she escorted them out.

When Morgan returned to the living room she carried a large box. "Ready to start?"

"You don't waste any time, do you?"

"We don't have time to waste." She took the cover off the box to reveal four large binders. "I'm sure it's organized. All we have to do is figure out where it starts." She handed a binder to me and then chose one for herself.

We began to read.

"Morgan?" I looked at her and saw she had the same scrunched up, confused look on her face I imagined I had. "I have no idea what I'm reading about. All I can decipher is that this explains how to put some kind of bacteria into a squash."

"I know what you mean. I think I have the notes on the gene for potatoes. Like the ones you wrote about in your article. We're going to have to make notes on which binders we don't understand and get Ivan to explain them to us." She made some notes on a pad beside her.

"It looks like we may need Ivan and Bill's help full time." I shook my head as I flipped through the pages.

"That may be difficult." She pursed her lips. "They're both flying home this afternoon. Ivan lives in a small town called Nelson, in southern British Columbia and Bill lives in London."

"They don't even live in the U.S.?"

"No, but Ivan's only a ten hour drive away."

"Only ten hours." I raised both hands for theatrical effect. "Well no problem then."

Morgan smiled as she made some more notes. "I won't be

able to reach Ivan until tomorrow. I'll ask him whether it'd be better for him to come back here or for us to go there. Let's just catalogue the binders for now."

"That'll be easy, there's only two left in the box."

She shook her head. "Follow me. I'll need your help."

We walked over to a storage room off the kitchen. There were about ten more boxes.

"That's half of them," she said. "The others are in a safe place. I'll get them when we finish with these."

"That's a lot of information."

"Make yourself useful and grab one."

The next binder I looked at was about soybeans; hers, papayas.

"Is no food sacred?" I passed it to her to index.

When I opened the third one, there was a diagram on the first page. "I think I have something interesting here."

Morgan slid over to me. "What is it?"

"It's titled *World Health Hierarchy*. There's a pyramid with eight numbered rungs."

I placed the binder half on her lap, half on mine. On the following pages there was a title at each level and a brief description. The order went from the bottom, up.

The first page was titled *General Population*. "That's us," I said.

"Obviously." Morgan read the next page, "*Alternative Health Care*. That's all the herbs and natural stuff."

"Obviously." I turned the page, "*Western Medical Profession*. This pyramid explains who makes the decisions for the world's health?"

Morgan raised an eyebrow. "That's why the title is *World Health Hierarchy*."

"What I'm trying to say is that if this shows who makes the decisions for our health, don't you think the medical profession should be close to the top, instead of the bottom?"

"Good point." She turned to the next page. "*Governments*. That's stupid. Why should the government have more say than the Medical Profession? What do they know?"

"It's all politics, I guess." I sighed. "What's next?"

Morgan's body went stiff. "Who the hell..."

"What's wrong?" I looked up and caught a glimpse of a man in a dark raincoat disappearing past the shrubs at the end of her patio. "Who was that?"

"I don't know. He was watching us."

"Really?" I jumped up and rushed to the patio door.

She came up beside me and put her hand on my arm. "Don't go out there."

I tried to mask a wave of nervousness. "Should we call the police?"

The faint click of an exterior door being opened was loud in the quiet.

"Didn't you lock the door?"

"I did." She stood rigid. "The whole house is locked up."

Without thinking, I strode toward the three stairs that lead to the foyer. What I saw stopped me dead in my tracks.

A small canister pouring out smoke rolled down the steps. Stunned, I watched it land right at my feet.

I turned back toward Morgan and saw the fear in her face.

I took a breath and a bitter acid taste burned my mouth. I began coughing so hard my eyes teared up.

With all my strength I managed to croak, "Run."

I tried to follow. My legs buckled. I spun around as I fell. A large figure came at me through the rolling cloud of smoke.

Everything went black.

CHAPTER 11

My head pounded. I couldn't see.

After a moment of disorientation, I realized I was sitting in a chair. I tried to move. My arms were tied behind my back. My legs were bound. Something covered my eyes. What had happened to me?

A raspy male voice said, "He's awake."

I heard someone come toward me.

I pulled, but the constraints around my wrists were so tight, my hands were numb.

A deep voice said, "How are you feeling, Nick?" I could feel his breath on my cheek. It reeked of stale garlic.

"I have a headache," I managed to say. "What's going on?" I tried to move and discovered there was a bind around my waist as well.

"The headache will pass soon," the deep voice said. "It's an after effect of the gas."

"Where am I?" My panic intensified by the second. "Why've you done this to me? Where is Morgan? How do you know my name?"

"Just relax and answer my questions. If you answer them honestly, nothing bad will happen."

"But I don't know anything." I was hyperventilating and getting dizzy.

"Just focus," the raspy voice threatened, "and answer his questions, before I shit kick you."

I felt claustrophobic. Darkness was closing in from the inside.

"Why were you and Ms. Elles' going through the Doctor's notes?" Deep voice spoke in an authoritative tone.

I had to calm down so I could think. I tried as hard as I could to take deep breaths and get a grip on my terror.

I felt a sudden hard jolt of pain on my right cheek, as something made hard contact. My jaw almost snapped. Blood instantly began to pool in my mouth.

"Did you hear my question?"

I spit in a weak attempt at defiance, hoping it'd land on whoever hit me. "What'd you do that for?" The high pitch of my voice admitted my fear. "I'll answer."

"You'd better or I'll break your jaw next time." The raspy voice was next to me now too.

Blood spewed out of my mouth when I opened it. "We wanted...we wanted to know what his work was about." It was hard to speak. "He's dead, you know?"

"What'd you find?" He was so close that every time he exhaled I got a blast of garlic up my nose.

"Just a bunch of formulas. He was studying fruits and vegetables. He never told Morgan much about what he did, so we were curious." I swallowed thick fluid. The copper taste made me gag.

"Where'd she get the notes?"

"She said her Dad was storing them there."

"Why'd you all of a sudden become friends with Dr. Elles and now his daughter?"

"He liked some of the articles I'd written and wanted to talk about them." I fought my immobilizing panic and tried to make my answers sound logical. "He was retired and had nothing better to do. He introduced me to his daughter because he thought we'd have a lot in common."

"Weren't you going to write something for your paper about Dr. Elles' research?"

"No. We never talked about that." My jaw was tightening up, making it hurt even more to speak. "Besides, I already wrote an article about all the good things Naintosa is doing for agriculture. What little I read of Dr. Elles' notes seemed to confirm that."

"What do you know about Naintosa?" A hand touched my forehead.

"I just told you. They're doing good things with farming. Dr. Elles used to work for them and he said my article was accurate." I hoped they'd buy that answer.

There was silence in the room and the hand left my forehead.

After a moment, the deep voice spoke up, "Dr. Elles had no right to have the notes and you had no right to read them. Are you aware of any other copies?"

His voice sounded vaguely familiar, but I couldn't place it. That scared me even more. Who was he? "No, I don't know of any other copies. I promise not to read anymore, all right?"

"For your own well-being and Morgan Elles', you'd better get amnesia and go on with your life like none of this ever happened."

I felt the prick of a needle in my left arm.

"What about Morg...?"

CHAPTER 12

My eyelids felt heavy and I raised them slowly.

It was dark except for a distant streetlight shining faintly through a window. I focused and saw the outline of a fireplace with pictures on the mantle. I was on Morgan's sofa.

I sat up quickly. "Ouch. Shit." My head hurt. I touched my face; my jaw was sore, right cheek swollen and tender and a tooth was loose.

Where was Morgan?

I got up and found a light switch.

The two boxes weren't on the coffee table any more. I went through the kitchen to the storage room. All the other boxes of notes were gone too.

"Morgan, are you here?"

No answer.

I cautiously went upstairs and searched, turning on every light I could find as I did. There turned out to be three bedrooms and a bathroom. Everything was neat and appeared to be in its proper place.

The master was at the end of the hall. It was tidy. Only a sapphire blue robe looked out of place. It was carelessly tossed over a white chair, in front of a dressing table with makeup on it. I touched the silky robe, as I quickly scanned the room. The emerald and teal patterned duvet was unruffled. The four post bed hadn't been slept in.

Turning off every light as I backtracked, I went downstairs to the dining room.

Examining the dark hardwood chairs, I noticed one had

scuffmarks and the finish had rubbed off part of the two front legs. That must've been the chair they'd tied me to. I sat down on it and rested my elbows on the table. "This is too much to handle."

Did they get Morgan too or had she gotten away? My memory was fuzzy, but I remembered seeing her run out the patio door before I blacked out.

I had to get out of there. The clock on the wall read 2:14am. If Morgan had escaped, I doubted she'd come back tonight.

There were a pair of keys on a hanger by the front entrance; I grabbed them. When I opened the door I examined the area around the lock. I wasn't an expert, but I couldn't see any sign of forced entry. I locked the deadbolt behind me and headed off.

The night was still and quiet. I walked tensely down the pathway to my Blazer, watching for any sign of the men who interrogated me.

There was movement in the bushes to my right. I froze and my heart jumped. I tried to sound intimidating, but all that came out was a weak, "Who's there?"

No answer.

I was about to make a run for it, when the masked face of a raccoon appeared from the bush. It stepped out onto the path and looked at me defiantly, before slowly waddling on its way. I exhaled and hoped I could make it back to my apartment without having a heart attack.

۞

I couldn't sleep at all when I got home. I was too worried about Morgan and what I'd gotten myself into.

At 7:30am I left a message on Dan's voicemail, saying I was sick and wouldn't be in. I made sure I called before he got to work. I didn't want to deal with his crap today.

I paced around my apartment all morning. Angry thoughts mixed with fear and guilt raced through me. How could those men just walk in, do what they did and get away with it? What could I have done to help protect Morgan?

Finally, I decided to write out everything I could remember about last night. As I wrote, it became clear that the questions the men had asked about Morgan meant they hadn't caught her. I put down the pen and thought about it. Or had they killed her? I didn't even want to entertain that theory.

It was time to call the cops.

At that moment the phone rang. I jumped to get it, "Hello?"

"I heard you were sick. I haven't talked to you since you went to that funeral, so I thought I'd check in. What's wrong?"

Well, it wasn't Morgan, but I was happy to hear Sue's voice. "It was a bad weekend. Do you have time to come over?"

"I can be there in an hour."

Sue would help me figure out what to do. I'd wait to call the police until after I talked to her.

⚡

When Sue arrived, I gave her a big hug before she even got through the door.

"Wow, something really bad must've happened to get a hug from you." She pulled back and examined me. "Did you get in a fight? You look like shit."

"I'll explain."

She went to the couch. "Grab a couple cold ones and tell me what happened."

"I wrote down what happened." I handed the legal pad to her and then went to the fridge. "I think you should just read it. I don't want to go over it again."

She sat back and began to read.

I handed over a beer and sat down next to her, holding the cold bottle I got for myself against my cheek. It numbed the constant dull pain.

Half way through she looked up, "Is this for real?"

"It's not fiction."

"Shit."

"Read on, it gets worse."

When she came to the end, Sue placed the pad on the coffee

table. "Wow, I can't believe that happened. Are you sure you're okay? Maybe you should go see a doctor."

"No, it's not that bad."

"Well then, you gotta go to the police. You have to find Morgan."

"Morgan and the two scientist guys told me not to go to the police."

"Screw them." Her tone was forceful. "Circumstances have changed."

I reached for my phone. "I just wanted to get your opinion first."

There was a faint knock on the door.

"Are you expecting anyone?" she asked.

I hesitated. "No."

"Maybe it's the men who interrogated you."

"They don't knock." I went to get the door and yanked it open. "Morgan, you're alive." I pulled her through the doorway in an embrace.

"You're alive, too." Morgan hugged back hard. "I was so worried. I wish I could've helped you."

"Don't worry. As long as you're safe."

I introduced Morgan and Sue. They smiled politely at each other, but there was a subtle tension. I recognized Sue's quick up and down look of sizing someone up. Morgan's face turned a pale shade of pink and she stood taller. She had a good four inches on Sue.

Even after thirty years of experience, there were things women did that were still alien to me.

I tried to steer them past whatever was going on. "So what happened?"

"Maybe I shouldn't say anything," Morgan glanced tentatively at Sue.

Sue raised her chin and her eyes narrowed. "Nick already told me his side of the events."

"I just don't want anyone else to get into trouble." Morgan turned away from Sue. "Oh Nick, your face."

"It's nothing I can't handle." I set my jaw and tried to look tough, but winced at the pain.

Sue rolled her eyes, but said nothing.

"I haven't been home yet. I hope it's still in one piece?"

"Your place is fine." I motioned toward the couch. "Come sit down."

Morgan sat down on the sofa. "So what happened?"

For whatever reason I decided to tell Morgan about the interrogation, instead of making her read it, too.

Morgan looked sympathetic throughout the story.

Sue was patient after she returned from the fridge with more beer and didn't complain about not getting the verbal version.

"I'm so sorry," Morgan said, at the end. "I feel so guilty."

"Don't." I made it sound as nonchalant as I could. "How'd you get away?"

Morgan looked at Sue again.

"You can trust her," I said. "She's my best friend."

Morgan sat back where she could see both Sue and me. "When you said run, I just bolted. I went out the door, hoping you'd follow. But when I looked back, you were lying on the floor and two men in gas masks were coming down the stairs. I thought they'd spotted me, so I ran across the street to the woods."

Sue sat forward. "Did they come after you?"

"To be honest, I'm not sure." Morgan turned pink again. "I scrambled into a gully with a dried up creek bed at the bottom and hid behind a tree in some underbrush. At times I thought I heard movement, but I couldn't see very well."

"How long did you hide for?" I asked.

"It seemed like half an hour."

Sue was frowning. "Then what'd you do?"

"I followed the dry creek bed down to the next development, snuck through someone's yard and onto the street. I was in my socks and didn't have a jacket or money." Morgan shivered. "By then it was raining hard."

"That must've sucked." Well, maybe not as much as getting tied up and beaten.

"I got lucky. I found a quarter on the sidewalk and walked until I saw a phone booth. I called a girlfriend who lives nearby and she came to get me. I was so paranoid we drove forty minutes to Edmonds and checked into a motel. I had to tell her everything." She paused for a second. "That reminds me, my friend's still waiting in her car."

I reached over and patted Morgan's shoulder. "I'm just glad you're safe." It felt awkward, so I pulled my hand away.

Out of the corner of my eye I saw Sue trying to hide a smile. That quickly turned to a questioning squint. "Hold on. How'd you know where Nick lives?"

"I looked in the phone book."

A burst of tension ran through me. Those men knew who I was, so they could find out where I lived just as easily.

Morgan shrugged. "Your buzzer's broken, but the main door was open. So I just came up."

What? I didn't know the buzzer was broken; just my horrible luck. "Did you see anyone suspicious outside?"

Morgan shook her head. "I should go tell my friend that everything's all right. Is it okay for me to let her leave?"

"Yeah, of course."

"So you'll help me get back to my place tonight? I'll need some stuff before we take off."

I stiffened. "What do you mean, take off?"

"I'll explain in a minute." She was already on her way out of the apartment.

"Are you sure you're still up for this?" Sue asked, looking hard at me. "It's too dangerous. If they find out that you're still going through Morgan's dad's notes, they could *really* hurt you."

I hesitated. The last words of the deep voiced interrogator repeated in my mind – "*You'd better get amnesia and go on with your life like none of this ever happened.*"

"They took the notes, so I don't know what we'd do. But I can't just abandon her. They might still be after her." I touched my face to remind me of how it would feel to be interrogated again.

"You like her, don't you? If you didn't, you'd run away as fast as you could." Sue had that critical look on her face. The one she always had when she judged me.

"No I wouldn't. And quit looking at me like that. Besides, she seems like a nice person." Wow, that was the best I could come up with?

"Yeah, she's a nice person with long legs, big perky boobs and a constant sultry look on her face," Sue was flat-out smirking. "Her eyes are a really unique color, though."

"Jealous, shorty?" I found myself smiling. Sue had managed to distract my inner panic for a second.

She went back to serious. "Just make sure you're doing this for the right reasons."

"What do you expect me to do?" I shrugged. "Her looks don't have anything to do with it. I'll just help her get to a safe place."

"Okay, I'm just concerned about what happens to you."

"Thanks." I reached over and gave her a hug.

"Enough," Sue said, but didn't pull away. "I don't know if I could take two hugs from you in one day."

Within a few minutes Morgan returned.

"So what's the plan?" I peered down the hall before locking the door. All clear.

Morgan made her way to the couch. "First, after dark we'll go back to my place so I can get some clothes." She gestured as she spoke, revealing two jagged fingernails with chipped red polish. That must've happened while she was scrambling around in the gully. "Second, we pick up another set of notes. Third, we drive up to a place near Ivan's. Hopefully it'll be safe to write there."

"Hold on," I said. "I thought I was just going to help you get out of trouble and what's this about another set of notes?"

"We can't stop now, Nick." Morgan looked determined. "I've talked to Ivan. He's going to start putting the formulas into layman's terms and arrange a place for us to stay."

"When did you do that?"

"I called him on my friend's cell phone on the way here." Morgan turned and our knees touched.

I felt flushed immediately, but consciously didn't pull my knee away.

"Hopefully we can stay at Ivan's friend's cabin on a lake,

about an hour and a half from where he lives. Summer's over, so no one will be around."

"I'm not sure I want to continue writing the manuscript. I'd sooner just forget all of this happened."

"Nick, can't you see that's exactly what they want you to do?" Morgan's beautiful blue eyes shone with conviction. "They're just trying to scare us so we'll stop."

"And it's working."

"I think you'll be safer going to Canada with me than staying here. What if they come after you again? They might really hurt you next time."

Sue cleared her throat. "If they really wanted to hurt Nick, they'd have already done it. I'm sure they know where he lives. Look how easy it was for you to find him. But if Nick continues to work on this, that's altogether different."

"I agree with Sue." I finally tore my eyes from Morgan's. "I'm not too big of a man to admit that I don't like pain."

Morgan took a moment to reply. Her determined look grew even stronger. "What about helping the world by exposing these criminals and preventing them from doing further damage?"

I got up, walked to the window and looked at the tree I sat next to when I meditated. Like it or not, this is what I'd been searching for; something of meaning. People would *have to* listen to this.

Was it possible to ask for a quest, then say *I don't like this, give me another one please*? No. It all solidified to me at once. Even if I didn't review much of the research yet or check out Ivan, Bill and Morgan. This was the right thing to do. I could feel it.

I turned to face the women on the couch. "Okay, let's do it."

Sue looked worried. "Nick, it's too dangerous."

I walked over and sat down on the coffee table directly in front of Sue. "I know, but you have to understand. When I picture myself going back to my old life, it feels depressing. When I think about going to Canada with Morgan and writing the manuscript, it feels exciting. This story could really help people. I don't think I'd be able to live with myself if I didn't continue." The sudden conviction I felt was good and scary at the same time. "I've got to go with my gut."

CHAPTER 13

"How many more copies of the research are there?" I asked.

Morgan raised three fingers. "Ivan has one, Bill is hiding another and one's in a safety deposit box here in Seattle. We'll get that set on our way out of town tomorrow."

Sue raised an eyebrow. "Good backup."

"Nick, you'd better pack," Morgan said. "We should get a motel room before we go get my stuff. I think it'll be safer."

"You're already giving him orders, huh." Sue smiled after she said it, but I heard the underlying cynicism in her tone.

Morgan half smiled back, but didn't say anything.

I was halfway to my bedroom when a few realities dawned on me. I turned back to Sue, "If I'm gone for a while, can you take care of my bills and rent? I'll send you the money."

"Sure, no problem."

"Oh, don't bother watering my plant." I gestured at the spider plant on the windowsill. The lone shoot hung almost to the floor, with only three green leaves at the tip. All the leaves higher up were brown and dry, waiting to fall. "If I water it before I go, I'm sure it'll be fine."

The girls looked at the plant, then each other, and shook their heads. I'd managed to relieve the uncomfortable tension in the room.

"One other thing, Sue," Morgan said. "Could we use your car tonight and can you be our lookout? If those men are watching my place, they won't recognize you or your car."

"At your service." Sue answered Morgan, but was looking at me.

꒰꒱

I locked the apartment, with a sense of finality. I had no idea when or if I'd be coming back to the life I had there.

I looked at Sue as I pressed the lobby button in the elevator. "So, for sure you remember the motel by the bank we're going to in the morning?"

"Yes, I already told you."

"Okay. Where are you parked?"

"I'm at the end of the block." As the door opened, Sue stepped out. "See you two at the motel."

At that instant, I looked through the glass entry way door and saw a gray Chevy sedan parked right across the street. Without thinking I reached out and grabbed the back of Sue's collar and pulled her hard into the elevator.

Sue's shoulders and head hit the side elevator wall. "What the fuck, Nick!"

"Morgan, move to the side."

Morgan stared in disbelief at my assertiveness, but obeyed.

"The car that's been following me is right outside the lobby." I pressed back out of sight and jammed my finger against the P button.

The elevator door began to close. A man's voice said, "Hold it."

A hand reached out to get in between the doors.

He was too late. The elevator door closed and we descended.

"Who was that?" Sue's voice was high and tight. "Was that one of them?"

I shook my head. "I didn't recognize the voice."

"I didn't notice anyone suspicious before." Morgan's voice had a tremble.

Sue rubbed the back of her head. "What do we do now?"

"Sorry if I hurt you."

"I'm okay. I'm just not used to watching my every move."

The elevator opened to the underground parking. We cautiously walked out into the open garage. As soon as the door closed behind us, the elevator began to ascend.

"We'd better get moving," Morgan said.

The light was dim and the cool musty air smelled of concrete dust. Our quick steps echoed off the walls as I led the women to my Blazer.

I opened the rear latch and flung my luggage in. "Do you think you could get to your car without them seeing you, Sue?"

"I hope so. It's a ways behind them, on the other side of the street."

"Okay, go around through the alley. If they follow you, just go home. I'll call you in an hour and we can figure out another way of meeting up."

Morgan squinted. "Be careful, Sue."

"Wish me luck." Sue jogged to the exit. She poked her head out the door, gave us the thumbs up and disappeared.

We got in my truck, drove up and onto the black hose on the concrete floor and waited for the door to rise. I never realized how slow it was before.

Inching out into the alley, the only movement we could spot was a kid dribbling a basketball near the end of the block.

"I think we're safe." Morgan's body was rigid in the seat.

Maybe it wasn't one of them trying to get into the elevator and just some guy in a hurry. If so, and they didn't notice Sue in her car, the men in the grey Chevy could sit there for days. My apartment faced the courtyard, so they couldn't see if my lights were on at night. This could be an easy getaway.

❧

"I'm sure they didn't follow me," Sue said, as she got out of her red Honda Civic in the motel parking lot. "I put on a hat and sunglasses that I had lying around. There were two guys in the car, but they didn't notice me." She sounded like she got a kick out of it.

"I'm not sure how to get into my place," Morgan said. "When I ran out I didn't take a key. Maybe the place is unlocked."

I reached into my pocket and produced a keychain with six keys. "Will one of these work?"

Morgan's dazzling blue eyes looked at me with approval. "Oh, you're an angel."

Sue gestured for us to move with the palms of her hands. "It's getting dark outside."

Morgan shot Sue an annoyed look.

I was proud of myself for having the insight to lock up Morgan's place. "Let's get a room before we go to your place."

CHAPTER 14

When we turned onto the street beside Morgan's townhome, Sue slowed down.

I pointed. "There's that Chevy. Morgan, get down."

We both put our heads in our laps as we drove by the gray car.

"I only saw one guy," Sue said. "Where do you want me to go? It's a dead end."

Morgan peered up from behind the seat. "Turn left up ahead and park in a visitor's spot."

Sue parked in an open stall. "Okay, he can't see us from here."

Morgan sat up. "The guy in the car would only have a partial view of the front of my place."

"I wonder if there's a second man?" I said.

"Hopefully not." Morgan opened the door and got out.

We snuck around the back of the complex, sticking close to the buildings and barely avoiding people's patios.

As we came to a corner, we heard voices. Morgan was in the lead and motioned for us to get down.

We ducked behind a wall of large shrubs, about forty yards from her home.

Two men were standing on the walkway to the side of her front door.

I recognized one of them immediately. He was the Lieutenant who had interviewed me at Dr. Elles' office on the night of his death. He was a tall, imposing figure, wearing the same trench coat over a suit. The other was a hefty, middle aged man, wearing khakis and a golf shirt.

"The one with the blue shirt's my neighbor," Morgan whispered. "I don't know the guy in the trench coat."

"But, you've been standing out here for awhile." The neighbor's British accent carried.

"Just waiting for Ms. Elles." The Lieutenant stuffed his hands into his dark coat pockets. "I'm a friend from out of town. Do you know where she is?"

"Don't fall for that bullshit," I said, under my breath.

The neighbor looked the man in front of him over. "Have you known her for very long?"

"I was more a friend of her father's."

"Then you must've seen her at the funeral? Didn't you tell her you'd be visiting?"

The questions were clearly irritating the Lieutenant. "Listen pal, I don't see what this has to do with you. Just go back to your home."

The neighbor wasn't backing down. "Maybe you should leave your name with me and I'll tell her you were here."

"Maybe you should mind your own business." He took a step toward the neighbor.

The neighbor didn't budge. "Perhaps I should call the police."

Sue crouched even lower. "This doesn't look good."

A man wearing a gray suit and carrying a briefcase walked up to the two men. "Hey Harry, everything all right?"

"I'm not sure Walter. This fellow's been standing outside Morgan's place for quite some time. He claims to be her friend, but he certainly doesn't act like it."

The Lieutenant gave Harry a poisonous glare. "I'll try back later." He strode off toward where the gray Chevy was parked.

"That was odd. Thanks for coming up when you did, Walter. He didn't seem like a very nice chap."

"Well, I heard you say something about calling the police, so I thought you might need some help."

"Thanks, mate. Let's keep an eye out for that guy."

"You've got nice neighbors," Sue whispered to Morgan.

"Most of the people here are really friendly and look out for each other." Morgan pointed to a large row of mailboxes about seventy yards away. "Sue, can you go over there and see where the guy went? Act like you're checking your mail."

"Sure." She looked over at me, then stood up and walked over to the boxes trying to look as casual as possible. She pretended to open one as she glanced over her left shoulder.

Still acting relaxed on her way back, Sue ruined the effect by tripping up on a loose stone on the sidewalk. Luckily she recovered quickly.

Back beside us she squatted down. Her accusing frown dared me to smile. I couldn't help but grin a little, even under those circumstances.

"It looks like he's back in the gray car."

"Okay, sneak back and hide behind the mailboxes to keep an eye on them." Morgan stood up. "We'll go get my things."

Sue saluted Morgan and crept back over to the boxes. Once in position, she gave us the okay signal.

We moved quickly around the bushes and plants to Morgan's front door. Inside we headed directly upstairs to her bedroom. I stumbled trying to keep up with her in the dark.

"Grab my duffle bag out of the closet," Morgan said, as she clicked on a small lamp on her dresser.

Within a minute the bag was stuffed with clothes and toiletries.

"That should be enough," Morgan said. "I need jackets and shoes from the hall closet. Follow me."

Half way down the stairs we heard the thud of the front door closing and the click of the lock.

We froze.

Sue came bolting by and tripped down the three stairs to the living room.

"What the hell?" I raced down to her, pulling the duffle bag with me.

She jumped to her feet. "They're right behind me."

I could hear a rough pull on the front door.

Morgan went past us and flung the patio door open. "Come on." She made sure to lock it behind us.

Sue and I ran behind Morgan through the maze of a courtyard.

We rounded the side of the building, in full view of the two men. Only a hundred feet separated us.

The Lieutenant turned and made direct eye contact with me.

"Oh fuck," I gasped.

We sprinted. Morgan's long legs could really move. Sue kept pace with sheer will and athleticism. I kept snagging the duffle bag on small trees and plants, but managed to muscle my way through.

By the time we reached the car we'd distanced ourselves from our pursuers.

Sue fumbled and dropped her keys.

I motioned toward the approaching men. "Hurry, they're coming."

"I know! Shit." She finally unlocked the doors.

I flung the front seat down and jammed the duffle bag into the back. With one hand I pushed the seat back upright and with the other I pulled Morgan onto my lap as I got in. She hit her head on the door jam, but managed to wedge herself inside.

The engine lit and revved.

I hit the door lock with my elbow, just as the men got to us. "Go, go, go!"

Sue turned the wheel, reversed, and clipped the man grabbing the door handle. He twisted around the side of the car and the bumper took his legs out from under him.

The Lieutenant reached into his coat.

Sue ground the gears into first and pushed the pedal to the floor. The tires spun on the wet pavement, then caught with a loud squeal. Our heads flew back by the sudden traction.

Then, the windows exploded.

Morgan screamed and pushed back hard against me.

"They're shooting at us," Sue cried out.

Glass sprayed everywhere. The bullet passed right through, blowing out both side windows.

I'd never been shot at before. I was terrified, but my mind registered tiny details. A shard of glass landed on my shoulder. It was square, except for a protruding point. I turned my attention to the passenger side mirror and saw the Lieutenant.

He was picking up the man on the ground. The pistol was still in his right hand. It looked like a silver cannon.

"Turn right at the intersection, then left at the next." Morgan's tone was calm, but I could feel her trembling. "Is everyone okay? Sue your hand is bleeding."

"I'm okay." I'd never seen Sue's eyes so wide. "A piece of glass cut it."

"Look this way." Morgan turned her head toward me. She had three small cuts on her face and blood was starting to trickle down. One cut on her cheek still had glass in it. "Your face is cut."

She pulled down the visor and looked in the mirror. "Hell." She pulled the glass out of her cheek and threw it out the window.

"There are tissues in the glove box." Sue was looking in the rearview mirror. "I can't see them, so I'm heading for the motel."

A police car passed us in the opposite direction, lights flashing.

"My neighbors must've called them." Morgan pulled out a tissue and held it to her right cheek.

My legs finally noticed the weight of Morgan's body. They were turning numb, but at that moment I really didn't care.

Sue's voice trembled. "Those men are going to have to stay out of sight if the police show up. It'll buy us time."

"I can't believe they actually shot at us." My own voice wasn't so steady.

Sue braked for a corner. "This is serious."

"I'm sorry I got you two into this."

"It's too late now," Sue responded.

I could hear the note of defensiveness in Sue's voice. I wanted to say something to support Morgan, but Sue was in shock and worried about me.

Morgan just looked straight ahead.

❧

Once in the motel room, the girls went into the bathroom to clean up their cuts.

I went to the desk and found a piece of motel stationery and a pen. My hands were vibrating in jerks and it was difficult to keep the pen on the paper. I was shaken right down to my central nervous system. I used both hands and scribbled: Dr. Ivan Popov, Dr. William Clancy and Morgan Elles. I roughly folded the paper and put it into my pocket.

I could hear the girls talking, so I sat down on the edge of the nearest bed and listened.

"You know, Morgan, this could've been a lot more serious."

"Yeah Sue, I know."

"Is it really worth it?"

"There's nothing more important in my life."

"Except your life."

It was quiet for a moment before Morgan changed the subject. "You need to get a four door car. Nick banged my head pretty good when he pulled me in."

When I leaned forward I could see them in the bathroom mirror.

Morgan finished sticking three small bandages on her face.

"I wish I could be as calm as you," Sue said.

"Believe me I'm not so calm on the inside."

Sue placed a bandage on her hand and removed pieces of glass from her hair. "I better get my car out of here. It looks suspicious."

As Sue came out of the bathroom, I sat up straight. "Where are you planning to go?"

"I'll spend the night at my parents. My dad has a shop vac and I can leave the car in their garage."

"Sounds good."

Sue turned to Morgan and gave her a weak hug. As Sue pulled away, she gave Morgan a stern look. "You better get him back safe."

Morgan stared straight back. "I'll do my best."

I got up and walked Sue outside.

"You sure about this?" Sue squeezed hard as she hugged me. "Last chance."

"Like you said earlier, it's too late now." I pulled back. "What about you? Are you going to be okay?"

"They're after you, not me. I should be all right."

I took the paper from my pocket. "Can you do me a favor and see if you can find out any information on them?"

She read the names. "I'll do a background check."

"I appreciate it. This all happened so fast, I didn't have time to do it myself."

Sue gave me a reflective smile. "Remember what I said; keep in touch so I know you're safe."

"I'll call you when I can." I forced a grin to try hide how uneasy I felt.

When I came back into the room, Morgan was getting into a bed fully dressed. Her moist eyes indicated she'd been crying. "Good night." She pulled the covers over herself and turned away.

⚓

I tossed and turned, thinking about what'd happened, anxious about what was to come.

I looked over at the silhouette in the other bed. I barely knew Morgan, yet here I was going on a dangerous journey with her. We had to put our lives in each other's hands.

She opened her eyes and looked over at me. Even though she didn't say a word, I knew she was thinking the same thing.

CHAPTER 15

I poked at the unfinished scrambled eggs on my plate. It felt like a thousand bats were flying around in my stomach. My hands jerked in an uncontrolled spasm every few moments. I knew Morgan had noticed, but hadn't commented on it. I was a wreck inside; thinking about how we were almost killed last night and anxious about the trip ahead of us.

"I guess I'm just not hungry." Morgan pushed her fresh fruit plate and half eaten bagel to the side. She lifted her cup with two hands. The coffee inside rippled with vibration.

She'd taken the bandages off her face before we'd left the room and had done her best to cover the cuts with makeup. The one on her left cheek, where the glass had been imbedded, was still noticeable. It looked like it stung. Hopefully it wouldn't leave a scar.

"It's almost nine. Let's go, Nick."

Before we left the motel parking lot, I scanned the street around us. No gray car or suspicious looking men.

It was already warm, with a high overcast sky. I wondered what the weather in Canada would be like.

It was only a block to the bank.

"I'll only be a minute." Morgan had the door open before I fully stopped.

"Aren't you going to need help with all the boxes?" I asked.

"Oh, you thought it was on paper, like the original set?"

"Ah, yeah."

"My father spent the last few months putting it on disks. He hadn't finished, so we've lost some of it. Unfortunately I don't know what part." Morgan closed the Blazer door harder than she needed to.

She wore a jean jacket. Her backside had a wiggle under her short white skirt, as she walked in her platform sandals to the bank's front glass doors.

After Morgan went inside, I watched the street.

I wondered what had happened after we left Morgan's place last night. Were the Lieutenant and his partner still there when the police arrived? Was the Lieutenant really a cop? Not likely. Had they been arrested? Could the police be looking for us now?

I felt some relief I hadn't gone to the police. Ivan and Bill were right; we couldn't trust anyone right now. Disappearing to a safe place really was the best thing. I hoped Dr. Elles notes would give us some insight on how to get out of this mess.

"Did everything go all right?" I asked, when Morgan returned after ten minutes. "Did you get the disks?"

"Yep." She opened her jacket and revealed a small carrying case with around ten disks in it. "I also changed some money into Canadian, so we'll blend in better. The Canadian dollar sure is cheap. It's almost half price. We'll be able to last a long time up there."

My hand spasmed as I shifted the vehicle into drive.

Morgan looked sympathetic. "Are you going to be okay?"

"My body's never reacted like this before."

"We're both on edge."

We got on the I-5 heading north.

"We have to stop at the mall in Bellingham and buy two laptops," Morgan said.

"I didn't even think of that, great." Then I remembered, "Shit, I forgot to call work."

"You better take care of that." Morgan reached for her black bag on the floor and pulled out a cell phone. "I'd better call my friend and tell her we're taking off. She's the one who dropped me off at your place."

Morgan got a hold of her friend and told her she was leaving, but didn't say where she was going.

I obviously wasn't thinking straight, because it didn't dawn on me until she ended her conversation, that cell phones were traceable.

"Here, call your boss." She held out the phone.

"I don't think that's a good idea. I'm sure the guys we're dealing with are sophisticated enough to trace calls."

Morgan looked at the phone for a second. "I'm new at this." She opened the window and flung it out. "Why didn't you tell me sooner?"

I looked in the rearview mirror and saw the phone burst into pieces as it bounced on the pavement. "Sorry, I didn't realize that until you'd finished talking." The way she disposed of it jarred me.

She looked at the road ahead and took a deep breath.

❧

In less than an hour, we reached Bellingham.

It had turned out to be a nice fall day. The sun poked through the clouds and even in a parking lot you could smell the cool scents of the seasons changing.

"There's a computer store." Morgan pointed. "Go find a phone, then meet me in there." Before I could answer, she walked off.

She could be kind of bossy, I thought, as I proceeded to a bank of pay phones.

I stood there with the receiver in my hand, not a hundred percent sure I knew what I was going to say. Asking for a leave of absence with no notice wasn't going to go over well. "Well, here goes nothing."

"Hello, Dan here."

"Hi Dan, it's Nick."

"Where the hell are you? It's almost eleven."

"It's a long story and I'm really sorry for the short notice." I wanted to get straight to the point. "Is it possible to take a six month leave of absence?"

"Starting when?"

"Now."

"What? Are you crazy? You can't just take a leave of absence without any warning. We have to find a replacement and I have to get the publisher's approval. And you need a good reason."

"I know. Normally…"

"If you know, then why are you doing this? I'm fucking busy. I can't just drop everything."

"Sorry, but…"

"Sorry my ass. Get your big butt down here right now. Then if you really work hard for a few months and quit sulking around, I'll think about giving you a leave of absence."

"But I can't wait a few months." His confrontational, mocking, high-pitched whine was pissing me off.

"What? Do you need to *find yourself*? Do you want us to write a letter to all of our readers and tell them that there will be no more papers until Nick gets in touch with his feelings and discovers his inner child? This is a business and I expect you to act professionally."

"Well then do whatever you want. I can't come in right now. I'm out of town on a personal emergency."

"I'm going to talk to the publisher. Call me back in two hours." He hung up.

What a little prick. He was justified in being mad, because of the short notice, but that tone and abuse was totally uncalled for. What an ass. I walked over to the computer store, muttering obscenities under my breath. The good thing was that focusing on Dan had managed to distract me and my hands had stopped jerking.

Morgan was browsing with a salesman in tow.

The guy must've thought that when he'd rolled up the sleeves of his white dress shirt that he meant business. But he was so skinny that his brown belt couldn't hold the shirt tucked into his tan slacks. So the shirt was half hanging out in the back.

When she saw me, Morgan pointed to a laptop on display. "Rick here says he can give us a super deal if we buy two of these."

"I bet he can." I looked Rick straight in the eyes, while thinking, don't you screw with us.

Rick took a step backward and gave me a nervous grin.

Morgan looked closely at me. "The call didn't go so well, huh?"

I shrugged. "Whatever. I'll tell you about it later."

She gave me a sympathetic smile. "Okay."

Rick cleared his throat. "Is there anything else you need?"

"How about a printer?" I said.

Morgan nodded. "Yeah, we need a printer."

"Morgan, do we really need two computers?"

"How else are we going to be able to work at the same time?"

When we got out to the parking lot, Morgan faced me. "Tell me about your call? You obviously got through to your boss?"

"I talked to him, but I didn't get through to him." I muscled the wheel of the cart with our purchases out of a groove in the pavement.

"That bad? How did it end?"

"I'm supposed to call him back in two hours for a verdict. I'm sure he's checking with the publisher and the company's lawyers, to see if they can legally fire me."

"You can call him once we get across the border." Morgan looked consoling. "I'm sure it'll all work out."

As we continued to walk, it sunk in that it didn't really matter if I got the leave of absence or not. I'd go through the motions and call Dan back, out of courtesy; even though he didn't deserve it. What did matter was that I'd committed to a dangerous project that I might not be able to handle and now couldn't get out of, even if I wanted to.

We hid the boxes containing the computers and printer under the luggage in the back of the Blazer. They didn't usually search vehicles at the Canadian border. We just wanted to avoid any hassles of having to explain why we were bringing brand new equipment across.

Once we were back onto the I-5, there was very little traffic.

I figured it was a good time to fill Morgan in. "Remember when I told you about the night I found your father? There was the Lieutenant guy who showed up before the paramedics?"

She turned to look at me. "Yeah, you thought he was acting strange. He just disappeared, right?"

"Yeah. The guy that was standing in front of your door, the one that shot at us last night, was the Lieutenant."

Her blue eyes opened wide. "Why didn't you tell me this before?"

"Sorry, I guess I needed time to internally process it."

"So what you're saying is that you think the guys chasing us are cops?"

"I'm not sure. They could be bad cops or the guy could've been posing as a Lieutenant. He could actually be the one responsible for your father's death."

Morgan gasped and her face drained of color. She slowly turned to face forward.

I left her alone to absorb the information before I told her the last part. Morgan had been trying to act strong through this whole ordeal, but her shield was breaking down. I wondered how much longer she'd be able to hold everything in, before she lost it.

After a few minutes she turned back to look at me. "He was asking you questions to see how much you knew. He could've killed you if he thought you knew too much."

"Probably, I mean, if the paramedics hadn't shown up when they did."

"Wow."

"I'm pretty sure I recognized the Lieutenant's voice when I was being interrogated at your place, too."

"It's starting to make more sense," she said. "But, is he a cop or does he work for Naintosa?"

"Or both?" I looked in my rear view mirror and watched a large, dark SUV coming up behind us. Something about it didn't feel right. I tensed and stopped listening to what Morgan was saying.

I sped up and passed two cars. The SUV followed.

I moved into the right lane and slowed down to the speed limit. They did the same. "They're not being subtle."

"What do you mean?" Morgan asked.

"I might be being paranoid, but I think they've found us."

She jumped up in her seat. "Where?"

"Behind us. That black Suburban caught up to us really fast. Now it's just following."

"I was wondering why you were speeding up and then slowing down." She looked in her side passenger mirror. "But it's not a grey Chevy."

"They could've changed vehicles."

"We're almost at the border. What should we do if it's really them?" She unhooked her seatbelt and twisted around to look back. "I can't make out the drivers' face through the tinted windows."

"This may sound weird to you, but I can feel that it's those thugs." My palms were sweating.

"Let's not take any chances."

I sped up and watched the Suburban speed up as well.

"This might work." I stopped pressing the gas and coasted, focusing on the exit coming up.

The vehicle was almost on our back bumper.

"Hold on." At the last second before we would've passed the turn off, I hammered the gas pedal and cranked the wheel to the right. The tires howled and began to lose their grip on the road, but we managed to make the exit. We hit a curb with our back left tire, throwing us sliding to the right across the road and onto the gravel shoulder. I just got control of the slide before we went off the road. The Blazer straightened out.

"Hell." Morgan had been bounced into the door pretty hard. She was hugging the seat, looking back. "You did it."

I looked in the rearview mirror. No black Suburban.

Morgan turned around. "Where are we going?" She fumbled with the seatbelt.

"We're going to another crossing. My dad used to go this way when there was too much traffic at the main one. It goes around Blaine. It won't put us far off track."

We pulled into the line-up at the Pacific Highway Border Crossing.

I kept looking in the rearview mirror and within minutes saw the black Suburban at the last intersection before the line.

It turned toward the border, but pulled over onto the shoulder of the road.

"What are they doing?" Morgan was watching her side mirror.

The line inched forward.

"How'd they find us?" she asked.

"Did you use your credit card to pay for the computers?"

"Yes." She thought for a second. "They couldn't trace us that quickly?"

"I'm not sure, but don't use your credit cards anymore." Then it dawned on me. "It was the cell call."

Morgan frowned and looked upset at herself. "I promise to be more careful."

I couldn't fault her for it. "Like you said, we're new at this."

"No more cell phones and if we make it to Vancouver I'll get more cash."

I felt a bead of sweat run from my left temple into my ear. "Do you have a plan for that?"

"I have a second account all set up. After I get more money in Vancouver, we'll use that account when we need more. They can't trace it to me."

"What do you mean?"

"Don't worry, some things it's best you don't know about."

"You have a lot of money?"

"You know my parents were well off."

"I'd guessed." I didn't want to pry and ask how much, so I thought we'd leave it at that.

The vehicle in front of us moved a car length up and I followed.

"Look, the door's opening." Morgan hadn't taken her eyes off the side mirror.

A man got out of the driver side of the Suburban. He lifted a pair of binoculars and pointed them in our direction.

"I can't tell if that's the Lieutenant," I said, leaning forward to get a closer view through my mirror. "He's too far away, but his build seems the same."

"I bet it's him," Morgan said.

"It's like this time he *wants* us to know they were onto us."

"You mean to scare us?" Morgan turned to look at me. "Nick, your hands."

I was gripping the steering wheel so hard they'd turned white. I let go and shook them to regain feeling.

Within a few more minutes we were one vehicle away from the customs booth. The man with the binoculars got back in the Suburban. The SUV waited until there was an opening, did a u turn and disappeared.

"There might be someone waiting for us on the other side," Morgan said.

"That's what I was thinking."

After showing our I.D.'s and telling the border guard we were going on a week's vacation to Vancouver, she let us through without any problems.

As we drove off, I glanced at Morgan. There was a tear running down her left cheek. She quickly wiped it away.

I hoped we were going to make it through this.

CHAPTER 16

I was nervous and hyper-watchful. We had a few close traffic calls because I kept looking in the rear view mirror. Morgan held on tightly, but didn't complain; even when I almost rear-ended a semi. But we didn't encounter any suspicious vehicles on the way into Vancouver.

"Let's find a place downtown where there are more people and underground parking," Morgan said. "Easier to get lost."

Once in the downtown core it didn't take long to find a place to stay.

The hotel was a twelve story concrete tower. The lobby was finished in oak, brass, and tinted green glass. The accents were all decorated in shades of green. Since the name of the hotel was O'Sullivan's it was fitting to have green everywhere.

We were on the ninth floor in a two bedroom suite with a small living area. It was clean, comfortable and also very green.

"This is pretty fancy for being on the run," I said.

"I just figured that since we don't know each other well and we might be here for a while, we might want our own bedrooms. We can afford some comfort."

We stepped out onto the balcony into the crisp fall air.

Morgan crossed her arms and shivered. "The view's beautiful. I've never seen Vancouver from this vantage point."

"Yeah, it's a pretty cool place."

"It's like Seattle, but somehow more vibrant."

"Do you know what we're looking at?" I asked.

"Not really. You tell me, Mr. Geographer."

"My Dad loved Vancouver and took me sightseeing all

over." I pointed, "That's Stanley Park on the left. Straight ahead is Burrard Inlet and on the other side is the North Shore. See that mountain with the ski runs?"

"Grouse Mountain?" She smiled.

"Yep."

"Too bad we won't have time to go up there."

"Speaking of time." I glanced at my watch. "It's been over two hours. I'd better call work and see where my fate lies." I didn't want to do it, but needed to.

"Good luck." Morgan stayed on the balcony. "And try your best to be calm."

"I will." Emotional advice from Morgan was going to take some getting used to. I even had trouble listening to Sue when she made those kind of comments.

A bank of pay phones was in a hallway just to the right of the lobby.

Sharon, the editorial receptionist, told me to hold. I was forced to listen to a recording of the *News'* virtues while I waited.

The pre-taped voice suddenly cut off. "Nick?"

"Hi, Dan. Before you say anything, I just want to tell you I'm sorry for any inconvenience I've caused."

"It's a little late for that." He hadn't calmed down, but there was restraint in his voice. "I spoke with the publisher and one of our lawyers. They feel it's best to grant your leave of absence. But just between us, this isn't what I want. I'm giving your beat to Steve. If and when you get back, you'll start from the bottom. You got that?"

"No problem." I didn't have far to fall. "Thanks for giving me the leave of absence." I was being as polite as possible. One part of me didn't care, the other wanted to say; kiss my butt.

"Good. For our records, type out a request and fax it to me, from wherever the hell you are. In addition, if you do any freelancing for a competitor or are doing something illegal, it'll be my pleasure to fire your sorry ass."

"Why would you say that?"

"A cop came into the office looking for you first thing this morning."

"What did he want?" A sharp pang of fear raced through my body. My mouth went dry. "What'd you tell him?" It had to have been the Lieutenant.

"I told him the truth; that I didn't know where you were and you were late for work."

I tried to keep my voice calm. "Did he ask any other questions?"

"Just standard background ones, like how long you've worked here."

"What did he look like? Did you get his name?"

"Tall guy, with a scar. I didn't pay attention to what his I.D. said. Is there something you're not telling me?"

The Lieutenant. "He's probably just after me for all my parking tickets. You know they're clamping down on that." That was lame.

"Uhuh, sure." He paused and I visualized a light bulb go on over his head. "If there's a story in whatever you're doing, you'd better give it to me first. If you submit stories from time to time, I may make it easier on you when you get back."

"Sure, I'll keep in touch." That wasn't honest.

"Right then." He hung up.

When I got back to the room, Morgan looked over from the sofa in the sitting area where she was watching TV. "So, what happened?"

"I got the leave of absence, but he's pissed and going to make my life a living hell if I go back."

"It sounds like he was making your life a living hell up until now anyway."

I stopped in my tracks. "Good point."

"Then there's no use stressing out about it."

"Except that he said that a cop came in looking for me this morning."

Morgan clicked the TV off. "What did he want?"

"Dan told him that he didn't know where I was. Then he asked a few background questions and left."

Morgan's eyes showed concern. "It had to be the Lieutenant guy."

"Yeah, that's what I think too."

"Do you know what time it was?"

"Dan said, first thing. So, around nine, I guess."

Morgan thought for a moment. "He would've had time to catch up to us afterward."

CHAPTER 17

In the morning, Morgan went to get more cash.

My job was to get both new computers set up. As I waited for each part to load, I thumbed through Dr. Elles' disks, trying to figure out if there was a beginning or an order to them. The titles didn't help.

When the computers were finally ready, I randomly loaded a disk. It was full of formulas that might as well have been written in Swahili.

Flipping through the disks again, I saw that one contained the word *overview* in part of the title. I put it into the drive.

It contained some of Dr. Elles' thoughts on Naintosa and his research. One long paragraph caught my eye. It read: *I fear the actions taken by Naintosa regarding my team's research contradict everything we believe in and dishonor our work. They are not trying to help people by making food safer and crops grow faster. They want control. By falsifying results and planting the genetically altered seeds before they are properly tested, Naintosa could cause a worldwide catastrophe. When these crops are introduced into the food chain, they will cross-pollinate with the unaltered crops in the surrounding areas. The altered crops will eventually choke out the unaltered crops. Once in the food chain, you cannot recall genetically engineered organisms back to the laboratory.*

I sat back, feeling the frustration in the words. That was really disturbing. It's no wonder Naintosa wanted to keep this information a secret. And what exactly did Naintosa want *control* of?

A few paragraphs later, he made another profound

statement: *The long-term effect on humans and animals eating food grown from genetically engineered seed is inconclusive at this time. However, early results point in one specific direction. The findings show that a lack of nutrients combined with the chemical compositions compromise people's immune systems, making them more susceptible to disease.*

"But why?" I said, aloud. I knew I was missing most of the pieces to the puzzle. Reading this made me want to know more.

It was hard to believe that Naintosa or any company for that matter would knowingly introduce something into the environment that would make people more susceptible to disease. What was their reasoning?

I stared at the computer screen, as if waiting for it to answer my thoughts. That was when the book started to take shape in my mind. If I could figure out how to make the research more interesting and surround it with statements like the ones I had just looked at, it could read like a scientific thriller.

I made a file on the computer's hard drive and started copying information for the manuscript notes.

🖘

"I got a bunch of cash and some traveler's checks." Morgan placed her black leather bag and a white paper shopping bag on the table. The white cotton turtleneck and form fitting jeans she wore accentuated all her curves.

I tried not to stare. "Aren't traveler's checks traceable?" I suddenly felt like a slob in my sweat pants and t-shirt with a tear under my right arm pit.

"I don't think so."

"Let's use cash until we find out, okay?" I wished I knew more about that kind of stuff.

"Fine, I'll ask if Ivan knows."

I motioned to her. "Come here a second."

"Did you find something?"

"Uhuh. Read this." I got up from the chair and let her sit to read the information I had transferred.

As she read her eyes grew wide, "You see why it's so important that we write this thing?"

"I may be stupid, but I keep asking myself why Naintosa would purposely do something like this?"

"It's called money."

"How are they going to make lots of money by ruining the environment and making people sick?"

"We'll probably know by the time we finish going through the notes."

Morgan moved to the chair at the opposite side of the desk and randomly chose a disk to load onto her computer. "Thanks for getting these going."

"No problem." I sat back down in front of the computer that was to be mine.

"How about I write down a summary of what I find on the disks I look at," she said. "That'll help you save some time organizing."

"Good, then I can transfer what I need to the hard drive."

We got to work...or at least I did. Morgan seemed to have trouble concentrating. She kept shifting in her chair and glancing out the window. It was distracting.

She suddenly stood up. "I have to call my boyfriend."

Her quick movement made me flinch. "You haven't talked too much about him." I guessed that what I saw as fidgeting was really her psyching herself up.

"He's not around a lot."

"That's right; you said he's a flight engineer for an airline."

"We're not that serious." She'd been fiddling around, pushing a flat shoe back and forth with her toes. She slipped it on. "This is more important. I guess it's time to end it." She sounded so nonchalant about it.

"Does he know what's going on?"

"I tried to explain, but he's preoccupied with his ex-wife." She went to her bag. "Do you have any Canadian quarters for the pay phone?"

"Call him collect." I smiled at my wit.

"Yeah, right."

My wallet and some change were on the desk beside me. "Here are a few." I handed her some quarters. "Good luck."

After Morgan left I took the laptop to my bed, propped up the pillows and delved into the flax experiments.

⚬

"Working hard, I see."

I opened my eyes. Morgan stood in the doorway. I must've dozed off. I needed to be sitting in a chair when I read the experiments from now on. "Just resting my eyes."

"Yeah, sure." Morgan smiled. "I talked to Ivan. The cabin's ready. We can leave in the morning. He gave me the directions."

"Great." I got off the bed to get my map of British Columbia from my suitcase. "What about your boyfriend?"

"It's over. He didn't seem too sad. I think he's doing a stewardess on the side."

"That's too bad." I unfolded the map.

"Oh, whatever." Morgan came and sat on the bed next to where I was laying out the map. She gave an audible exhale and dropped her hands into her lap.

I knew she was trying to sound like she didn't care, but there was sadness on her face. I felt a sense of relief.

We plotted our course and figured it'd take approximately six hours. We had to go half way across the province.

That was a long way to be looking in the rearview mirror. I hoped Morgan was up for the experience. I wondered if I was.

CHAPTER 18

*P*erched atop a high cliff, I watched the dizzying rush of white water churning past on both sides. Behind me, it fell into the cool, moist vapor. I had no control over my body, as my arms spread, knees bent, and back arched. I pushed off, backwards. Sky bright, sun glistening, rocks coal black and trees luminous green. Paralyzed, I fell into the mist. Droplets of water on my naked body streaked away as I gained momentum...

I opened my eyes with a gasp and placed my hand over my pounding heart. What a dream. *Jump and trust* was the first thought that came into my mind.

The clock read 6:08am. I could hear Morgan in the shower.

I put on a hotel robe and walked out onto the balcony. The city was waking below, but the mountains in the distance were only a charcoal gray outline in the early October pre-dawn.

I made myself comfortable on a patio chair, closed my eyes and focused. I visualized the special sanctuary I'd created when I was first taught to meditate. The inner me sat down on my favorite leather recliner floating in the middle of the cosmos. I relaxed. Soon, even the sound of my breathing faded away.

After about twenty minutes I came out of my meditation, feeling calm.

Out in the harbor, a float plane left a silvery wake behind it as it took off. I thought about my dream. To me, it meant I had to release my fear and jump into this project hoping everything was going to turn out for the best. We'd embarked

on a quest. It sounded melodramatic, but at least I was thinking positively – like my old self.

We were on the road by 8:00am. Within twenty minutes
we were traveling on the Trans Canada highway. We kept
checking to see if we were being followed, but nothing seemed
out of the ordinary.

Within an hour and a half we were out of the Fraser Valley,
heading up into the sharp peaked mountains. Large cedar and
hemlock trees closed in on both sides of the highway.

We'd hardly said a word up until then. Morgan broke the
silence. "So you meditate?"

"I used to meditate almost every day." I checked once more
in the rearview mirror. "I'm trying to get back into it."

"Hmm, interesting."

"What do you mean?"

"Nothing...just that a thirty year old, single, American
man that meditates is kind of different."

"Do you think that the only people who meditate are sages
on mountain tops and Buddhists?"

She smiled. "No, it's just that most guys your age have other interests."

"I have those interests." I heard the defensive tone in my
voice. A memory of my *used to be* golf buddy Mark flashed
across my mind. He once tried to discredit me in front of a girl
we both wanted to impress. He called me "Buddha boy" and
"Ohm." I told myself Morgan was just asking and I shouldn't
get bent up about it. "Meditation just helps me focus and
think clearer. Which is something I need right now."

Her smile broadened. "Oh, so you can focus on your other
interests with more clarity."

"Precisely." I decided to explain more and see how she reacted. "Meditation also helps me get answers to questions."

"Hmm...how?"

"You know how your mind is always filled with chatter; all
kinds of thoughts racing through your head at the same time?"

"You mean when you have a lot on your mind?"

"Exactly. Meditation's a way of clearing your thoughts. So, when you have questions, if your mind is calm you can pick up the answers easier. Otherwise, the answers come, but your head's too full of other stuff and you miss them."

"I didn't know that." She paused. "Where do you think the answers come from?"

"I picture them coming from a big, cosmic library."

"Interesting concept." She gave me a look that implied she wasn't quite sure if I was joking or serious.

I didn't want her to think I was crazy. "I haven't totally figured it all out yet. That's just how I envision it."

The road climbed to the Hope Slide. I'd heard it happened in the mid sixties. It was one of the largest landslides in Canadian history. The mountain remaining was sheer, stripped of vegetation. The part that came down had covered the entire valley floor. Trees and underbrush now hid the devastation. Past it the valley narrowed. The highway wound upward, with parts cut right into cliff faces.

Morgan glanced over at me. "Can you teach me how to meditate when we get to the cabin?"

"Sure." I was happy she was open to it.

We watched the rushing stream next to the road as we drove through Manning Park. The trees were a patchwork green, orange, yellow and red. Fresh snow gleamed on the summits.

After we went through the Coastal Mountain Range, we came down into Princeton. A large sawmill stood right in the heart of the town. The climate had become drier; no longer lush, like the coast had been.

From there the road followed a narrow, rocky, river valley to Keremeos. It was a small village with a grocery store and a pub as its focal points. The surrounding area was covered with orchards.

Then the road climbed again and the trees became sparse. We'd entered high desert country. Green-gray sagebrush covered the landscape.

We came over the crest of a hill and saw a beautiful oasis

below. A deep blue lake sparkled amidst groves of fruit trees and vineyards. A Spanish themed village sat on the west shore.

A road sign said, *Welcome to Osoyoos.*

I tried to pronounce it, "Os...oye...oos. That right?"

"How would I know?" Morgan shrugged. "Pretty, how most of the buildings are white, with the rounded corners. It's a touch of Mexico in Canada."

We pulled into a gas station. Morgan went inside to use the restroom while I filled the tank. Just as I finished, a gray Chevy pulled over and parked a short distance away. I could make out Washington plates. My heart jumped. Holy shit, that couldn't be? How did they find us?

I turned and saw Morgan walking back to the truck. I waved my hand frantically at my side, hoping to get only her attention.

She stopped and looked at me like I was an idiot. Then she realized I was serious and hurried to the truck. "What's wrong?"

I pointed behind me. "That car, over there."

She peered around the back of the Blazer. "Are you sure it's them?"

"The car looks exactly the same, but I couldn't make out who was inside when it drove by." I was still holding the gas nozzle. "I know there're lots of those cars around, I just don't want to take any chances."

Morgan thought for a second. "Let's start driving and see if they follow us."

"Okay." I replaced the nozzle. Then as casually as I could, walked over to the station store and paid for the gas.

The gray car hadn't moved.

"Which way do we go?" Morgan fidgeted in her seat.

"If we drive away in the opposite direction, they'll have to turn around on the street. That'll give us a head start."

We pulled out and turned left at the intersection.

Morgan watched. "Their backup lights are on. They're pulling out."

We lost sight of the car when the road jagged. That was the perfect time to get off the main road. We turned right, into a residential area. We went right again at the end of one block and then left twice. After a few more streets we reached the lake. A left turn took us gradually back to the main highway.

Morgan turned to face forward. "I think we lost them."

I checked the rear view mirror again. "If that was even them."

We were stuck behind an old one ton truck carrying crates of apples. After a few slow moving minutes it turned off on the outskirts of town.

I sped up and drove as fast as I could without drawing the attention of any passing police cars. We climbed up the steep, winding highway. The engine worked hard and I had to concentrate to navigate the switchbacks.

"Every time we start to relax, even for a second, they come after us." Morgan placed her hands over her eyes and leaned her head back against the seat. "Hell."

My mind said we were wrong about the gray Chevy and had overreacted. The knot in my stomach wasn't listening.

We got over the mountain and followed another river valley, then up over another pass. The whole way I pushed the Blazer harder than it was meant to be driven. There was a lot of lean in the corners and twice the tires squealed.

After over an hour, we turned a corner and saw a long valley with a town spread out in the middle of it. Descending, we passed a large sign with caricatures of Russian peasants dancing. It read *Welcome to Grand Forks*.

"This is where Ivan said to stop, get supplies and call him before we go to the cabin," Morgan said.

The town had an old-fashioned quaintness. The sun shone on large maples lining the main street, their orange and red leaves gently falling in the breeze. Behind the trees were blocks of heritage homes with the occasional newer structure mixed in.

We stopped at a small strip mall that had a supermarket. I followed Morgan over to a phone booth. It was at the corner of the parking lot, facing the street. I watched the road while trying to listen to her.

She told Ivan about seeing what may have been *the* car in Osoyoos. I gathered by the tone of Morgan's "uhuh's" that

Ivan was concerned. She reached into the black bag hanging from her shoulder and pulled out a pad.

Watching the road, I noticed the vast majority of vehicles on the street were pickups.

"The cabin is ready," Morgan said, stepping out of the booth.

Just then I spotted a gray Chevy coming up the street from the same direction we'd come. "Oh shit, look."

We watched the car stop at the intersection. It waited for a truck to pass in the opposite direction, before it turned into the parking lot.

"False alarm," Morgan said.

I could make out an elderly couple inside. "Let's get some supplies and get out of here."

As we walked toward the market, I watched the gray car park in front of a Chinese restaurant. I asked myself if I was getting too paranoid. Maybe, but I didn't want to let my guard down. "What did he say about the car following us?"

"He gave me a different road to take when we get near the cabin. A secret entrance."

We bought a week's supply of groceries and got back on the road.

Within twenty minutes, we drove down a hill and saw Christina Lake for the first time.

"Sweet," I said.

It was beautiful. A small village stood on the south shore. Cabins set amidst large ponderosa pines lined the edges of the blue water. A rocky mountain on the east and a heavily treed mountain on the west perfectly framed the valley.

"It looks great, doesn't it?" Morgan said.

"Yeah, I can hang out here for a while. Now where do we go?"

Morgan scanned her directions and started looking for landmarks. "We drive past the town and follow the lake for about five miles. Then we go up a hill, around a switchback, and take a quick left. That way, if we're being followed from a distance, they won't see us turn and they'll think we've stayed on the highway."

"The secret entrance." For the first time on this trip I felt excited, instead of tense and scared. "Crafty."

As we passed through the village, I took mental note of the small grocery store, restaurant, gas station, bar and bakery for future reference. Farther along was the touristy stuff; a go-kart track, mini golf, arcade, ice cream and hamburger stands. They were all closed up for the season.

Once past the town we drove alongside the clear, calm lake before climbing up a hill to a switchback.

"There it is." Morgan pointed.

I hit the brakes. "I almost missed it. It's hard to see the narrow turn off in the trees."

We drove a few miles along the winding, narrow road to the lakeshore. There were quite a few cabins nestled between the road and the water. The area was covered in ponderosa pine, birch and alder. Pine needles and dried leaves blanketed parts of the road.

Morgan checked her directions. "It should be right along here somewhere."

I slowed to a crawl as we turned a corner. The next cabin didn't have a number in front of it, or the next. A short distance ahead, we could barely make out the roof of a third cabin. All that was visible from the road was a set of stairs. On the post were the numbers 2166.

"That's it," she said.

We pulled onto a narrow strip of dirt, just wide enough to park on. We jumped out, eager to see our hideout.

A large raven took flight from the green tin roof below. The air was crisp and smelled of burning leaves. It was calm. Only the sounds of water gently lapping against the rocky shore and the chirp of scurrying chipmunks broke the quiet. Through the trees, down the steep embankment, I spotted a wharf with a diving board.

"We better not have to use that thing." Morgan pointed down to the right.

"What?" I realized what she was referring to. A small, green outhouse was barely visible in the overgrown bushes. It looked old and had the classic half moon and star cut into the door. "Jeez, I sure hope not."

The cabin was a rustic two-story building with dark brown stained cedar siding. There was a screened-in balcony on the second floor and a large, open balcony on the first. Its weathered look made it seem like it'd been there for a hundred years.

I touched Morgan's shoulder. "Let's get unpacked."

She was still distracted by the outhouse, but followed my lead. We each grabbed a load and walked down the stairs. Morgan found the key hidden exactly where Ivan told her it'd be.

When we opened the door a musty smell greeted us.

The first thing we noticed was a fully functioning bathroom on our right. Morgan sighed in relief.

The inside was finished in red cedar. A wood stove sat in the middle of the main room as the focal point. The kitchen had all the modern amenities and opened onto a dining area with a big old oak table.

Past the dining room a set of green carpeted stairs led down to two moderate sized bedrooms. Each had a closet, dresser, and thick down quilts on the beds.

All of the furniture was mismatched and dated; obvious hand-me-downs from the owner's primary home.

We walked out onto the large, open balcony and admired the view. The sun had just set on the opposite side of the lake. Deep tones of orange and red reflected over the water against the blackness of the mountain.

"It feels good here." Morgan turned away. "But, we need to finish packing our stuff down."

I took a deep, refreshing breath.

After the truck was unloaded, I drove it a few hundred yards from the cabin and found an overgrown, abandoned driveway. If I drove it in a little ways, the Blazer wouldn't be visible from the road.

As I walked back to the cabin, I could hear the faint hum of a power transformer on a nearby pole. It was in harmony with a choir of crickets.

I breathed the clean air. It was the first time I felt calm since the whole ordeal began.

INTERLOGUE 1

The study's opulence befitted the estate. Grand traditional furniture was complimented by a large Persian rug atop a polished granite floor. All was surrounded by rich, stained cherry wood paneled walls.

Peter Bail sat in a deep, stiffly padded, blood red leather chair and waited. He faced a hand carved, oversized mahogany desk, near the crackling fire in the black slate fireplace. Long, thick, crimson velvet drapes framed a view of immaculately kept gardens alight in rich fall colors.

A butler in a flat black suit and crisp white shirt entered. His slicked-back grey hair and pencil-thin moustache were a throwback to the past.

He placed a silver tray on the desk in front of Peter. It held a decanter of dark liquid, a silver bowl of ice, a crystal water carafe and two glasses.

Peter raised his hand. "Neat, please."

"As you wish." The butler poured the bourbon from the decanter into a crystal glass until it was a third full and handed it to Peter.

Peter didn't care much for the pomp of aristocrats and their servants, but he was courteous. He also didn't like wearing ties. He gave a tug between his shirt collar and Adams apple. He rarely had to wear them in the field. Now that he was stuck in an office it was more of a common occurrence.

"Dr. Schmidt will join you shortly." With a slight bow, the butler retreated from the room.

Peter had only met Dr. Hendrick Schmidt IV in person on two occasions: once at the London headquarters and once at the Boston lab, where Peter had his office. All other communication had been by email or through his personal assistant. Dr. Schmidt wasn't very patient and Peter wasn't looking forward to this meeting. But, when the chairman wanted to meet, you met. Even if it meant flying to Germany for what would probably be a fifteen-minute one sided discussion.

He took a lingering sip. The liquid brought a sweet and bitter sensation to his mouth. It warmed his throat and chest on the way down. Peter sighed, now that was good bourbon. He'd grown up in Nebraska, where men drank the hard stuff. His dad even had his own still. Now in his forties he'd developed a more refined appreciation for good liquor. He took a second sip and tried to identify the brand.

The door opened behind him. Peter stood and turned to meet his host.

"Good afternoon, Mr. Bail." Dr. Schmidt spoke in a thick German accent, "I trust your flight was adequate?" He wore navy slacks and a light blue French cuffed shirt. Each cuff had a gold link set with a large diamond. A thick gold bracelet peeked out at his right wrist. His wide, yet simple wedding band looked like it was choking his pudgy finger.

"Yes, Dr. Schmidt."

As they shook hands, Peter noticed how hot Dr. Schmidt's palm was.

Dr. Schmidt took his place at the work side of the desk. He was in his sixties and despite his round stature and what Peter estimated to be his five foot eight inch height, he was an intimidating figure.

Dr. Schmidt opened a white folder in front of him. "I have read your security brief and am not satisfied with the results. Do you have anything new to add?"

"No sir."

"So you don't know where they are?"

"As it states in the brief, the last record we have of their movement was the removal of $20,000 from Ms. Elles' checking account at a bank in Vancouver."

Dr. Schmidt looked Peter directly in the eyes.

"That was two days ago," Peter continued. "Border records

don't show them crossing back into the States. They haven't used their passports to fly anywhere, so they haven't left Canada; unless, of course, they have new passports under aliases. We presume they're either still in Vancouver or heading toward Ivan Popov's home in Nelson, British Columbia."

Dr. Schmidt turned a page in the folder. "Mr. Bail, explain to me how your people lost Mr. Barnes and Ms. Elles in Canada? Your report didn't cover that."

Peter shifted in his chair and tensed. "We weren't able to dispatch Canadian operatives. There were none available in Vancouver on that short notice. They were all on higher priority assignments."

Dr. Schmidt raised his gaze. "This is now considered high priority."

"Yes sir. My two main operatives on this case are now in Canada."

"I am not familiar with these operatives. How competent can they be if Mr. Barnes and Ms. Elles eluded them so easily? And they discharged a firearm in a residential neighborhood."

"Operatives Koffman and Thompson are very competent. However, I will say that they initially underestimated Mr. Barnes and Ms. Elles' abilities. Also, they explained that the shot was a scare tactic to stop them. It wasn't proper procedure, but in any case that's what happened. It's only a matter of time before the operatives find them."

Dr. Schmidt leaned forward in his chair and placed his hands on the desk. His bracelet clanked against the mahogany edge. "Mr. Bail, I cannot stress enough to you the importance of finding these people and any other existing copies of Dr. Elles' research. I have read the notes your operatives retrieved. The information definitely cannot become public knowledge. Our intentions would be misinterpreted. Do I make myself clear?"

"Yes sir." As chief of Naintosa's security, Peter would comply with his CEO's wishes. But he wouldn't be intimidated. He consciously sat up straighter and didn't flinch.

The butler entered to place a snifter of dark amber liquid on the desk in front of Dr. Schmidt. He also placed a silver serving plate at an equal distance between the men. On it were six colorful rows: one each of bright red tomato slices, deep green skinned pickled cucumbers, rich brown figs, whiter than white cheese, prosciutto, and crackers. He then placed a small white china plate, silver fork and linen napkin to the side of each of them, before quietly departing.

"Did you know that I possess the largest and oldest seed bank in the world? I use those seeds to produce the majority of my food. It's amazing, the taste of the most simple vegetable or fruit in its original unaltered state." He picked up a tomato slice with his hand and placed it whole into his mouth. "The tomato for instance, so flavorful and sweet. Are you hungry? Help yourself."

"No thank you."

"Suit yourself." Dr. Schmidt shifted. He wrapped his hands around his glass to warm the liquor and brought it up to his nose. He inhaled audibly. After a few swirls and another long inhalation, he sipped.

Peter knew exactly what Schmidt was doing, but patiently ignored it. Let him have his power trip.

Dr. Schmidt set his glass down. "How familiar are you with Dr. Ivan Popov and Dr. William Clancy?"

"They were at Dr. Elles' funeral and spoke with Nick Barnes."

"Yes, I read that in your report. Do you have any more information on them?"

"Not much since they left Naintosa; the regular follow up showed nothing unusual. I didn't feel that any further surveillance was necessary." At that moment, Peter realized that he hadn't taken the retrieval of the notes seriously enough. Deep down he hadn't seen it as that much of a priority.

"I was instrumental in arranging the original team." Dr. Schmidt swirled the liquor in his glass. "I know these men. They have a vested interest in the research. You must resume surveillance and determine their level of involvement. Their actions may provide clues to where Ms. Elles and Mr. Barnes are, especially because Dr. Popov lives in British Columbia."

"Yes sir." Peter organized people in his mind. "I'll have

operatives in London locate Dr. Clancy. The two watching Sue Clark in Seattle can relocate to watch Dr. Popov."

"Is it wise to cease surveillance on Ms. Clark?"

"A newly acquired informant can keep an eye on her. Ms. Clark seems to be playing a mere supporting role in this."

Dr. Schmidt's eyes widened and his jaw firmed. "Finding Mr. Barnes and Ms. Elles should not be difficult. They are not trained agents, only common citizens. Once you are absolutely sure all of the copies are in our possession, only then may you dispose of them and their accomplices. Do I make myself clear?"

"Yes sir."

Dr. Schmidt rose from his chair, his robust stomach pressed against the edge of the desk. "Just make sure they don't elude you again. And Mr. Bail, make sure there are no witnesses, unlike the incident three years ago."

"Yes sir." Peter looked straight at Dr. Schmidt, anticipating the next question. His one screw up in all the years in this business still haunted him.

"Do you have any new information on the witness's whereabouts?"

"Unfortunately no. But, she's simple; she'll eventually make a mistake and turn up."

"It's been three years."

Peter concentrated on not taking his eyes off Dr. Schmidt. "I understand your frustration, sir. All I ask is that you stay patient. This whole matter..."

"You do know the severity of these people joining forces with the witness, don't you?"

"Yes sir. But, the chances of that happening are slim. I'm sure they don't even know of each other's existence."

"We will not know for certain until everyone is located and their knowledge extracted."

"Yes, sir."

"It has not been that many years since you've been an operative. A man as athletic and physical as you might not be fitted to be a head of security. Perhaps it would be better if you went back to field operations where your strength and somewhat menacing manner would be more suitable. Of course, that would mean a seriously diminished salary. Consider the bright side, however." A thin smile appeared on his lips. "You'd be out of the office, traveling the world at our expense." The smile disappeared. "We'll re-examine that prospect when you've taken care of our present situation."

Peter knew Dr. Schmidt wasn't bluffing. Even though he'd reminisced about how things were easier when he'd been in the field, he liked his current position. And he knew he was good at it. "I will do everything in my power to resolve this matter."

Dr. Schmidt fixed Peter with one last steely stare. "Then I will leave you to the task at hand."

CHAPTER 19

As graying sky signaled dawn, I staggered sleepily up the stairs. I managed to stub the same toe twice before reaching the top. I put some coffee on and started a fire in the stove.

Sitting down at the kitchen table, I rubbed the stubble on my face. I went to scratch my knee and realized I was just in my boxers. I'd better put some clothes on before Morgan got up.

I found my old U of W sweatshirt in the suitcase and put on the same jeans I wore yesterday.

As quietly as I could, I opened the door and went out into the still, cool air. On the patio a folded old wooden lawn chair leaned against the cabin. I took it with me and made my way down to the wharf.

There was a wispy mist floating just above the glassy surface of the lake, like breath on a mirror. I placed the chair beside the short diving board and sat down.

I closed my eyes and let silent blackness engulf me. Within moments my consciousness sank into the gap – the empty space between thought and sound, where time didn't exist. My mind's eye saw two men. One was older and stout, the other slim with broad shoulders. They sat opposite each other at a large desk. I couldn't make out what they were saying. There was tension. They had something to do with our journey, but were far away. I got the feeling that even though we were safe for the time being, if we stayed too long we'd be found. Calmness evaporated and was replaced by anxiety. I tried to keep the vision, but that drove me out of the meditation.

It took me a moment to calm down. It was rare that I went into the gap, let alone have such a clear vision. This was big; a great sign. If I continued to meditate and trusted my intuition, I'd know when it was time to leave. It'd been a long time since I'd felt in the flow.

There were footsteps on the stairs. I turned to see Morgan coming onto the wharf in a tight gray tracksuit.

"Want to go for a run with me?" she asked.

"I…" I decided to keep what I'd seen in my meditation to myself. "I don't run."

"We'll have to change that." She had a playful grin. "How do you expect to get any exercise while we're out here?"

"I don't."

"Come on. We'll run till you get tired, then walk, and work up from there each time." Morgan obviously saw my lack of enthusiasm, so she upped the stakes. "Besides, I don't think it's a good idea for me to go out alone."

I sighed. "Let me go change."

"Isn't this place stunning?" She was speaking to me, but her eyes were focused on the lake and surrounding mountains. As if on cue, a fish jumped about twenty feet out from shore.

We headed north to explore the road that meandered along the edge of the lake.

I hadn't run in ten years, so it was painful. It must've been equally hard for Morgan having to watch me. However, she was encouraging and patiently went along at my speed. Whenever she said anything, all I could muster was a grunt.

⁍

After the morning's activity, we set up our work station.

We pulled a simple wooden table away from the wall and placed it near the stove in the middle of the living area. We borrowed two dark stained chairs from around the dining table.

We started our laptops, each picked a disk, and settled in.

"I found it again." I jumped up and pumped my arm, as if I just sunk a fifty-foot putt for birdie. "Yes."

"Found what?"

"The World Health Hierarchy."

Morgan brought her chair over and sat down beside me. "To be honest, I don't see why this is so important compared to the other stuff."

"Bear with me. I have a feeling this whole thing's a government plot to control everyone and Naintosa is just a research facility."

Morgan thought about it for a second. "Interesting. You kind of like drama and conspiracy theories."

I rubbed my hands together for effect. "Uh huh."

She pointed at the screen. "Let's start from the beginning again."

The base of the pyramid was *GENERAL POPULATION.*

"It makes sense that we'd be at the bottom," Morgan said.

The second level was *ALTERNATIVE HEALTH CARE.*

"That's stuff like ginseng, green tea, vitamins, minerals and that blue green algae stuff you take," she said.

"Also, Naturopaths, Chiropractors and Acupuncturists," I added.

The third level was *WESTERN MEDICAL PROFESSION.*

"Wow, you'd think they'd have more clout," Morgan said.

The fourth level was *GOVERNMENTS.*

"What? We're only half way up the pyramid," I said. "Who's more powerful than the government? There goes my theory."

"I'm not sure I believe this." Morgan took the mouse. "Let's see who's more powerful."

The fifth level was *C.O.D.E.X.*

"Oh, I remember Sue telling me about them," I said.

"A friend of mine is a member of a group called the Encompassing Life Foundation," Morgan said. "She told me that CODEX is a group of government officials, scientists and doctors from different countries and the largest pharmaceutical companies. They're quietly trying to control all of the world's natural health care products. It's called the Health Protection Act. If CODEX succeeds, things as harmless as garlic and vitamin C will be regulated and classified as drugs."

"The bottom of the pyramid wants to move up," I said. "So, the upper levels form a committee to keep them down."

The sixth level was WORLD HEALTH ORGANIZATION.

"I was wondering where they'd show up," Morgan said. "At least there's a governing body that has more power than CODEX."

"The W.H.O is a big part of CODEX." I shared what Sue had told me. "It's run by many of the same people and funded by...guess?"

"The drug companies."

I nodded. It started to make sense. "The World Health Organization is the tool the drug companies use to make the world governments do their bidding. It makes them seem legitimate."

Morgan stared at the screen, looking concerned. She clicked on the mouse.

The seventh level was PHARMACEUTICAL CORPORATIONS.

"Talk about the wrong people having that much power," I said. "For example, let's say the drug companies could have flu vaccine that they need to get rid of and want to make a lot of money, fast. So, they tell the media that there's going to be a flu epidemic this winter. Then everyone runs to get their flu shot. Who's monitoring them?"

Morgan slowly nodded. "Or, how about this; if they've found a cure for cancer or some other big disease, they could keep it quiet because they would sell fewer drugs if everyone were healthy. The sicker everyone is the more money they make."

"It's crazy." I didn't want to believe it. "Could this really be the way the system works?"

On the eighth and final level, the apex of the pyramid, there was nothing but a "?". Underneath the question mark was one line: Some theories, but no proven group or organization.

"Does that mean there is someone higher, but he didn't know who?" Morgan frowned. "Or he wasn't sure if there's someone higher?"

"I haven't got a clue."

CHAPTER 20

Dr. Popov arrived the next day at precisely 10:00am as promised.

He was dressed for cooler weather. Underneath a dark brown leather jacket he wore a light blue sweater and brown corduroy pants. His short hair and beard had more gray in it than I remembered. He seemed to be in pretty good shape for an older man.

After our welcome pleasantries, Morgan put her arm around Ivan and led him over to her computer. "We have a lot of questions."

"I will do my best to answer them," he said, his Russian accent making *answer* come out as *awn-zerr.* Yet he pronounced each word articulately.

Morgan brought up the World Health Hierarchy on the screen. "Does this look familiar? Have you seen it before?"

"Yes." Ivan seemed to drift away for a second. "It has been a long time."

"We need proof that this is the *real* way the health hierarchy works," I said, as I came up to stand beside them.

"In my opinion, it is. Acquiring tangible proof has been the challenge." Ivan reached for a pad of paper and drew two pyramids.

I was curious to see the hierarchies side by side.

"Here is the way most people think it works." Ivan placed his hand next to the pyramid on the right. "The top two are interchangeable. Some people think the Governments have the final say, some think the World Health Organization."

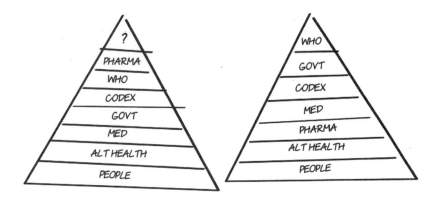

Morgan pointed at the pyramid on the right. "This one makes more sense to me."

Ivan tapped his pen on the paper. "You see, the big difference between them is the importance of the government and the pharmaceutical corporations."

I put my finger on the left side of the page. "Dr. Elles left the top of this pyramid blank, with a question mark."

"Well..." Ivan was silent for a moment, before continuing, "Some people, including Carl, Bill and I, think there might be a group at the top that controls the Pharmaceutical Corporations. For example, there have been times where it *seemed* obvious that decisions came from even higher up than Pharmalin – the company that owns Naintosa. We called it the Cartel, not sure if it had a name or who was part of it."

"So, what's that mean?" I asked.

"I do not think it affects what we are doing now."

Morgan looked skeptical.

I'd heard the conspiracy theories about a group of families that secretly ran the world, but I'd always thought it was too far-fetched. Was it possible? I wanted to stay open minded. "So, how could the Pharmaceutical Corporations have all that power?"

"It is all about who controls the money." Ivan's Russian accent made the statement sound even stronger.

Morgan nodded at me. "Of course."

Ivan gestured at the paper. "The Pharmaceutical Corporations control the inflow and outflow of money from everyone below."

Studying both drawings, I could see it. "From a money control perspective the conventional pyramid couldn't work."

Morgan interjected. "But, the governing bodies should oversee the industry, no matter where the money comes from."

"Yes, that *should* be the way it works," Ivan said. "However, the governments rely on the money from the Pharmaceutical Corporations. *And* the World Health Organization is mainly comprised of people who control the Pharmaceutical Corporations."

I was still fighting to let go of my old beliefs, but it did make sense.

"We are getting ahead of ourselves," Ivan said. "We have to focus on Naintosa. After we expose them, then maybe we can delve more into proving the reality of the whole pyramid. For now it is just something to keep in the back of our minds."

I had more questions, but Ivan was right. We needed to focus on the proof we had.

Ivan gestured to the living room. "Let's have a discussion where it is more comfortable."

We moved to the couch.

Ivan asked, "Morgan, do you remember your move from England to the United States?"

"Mostly, I guess. I was only eight."

Ivan shifted to face us both. "I will give you the background, so Nick has a better understanding and hopefully you will remember."

Morgan nodded.

"In the seventies, Carl and Claudia Elles worked for a small biology lab that was funded by Oxford University. They wanted to find a better way of growing food. Long-term use of chemical fertilizers has depleted the soil of nutrients or even made it sterile. Commercial fertilizer has not replaced all of the nutrients needed. So, over the years the plants have leached out most of the micronutrients from the soil."

I asked, "Is that why tomatoes from the supermarket barely have any taste?"

"Yes, because minerals provide the flavor."

I thought back to when I was at McMynn's with Sue. The news on TV was about the soil's depleted nutrients.

"Now plants are weaker and much more susceptible to disease and insect infestation." Ivan went on. "Farmers have to use more and more pesticides. Because of this, the foods that plants provide have much less nutritional value. Also, people are ingesting the pesticide residue. Since this practice began in 1948, people's immune systems have been getting weaker and weaker. We may be living longer, but we are more susceptible to disease. That makes people more dependent on pharmaceuticals and health care."

Morgan was looking at the floor and shaking her head. "About ten years ago I remember asking them why they just didn't focus on organics. I never got a clear answer back."

Ivan reached out and patted Morgan's knee. "Your parents wanted to see if they could make the plants genetically stronger. Their goal was to take favorable genes from one species and insert them into the DNA of another. No one else had attempted this. In time they discovered that they could not only splice genes from plant to plant, but also introduce genes taken from bacteria, insects, and even animals."

Morgan sighed. "Sometimes I wish they never started those experiments."

"Little did they know," I said.

"Yes, little did we all know." Ivan shook his head. "In 1981, they were told that a major benefactor would stop supporting the University if their experiments continued. The next day your parents were offered a large amount of money to continue the experiments at Naintosa. Using vast amounts of research capital Dr. Schmidt was positioning his company into the seed development business."

Morgan looked over at me. "Dr. Schmidt is the boss at Naintosa."

"Do you know much about him?"

"I'd just heard my parents mention him a few times."

I got up to get my pad and write Dr. Schmidt's name on it, then looked at Ivan. "If he's in charge of all of this, shouldn't we be going after him directly?"

"We must stick with the facts that we have and not make direct accusations."

I didn't like that answer, but decided to bide my time.

"Where were you and Bill at that time?" Morgan spoke up.

"Working in the fertilizer lab at Naintosa. We were transferred to work with your parents. It was very exciting at the time. Within a year, we had successfully altered genomes. By 1983 we were growing plants with genetically engineered traits. For eight years we worked on modifying different vegetables and fruit. However, as time went on we found that there were side effects and repercussions."

"So why didn't you stop at that point?" I asked.

"You could say we were obsessed with fixing the negatives."

Morgan's voice went up an octave. "Really?"

"However, in the end we became convinced that the only way to produce stronger, nutrient rich food was the old fashioned way – organically. Mother Nature had already figured it out."

"What did Naintosa have to say about that?" I already knew the answer.

Ivan frowned and slowly shook his head. "Naintosa went ahead and started field-tests. The director in charge told us not to worry about what they did, just to keep working."

Wow. "Does anyone there have a conscience?"

"By the time you finish reading the notes, you will have a better understanding."

Morgan and I nodded.

"There is something else I should explain to you now, that is not contained in Carl's notes." Ivan leaned forward. "In 1995, Bill, your mother and I were forced into retirement. The field tests were proving our conclusions right. They brought in a new senior scientist your father had to answer to."

"Why didn't my father just quit?"

"By that time he had decided to write the memoir. He wanted to stay so he could compile more information."

I admired Dr. Elles for being able to hang in there. I know I couldn't have. "Four extra years is a long time."

Ivan nodded agreement. "It was difficult for him, but that time revealed much information."

"I'd never known why the funding at Oxford was cancelled in the first place," Morgan said. "That was the catalyst for all of this."

"Your father did not find out until six months before he retired."

"Wow, that's..." I counted in my head. "Eighteen years after it happened."

"Carl had to go to London on business. After, he stayed a few extra days to visit Bill. Bill had been classmates at Oxford with the eventual Chancellor while Carl and Claudia had the lab there. His name was Charles Underhill. Bill had purposely rekindled their friendship to try to obtain information. Charles was about to retire and we knew he always felt guilty about what happened. We hoped he was willing to talk. Carl and Bill also found out that Charles had information about Claudia's car accident."

Morgan sat bolt upright. "What does my mother's accident have to do with any of this?"

Ivan hesitated. He was obviously choosing his words carefully. "Your father never told you, because he did not want to upset you more. However, under the circumstances I think you should know. We suspect your mother's car accident was not an accident."

Morgan's eyes opened wide. "You mean she was murdered?"

"It is a possibility." Ivan reached out and took Morgan's hand.

Morgan's eyes pleaded. "Why? She had nothing to do with the experiments at that point. She...she...did nothing wrong. Why?"

For the first time I noticed frown wrinkles on Ivan's forehead. "There is no evidence. Charles confessed that shortly after your mother died he was having trouble with another project. The representative at the time was aggressive. He told Charles they had ways of making sure their objectives were reached; like sacrificing Dr. Claudia Elles to control Dr. Carl Elles. He threatened that Charles was just as dispensable as Claudia."

"What? Dispensable?" Morgan pulled back from Ivan and clenched her fists.

Ivan leaned forward to take her hand again, but she turned away. "I am truly sorry Morgan. But, it was said as a threat and may just have been that. There is no way of knowing for sure."

Morgan's voice was shaky. "I knew it wasn't an accident... deep down. Something wasn't right. My father told me there was a witness to the accident, but no one could find the person. Do you know anything about a witness?"

He shook his head. "I am sure the people that caused it would have taken care of any loose ends."

"Did Dr. Elles go to the police?"

"Yes he did. They listened, but nothing ever came of it. That is the reason we are not involving the police now. Either they did not believe him or Naintosa has the ability to influence them."

Morgan was on the verge of tears. "So he did nothing?"

"After much soul searching, he decided he had to continue on. The book would be his way of stopping Naintosa. It took great courage."

Morgan sobbed. "Until he became dispensable."

⋈

Morgan spread the food around her plate with her fork. Her slim shoulders were slumped and the corners of her mouth drawn down. "It could all be genetically altered; food that caused the death of my parents."

"You're right." I put my fork and knife down. "But we can't just stop eating?"

Ivan watched, as if testing us. "Of course, we cannot stop eating. But, you can see the precarious position the world is in. People do not know what is in their food anymore. If you cannot grow the food yourself, buy organic food. Stay away from processed and mass produced food."

I looked at the vegetables on my plate. "Organic isn't always an option."

Morgan pushed her plate away. "Even if it's organic, the crops could still be tainted. My Dad's notes said birds could drop genetically engineered seeds onto fields, the wind could carry them and even the manure they use could contain affected seeds that the cows ate."

"What about meat, Ivan?" I asked. "The animals are not only eating the genetically engineered feed, but they're injected with all those hormones and chemicals."

"It is not just the injections. Feeding them corn instead of grass makes them more susceptible to e-coli. Worst of all is the feeding of animal by-products to animals. That is why we have Mad Cow Disease."

Morgan rubbed her eyes from fatigue. "Who would be stupid enough to think that would be a good thing to do to livestock?"

"Naintosa is one of the world's biggest feed manufacturers," Ivan said. "Pharmalin is a large producer of growth hormones."

"Is there anything about it in the notes?" I asked.

"Unfortunately, no." Ivan reached for a pad of paper. "I will do my best to obtain information on animal by-products in feed. I know someone who may be able to help. The fact that the animal epidemics are already occurring will add credibility to our findings."

Our appetites gone, we cleared the table.

Ivan gestured toward the living room. "I would like to continue our discussion."

Morgan and I settled back onto the couch.

Ivan sat on the matching chair opposite us. His face was solemn. "As I was saying, the Chancellor at Oxford, Charles Underhill, felt badly about what happened to your parents. He wanted to clear his conscience before he retired."

"Did my father trust him?"

"Yes. Charles explained that of the private groups that made donations, the largest one was very demanding. Charles never knew exactly who these people were. They always contacted him through their representatives. They always seemed to know what was happening. If they did not like something, they would manage to put a stop to it. Charles tried to talk to the University Board of Directors, but their response was to do what the contributors asked of him."

"Sounds like he wasn't able to do his Chancellor job properly." Or have a lot of back bone.

"That is the case at many Universities," Ivan said. "It really disturbed Charles when he was instructed to end the Elles' project. They were so close to a breakthrough. But, the representative threatened to remove the University's funding. He had no choice."

Something bugged me about the Chancellor discussion. It seemed too simple. I felt a piece was missing. "Whatever happened to Charles? Can we interview him?"

"Unfortunately he died two weeks after he spoke with Bill and Carl. He was not able to enjoy his retirement."

"How did they kill him off?" I asked, not even considering *if.*

"He had a massive stroke. Of course, like you, we suspected foul play."

Morgan crossed her arms and scowled. "Everyone who opposes them dies, don't they?"

"The problem is we don't exactly know who *them* is, do we?" I looked from one to the other. "Is it just Naintosa or another group as well?"

CHAPTER 21

Ivan had left us the information he'd transcribed and agreed to be back in two weeks with more.

Morgan spent much of her time in her room, on the wharf and going for solitary walks. I told her I was there if she wanted to talk, but left her alone.

The contempt I felt for Naintosa and the phantom people in control turned into a strong desire to work.

I went through the disks Ivan had transcribed. Once I decided where each part would go, it was like fitting the pieces of a puzzle together and tying them up with strings of words. Ivan's notes were much more understandable than the originals, but still very dry. He also wrote like he spoke – articulate and unabbreviated. I tried not to change the intention of what he wrote, but made it easier to read.

❧

After three days of work, I decided to take a break.

The sun was setting as I walked through the crisp air down to the wharf. Morgan sat on a plastic white patio chair facing the lake, bundled in a faded blue and white blanket.

I was starting to worry about her. "How're you doing?"

She turned to look at me. "I'm okay." Her eyes were blood shot and she looked tired. "I'm really sorry I haven't been able to help you. I promise I will tomorrow."

"That's okay. I'd be the same way if I were in your shoes. Besides, I've just gone through Ivan's stuff and figured out a basic outline."

"How is it?"

"It's coming along." I gave her a reassuring smile. "I'm going into town to see if I can find some edible food. Do you need anything?"

"Just some toothpaste…and try your best with the food."

🜚

The drive into the village of Christina Lake took ten minutes. Being the off-season, it was quiet. Only three sets of headlights passed by. The sidewalks were deserted except for two dogs out on a stroll. I guessed the dogs walked themselves there.

I was the only shopper in the grocery store. Soft muzak provided the background. I managed to find some vegetables and fruit that were local and not on Ivan's altered list. I stayed away from processed food and meat. I decided it was time to become a health conscious vegetarian. We needed carbs and protein, so I picked up rice, local bread, beans and eggs. I also chose some pasta and the ingredients for my mom's home-made pesto sauce.

After the groceries were stowed in the back of my vehicle, I spotted a pay phone. I wanted to talk to someone in the world outside.

"Hello."

The sound of Sue's voice made me smile. It gave me comfort. "I just knew you'd be home tonight. I'm psychic, you know."

"Right. Nick, how are you?" The excitement was audible in Sue's voice. "So, how is it there? Is it nice? How is Morgan? Are you safe? How's the manuscript going? Is it…"

"Hold on. Give me a chance to answer."

"Sorry, I just haven't heard from you forever. I can't stop wondering what's going on."

"Everything's fine." I didn't want to worry her with details. "It's really beautiful here and I'm getting a good grip on the manuscript. How's everything there? Noticed anyone watching you?"

"I'm not positive, but sometimes I swear I'm being followed from a distance. Have you seen the two original guys?"

"I think we saw them a couple of times, but I'm pretty sure we lost them." I sighed. "Sorry to have gotten you into this."

"Don't worry, they don't want me. Otherwise they would've picked me up by now." Sue sounded cavalier. Maybe she was putting on a brave face for me.

"Did you have a chance to check the backgrounds of Dr. Clancy, Ivan, and Morgan?" I asked.

"Yep. All three are who they say they are. They're on the up and up from what I could find."

I had been pretty sure Sue wasn't going to find anything bad and it was good to hear her confirmation. "Can you do me another favor? When you have time, can you get any dirt on Naintosa? Especially a Dr. Hendrick Schmidt. He's supposed to be running the show."

"That shouldn't be too hard. I'm glad to be able to contribute."

"Just be careful."

"You know Nick, while we've been talking I've heard a change in you. You sound like your old self; more assertive and focused."

"Yeah, my slump is definitely over. I do feel like I've found my passion again." As I spoke, the words solidified like concrete in my own mind. "This is important stuff."

"It really is...and welcome back."

I couldn't help but smile. What would I do without Sue?

"How's Morgan? Are you working well together or are you just drooling over her all the time?"

"She's fine." I didn't want to get into what had probably happened to her mother. "And I'm not just staring at her body..." Shit I just screwed up. "I mean...it's strictly platonic."

Sue laughed. "I know it's platonic, jackass. What I meant was is she distracting you? But, you just answered that question. I don't know any guy who wouldn't be drooling over her."

"To be honest, we've been so focused on the manuscript and not getting caught, that I haven't been thinking about how good looking she is." Okay, that was almost true. "Plus she's smart and has a great personality."

"Next you're going to tell me she's a good cook."

"No, she's not a very good cook. But, don't tell her that."

Sue snickered.

"Take care and don't talk to any strange men carrying a gun."

"How am I ever going to get a date then?"

I felt better as I hung up and started back. I missed Sue.

Morgan looked up from her cup of tea as I entered the cabin and gave me a warm smile.

"How are you feeling?" I asked, as I put the grocery bags on the counter.

"I feel like I'll be able to start helping you tomorrow. Did you find anything for us to eat?"

"I hope so."

Morgan got up from the table and walked over to the bags. Her posture wasn't slumped like it had been for the last few days.

Morgan approved of everything until she got to the pasta. "Who knows what kind of grain was used to make this?" She held up the package and read the ingredients.

"We need more food with sustenance. Most of this stuff won't fill me up enough," I said, as I stowed the vegetables in the crisper.

"I guess it'll be all right. Thanks for going shopping. Anything interesting happen at the store?"

"No, the place was deserted. But I did call Sue."

"Oh...what'd she say?"

I filled her in, except for the part about her.

CHAPTER 22

I slowly opened the door leading to the lower balcony. A burst of cold air stung my face. It was going to snow soon; you could smell it.

I almost flipped on the wet leaves blanketing the stairs down to the dock. "Ouch." A sliver lodged itself into my hand when I grabbed the old wooden rail for balance. Luckily half of it was protruding, so I was able to pull it out easily.

The lake was calm and dark. A low layer of cloud hung in the sky. The whole scene felt surreal.

An opening door creaked behind me. I turned and looked up to see Morgan coming out of the cabin.

"Good morning." The normal volume of my voice boomed in the intense quiet.

"I heard you come outside. I want to learn how to meditate today." She crossed her arms and rubbed them. "It's cold out here. Can't we do it inside?"

"Yeah, but it's better outside. We'll do it inside when the weather gets too cold."

I was glad she wanted to learn. It could help her deal with life right now.

Morgan was wearing a blue fleece jacket I hadn't seen before and mittens.

Once we were seated on the patio chairs, I explained the basics. "All we're going to do is clear our minds of chatter. If a thought comes in, just let it pass through. Don't dwell on it. Focus on your breathing, in and out, in and out."

"You told me you get answers to questions when you meditate. When will I start getting them?"

"It doesn't happen all the time and for me only when I've gotten into the *gap*. That's when you achieve total silence in your mind. The *gap* was explained to me as the silence between notes in music; the small gaps between the chords. Over time, as well as answers to questions, some people even get visions or premonitions while in a meditative state. Anyone's capable of it. It's all about opening up that frequency within you."

"Wow. That's kind of freaky. Do you get visions?"

"I have." I didn't want to tell her that I saw her father before I met him and the shadow of a man over his body or the two tense men I saw a few days ago. I'd never had so many visions in such a short period of time. They used to be a rare occurrence for me.

"Hmm. Are you saying that's the only way you can get those messages?"

"No, it's just the best way I know of getting the clearest messages. You might find other ways that work for you, once you start paying more attention to receiving them."

Morgan looked quizzical. "It sounds a little airy fairy."

I couldn't help but smile. "Yeah, I admit it does. You'll understand after you do it for awhile."

"I'm willing to give it a shot." She shivered and slid her mittened hands into her pockets.

"Think of meditation as a way to help you relax and deal with all the emotion you're going through."

"Okay."

"Close your eyes and take slow, deep breaths."

She did as I asked. Her chest extended and released with the audible sound of her breathing.

"Keeping your eyes closed, feel the beauty of your surroundings. Imagine inhaling and exhaling that beauty."

I watched her breath deliberately in through her nose and out through the slight separation in her lips.

"Remember, if a thought comes in, don't hold onto it."

I closed my eyes and began to do the same as I had instructed. After a short time I could hear her fidgeting beside me. I opened my eyes and looked over at her.

"I couldn't do it." She looked defeated. "I keep thinking about stuff."

"Don't worry, it's going to take time. It's not as easy as it sounds. We'll try again tomorrow."

"On one condition."

"What?"

"After we meditate, we go for a run."

I slumped back into the chair. You'd think she'd give up after witnessing me crap out the other day. Running was such a pain.

"All you need is more practice." She stood and pulled me to my feet. "You need to be fit on the outside as well as inside, Nick."

After another dismal attempt at a run, a shower and healthy breakfast, we sat down in front of our computers.

"My shins still burn a little," I said, rubbing my legs below the knees.

"You'll get through it." Morgan's eyes were fixed on her screen.

"I might be getting shin splints."

Morgan wanted to look at everything I intended to use in the manuscript, so I passed her my backup disk. She seemed determined to catch up with my work.

⋈

I loaded the last disk. As I listened to the faint hum of the drive, it was as if the clarity of my mind wanted to match the speed of the computer.

The title of the disk was *Safety Issues and Side Effects*.

"You may want to read this with me," I said. "I think we may have saved the best for last."

Morgan dragged her chair over, next to me. She smelled as fresh as new snow, but warm. Her hair was still damp. I didn't want to dwell on her scent. I needed to focus on the business at hand.

Dr. Elles described an instance when he was asked by Naintosa to help a competitor. A company named DKKR genetically engineered a bacteria to produce tryptophan, an essential amino acid. Within eight months of their release of the new product it was discovered to have serious side effects.

In all the reported cases, the unforeseen toxin produced by the bacteria that had been engineered to produce tryptophan caused Eosinophilia Myalgia Syndrome. Initially, people experienced severe muscle pain. Over time other problems developed including neurological complications, heart problems, memory and cognitive deficits, and paralysis. Ten thousand people had suffered serious disability and there were thirty nine reported deaths.

DKKR needed help to isolate the problem. Right away Dr. Elles found they'd cut corners in their testing.

The Food and Drug Administration allowed DKKR to sell the tryptophan produced by genetically engineered bacteria without stringent testing. That was because for many years they had been producing it using a non-genetically engineered form. The engineered bacteria cut time and saved money.

Dr. Elles found that the genetically engineered bacteria used in the making of tryptophan produced a highly toxic contaminant called EBT. When EBT and tryptophan mixed, the results were deadly. DKKR would have discovered this if they had performed all the proper tests.

After he presented them with his findings, Dr. Elles wasn't allowed to let anyone else study his research. DKKR destroyed the engineered bacteria.

In the end, DKKR paid out a few million to some of the people they'd poisoned and got a slap on the wrist from the FDA. There were never any reports about it in the media, so the general public never found out what had happened.

"They didn't give a shit and they produce health products." I looked over at Morgan.

It was like a light bulb went on in her head. "That happened right before Naintosa took the potato and soybean research away from my father. I bet the guys from DKKR talked to the guys at Naintosa and told them that my dad might talk if he found something wrong."

"Yeah...for sure he knew too much by then."

"From that point on, they only allowed my dad's team to develop things to a certain point. Then someone else would take over."

"They took him out of the loop."

Morgan wrote a note on the "Things to ask Ivan" page of her notebook. She laid her pen down and muttered, "fucking assholes," under her breath.

Whether it was a temporary part of the grieving process or permanent from her recent life experiences, she was becoming harder. It was probably good, considering the precarious position we were in, but I wasn't sure it suited her. Not her looks anyhow.

I wiped the thought from my mind. "Let's keep going."

The next part was about an attempt to grow crops that were resistant to herbicides. The theory was that if plants were resistant, farmers could save money by spraying to control weeds and increase yield. Dr. Elles chose to test soybeans and used Naintosa's own herbicide. They began the experiments in the mid eighties. By 1989 they found that the hardiness of the soybeans had substantially decreased. Under the heat of the summer sun, many of the soybeans were cracking and drying up. This rendered half the crop useless. Meanwhile the strength of the surrounding weeds dramatically increased. The team considered the experiment a total failure.

Naintosa saw it a different way. They could sell more of the new seeds and twice the herbicide. By 1990 the soybean seeds were making their way to the growers.

"Is there no limit to their insanity?" Morgan gritted her teeth.

"Why am I not surprised?" After all the information we'd read in the notes, I felt I was becoming de-sensitized. The things Naintosa was doing were so blatantly bad it was nearly unbelievable.

What followed was the account of an occurrence that happened just before the soybean seeds became available to farmers. A new scientist was assigned to the team. She was hired at the insistence of the Vice President of the Naintosa Herbicide Division. She was supposed to be an objective asset in deciphering the results of the experiments. Yet she always defended the use of additional herbicide. The day before the soy research was taken away from Dr. Elles, she was transferred without an explanation. One month later she was working for the USDA. Two weeks after that, the USDA increased the allowable levels of herbicide use to double the previous limit.

"What a coincidence." Morgan spoke to the computer screen. "So if they don't like the rules, they just get them changed."

I crossed my arms and sighed. "I bet half the people at the USDA are on Naintosa's payroll."

Next came a report on an independent university study on the herbicide resistant soybeans, completed in 1996. The soy's deteriorated hardiness had remained the same since 1989, but it now took five times the amount of herbicide to control the weeds in the fields. The gene that was supposed to make the soybeans resistant had transferred to the weeds.

A series of pictures followed the report.

I ran my hand along the screen. "Look at the size of these weeds compared to the soy plants."

Morgan leaned in. "The trunks of the weeds look so thick. Wow."

According to the accompanying information, the weeds had mutated at a rapid rate and spread into adjacent fields. They had choked out every competing plant species, including genetically altered crops. They'd become super weeds and the scientists couldn't control them. That's when the study was stopped. The report was never released. The seeds were recalled.

"Of course it was never released," I said. "The weeds are now probably spreading across the U.S."

"Of course." Morgan was obviously reading at the same pace I was. "As these weeds spread, they're going to need a nuclear bomb to kill them."

"They've become the cockroaches of the plant world."

Next came the experiments on methods to eliminate insects and rodents that were eating the plants.

"Speaking of cockroaches," Morgan said.

By ingesting the genetically altered plants and herbicides the same university study found that multiple species were being permanently altered. The toxin-induced changes were traceable in their gene pool, effectively creating new sub-species. Like the weeds, stronger and stronger chemicals were used to control these pests, without success. The insect and rodent population would be reduced for a time, but then came back stronger than ever.

"Nick, have you heard about the super bugs in hospitals?"

I thought for a second. "You mean new strains of bacteria that are resistant to every known antibiotic?"

"Yeah...this weed and insect thing reminds me of that."

"Just a few months ago, there was an outbreak in New York. They had to quarantine a whole hospital wing." Then it came to me, "I wonder whatever happened to the infected people? The story just dropped out of the news."

"You're right." Morgan nodded. "I never heard what happened in the end, either."

"The environment is being ruined," I said. "We're going to be stuck with monster bacteria, weeds, and pests."

The last part of the disk listed the findings of several experiments that had been conducted in specific locations around the U.S. Genetically engineered food was grown and readily consumed. The test subjects were regular citizens who didn't know they were guinea pigs. They thought they were just eating local produce.

Dr. Elles wasn't part of these experiments, but had managed to obtain copies of the results.

The main and consistent side effect was weakened immune systems, which outwardly showed as allergies. Once the immune system had been compromised, negative effects were documented on the kidneys, brain, spleen, stomach, pancreas, lungs, intestines, skin, muscles, lymph, liver, heart and central nervous system.

The damage sometimes showed up on the outside. Pictures included showed rashes, skin discoloration, tumors under the skin, and eyes that looked as if life had been sucked out of them.

Naintosa concluded that the findings were within their definition of tolerable side effect risk levels and that people wouldn't link these problems to food, in any case.

That was the last straw and Dr. Elles resigned.

"All this information blows me away," I said. "They hope people won't link the problems to the food they're consuming. They know it's the problem."

Morgan threw her arms up in disgust. "*Within their tolerable side effect risk levels?* Fuckers."

CHAPTER 23

I was flat on my face. Trying to yell, I just spat sand and dead leaves from my mouth. Pain seared through my left ankle.

Morgan ran back. "They're right behind us. I can hear them."

I grit my teeth. "I twisted my ankle."

She wrapped my arm around her shoulder and pulled me up. "Don't think about it, just run!"

She supported my left side as we stumbled from the beach, into the jungle. The combination of humid heat, breathless fatigue and sharp pain brought me to the verge of blacking out. Morgan kept pulling me onward.

Sue appeared and supported my other side.

The jungle grew denser. Blood and sweat mixed on our exposed arms and legs as we pushed through the coarse underbrush. We couldn't stop.

We stumbled into a clearing where three dilapidated cabins stood around a larger decaying building.

My right foot caught on a root. Morgan lost her grip on me. I went down against a rock. Pain now shot through every part of my body and my mind blurred.

"Get up!" Morgan cried. "We can't quit now."

"I can see them." Sue pointed back into the jungle.

A deep male voice shouted, "Don't you even think about getting up."

"We're dead."

I half opened my eyes. My sheets were clammy and cold. I was shivering. I must've thrown the blanket off. My breath caught with surprise when I looked up.

A drowsy Morgan stood at the foot of my bed, a pink terry

robe cinched around her waist. "Are you all right? I heard you groaning. Then you shouted something about your ankle."

I reached for the corner of the blanket at my feet and pulled it over me. I tried to act nonchalant about Morgan seeing me lying there, wearing only my golf ball print boxers. But how fast I jerked the blanket up must've given me away. "I just had the worst dream."

She didn't seem to care about how she found me. "What was it about?" She went to the end of the bed and sat down on the edge. "Tell me before you forget."

When I finished, she looked thoughtful. "Do you know how to analyze dreams?"

I scratched my head, realized my hair was sticking up in tufts and quickly tried to mat it down. "All I know about dream analysis is that it can either be a premonition, something that's been buried in one's mind that's being revealed or it can be symbols..."

"Or just a silly dream."

"I guess?"

She got up. "It probably has something to do with the stuff we read about yesterday. I didn't sleep very well either."

I reflected on part of the dream. "You kept helping me up and pulling me forward."

"More like the other way around." She shrugged it off, but I could tell something was bothering her. "Now get up."

❦

The weather remained clear and cold for the next three days. We managed to meditate outside and run afterwards. Then we'd park ourselves in front of the computers and work. With the notes organized, I made excellent progress and was well into the first draft of the manuscript. Morgan edited. I was amazed at her natural ability; it was a real asset.

❦

On Friday morning we awoke to an overcast day. It was

calm, but the smell of snow was in the air. For the first time we meditated in the living room and decided to take a break from running. I really was getting shin splints.

"Besides, you shouldn't run every day," I pointed out.

Morgan snickered, "Wimp."

"What?" I pointed down at my over-exaggerated limp as I followed her to the kitchen.

At breakfast, Morgan turned on the radio on the counter and we listened to the local news and weather report. The first snow of the season was coming. It was already falling in Grand Forks, which was only thirteen miles west of us. There was supposed to be an accumulation of up to fifteen centimeters, which we translated into six inches.

"I don't know about this." Morgan looked uneasy as she crunched her granola. "In Seattle when it snows an inch the whole city goes into chaos. What'll happen here?"

"We're in Canada. Everyone's equipped for snow and used to it."

"It's not them I'm worried about. We should spend the morning making sure *we're* ready?"

"Living in the country takes much more effort," I said, as I went to get paper for a shopping list. "You can't just stroll over to the corner store and grab a few things."

"Yeah, you have to plan ahead here."

⚘

Morgan was an efficient grocery shopper. She quickly scoped out the safest food to eat.

While she was inspecting a bag of oatmeal I decided to browse the wine section. It'd been a while since I'd had anything to drink. I hadn't even felt like it, lately.

I reached for a bottle with a label that caught my eye. "Hmm." I gestured to Morgan. "Come here for a second. Look what I found."

She wheeled over the almost full shopping cart.

I showed her the bottle of local wine. "It's organic."

Morgan looked at the label. "I've had some of this before,

it's really good." She picked out another from the shelf. "Wine from the Okanagan is getting a good reputation."

"Let's get a couple bottles."

>&

On our way back, the odd snowflake began to hit the windshield.

"Soon this will all be white." Morgan looked past me to the left. "I wonder if the lake freezes?"

>&

Back at the cabin, we carried the groceries down and started to put them away.

By the look on Morgan's face I could tell she was deep in thought. "Whatcha thinking about?"

She pulled the rice out of the shopping bag and placed it in the cupboard. "How meditating is working for me."

"And?"

"I think it's making me more relaxed and focused on the editing. And it's helping me deal with my parents' deaths." She turned to face me, her brilliant blue eyes misty. "Thank you for teaching me."

She looked so beautiful and vulnerable. I had to turn away. "No problem." I quickly pulled the wine bottles from a bag and set them on the counter.

After everything was stowed away it was back to work.

As I waited for my laptop to boot up, I glanced out the window. Steady snow had begun to fall.

Morgan went over to the window.

"Let's go down and have a look," I said.

Big flakes casually descended. The taste of the air was like putting cold, clear water to your lips. Each breath filled your lungs with pure freshness. We couldn't see the other side of the lake through the thick, puffy whiteness. Nothing stirred, not even a breeze. In that silence you could almost hear the delicate petals of ice land.

We stood watching in awe for some time.

Finally Morgan broke the quiet, "I'm going back inside. I'm freezing." Her strawberry blond hair had developed a layer of white.

Back in front of the computers, Morgan started looking at what I had written the day before.

I tried to continue from where I left off, but kept looking out the window. The snow was accumulating and a light breeze came up, making it swirl. "I can't get into it. I'm too distracted."

"Well...we have been working pretty hard." She gave me a mischievous grin. "You know what? I'm going to have a glass of wine. Want some?"

"That'd be great." I hadn't wanted to let my guard down before, but I felt safe in this storm. Who was going to be looking for us in this weather? We could relax a little.

While Morgan went for the wine, I got our jackets and slid open the glass door to the enclosed patio on the main floor. It was cold, but there was a portable space heater that I plugged in.

"Here you go." She passed me the bottle of Meritage and a cork screw.

I'd been a waiter at a half-decent restaurant during my college days, so I knew how to properly open a bottle of wine.

Morgan held out two broad bowled glasses while I filled them with the plum colored liquid.

"Mmm, tastes good," Morgan said.

I swirled the wine, stuck my nose into the wide mouthed glass and sniffed. It smelled rich and inviting. I took a gulp. "It's chewy."

She smiled and rolled her eyes.

The breeze gusted, so that the snow fell at a forty-five degree angle at times. It started coming down so thick that we could only see about fifty yards over the lake.

Morgan pulled her zipper up until the collar covered her chin. "Why don't you tell me why you aren't married or at least have a serious girl friend?"

"Where did that come from?" I felt awkward and didn't

want to get into it. I didn't want to admit that the possibility of her and me together had crossed my mind more than once.

"So, are you going to answer my question?"

"Yeah, I was just thinking." I bit my lower lip and gave the standard response, "I guess I just haven't found the right girl."

"Why? You're handsome and intelligent, poor, but fairly sociable."

"Not all women are looking for a rich guy." I bristled, falling for her trap.

"I'm kidding." She slapped me playfully in the arm, with the back of her hand. "What about Sue?"

"I'd thought about it originally, but we turned out to be best buddies."

"I understand. Well, once this is over I've got a few friends I could set you up with." Her smile turned slight.

"Thanks anyway." I looked right into her beautiful blue eyes. "I'll manage."

CHAPTER 24

It was mid November, with more than a foot of snow on the ground. The Canadian winter had arrived.

There wasn't much else to do but write.

"Ivan's coming tomorrow," Morgan said, handing me a cup of steaming hot chocolate. "I think we're ready for him."

The scent of lavender from her hair mixed with the smell of chocolate and a hint of wood smoke from the stove. It felt like we'd created a cozy winter den for ourselves.

"The first draft's pretty much done."

Morgan pursed her lips and blew into the cup in a gentle and innocent way that made it seductive. "We've made real progress."

⋇

At precisely ten a.m. the next morning, while we were reviewing our work, there was a knock on the door.

"He's here." Morgan burst from her chair and headed toward the door.

A moment later Ivan entered the room with Morgan on his arm. "Good morning Nick. How are you?"

"Good to see you, Ivan."

"It's so good to see another person; especially you." Morgan squeezed his arm. "I'm going stir crazy cooped up in here."

Did that comment mean Morgan was sick of me? Maybe while I was feeling all comfy and cozy, she was itching to get out.

Ivan held a black briefcase in one hand and a brown paper grocery bag in the other. He placed the case on the table. "Have you two eaten?" He held out the bag to Morgan.

"I'm sure we could use a snack," I said. "What is it?"

Morgan peered into the bag. "Fresh croissants and honey."

"Great." I got up from my chair and stretched. "We haven't had much variety lately."

Morgan squeezed Ivan's arm a last time and took the bag into the kitchen.

"How were the roads?" I asked.

"The highway was not bad, but the road from the turn off was slippery because it has not been plowed." Ivan's deep Russian accent was succinct. "The all wheel drive of the Subaru I borrowed made it easier."

"Oh, what happened to your Explorer?"

Morgan walked into the room with a plate full of cut croissants, knives and the wild, un-pasteurized honey.

"My vehicle is fine." Ivan reached for a croissant. "Two men have been watching me. I had to switch cars to lose them."

Morgan dropped the knives on the carpet with a thud. "Have they interrogated you? Are you okay?"

"I am fine." He didn't look worried at all. "It is just surveillance. Otherwise they would do more than just sit in a car near my home. That indicates to me that they think you are in the area, but they do not know where."

"Did you recognize the men?" I asked.

"No."

Shit. "I bet they bugged your house or at least your phone."

"Yes, chances are they have. I have been very careful."

Morgan had turned white as the snow outside. "When was the last time I called you?"

"Ten days ago. They began their surveillance in the last six days, well after the phone conversation."

"Maybe they showed up because of the call. I distinctly remember speaking about the weather at the lake."

Morgan's concern was making me nervous.

"I am sure it did not have anything to do with that." Ivan

bent over and picked up the knives. "Besides, there are a hundred lakes in this area."

"Nevertheless," I said. "We can't call you at your home again."

"I agree." Ivan pulled a piece of paper from his pocket and gave it to Morgan. "The top number is for a fairly secluded phone booth in my area and the other is for a close friend. We can have set times to call at the phone booth. If you need to reach me on other occasions, you can call my friend and she will relay the message to me. Maggie is very trustworthy."

Ivan's plan for communication made me feel better.

"Now, how is the manuscript coming along?"

"Really well," I said. "We've just finished the first draft."

"Splendid. May I read it?"

❧

Ivan read right through the day and well into the evening. Morgan took notes for him. I worked on the edits Morgan had finished the day before. It was a marathon because Ivan needed to return home the following afternoon.

Around ten o'clock, Ivan leaned back in his chair and rubbed his eyes. "I am very impressed with your work, Nick. I can see why Carl chose you."

"Thanks." I stifled a yawn. "Morgan's been a huge help. She's a natural editor."

"That I already knew; fantastic work, Morgan." Ivan covered a yawn with his right hand. "I have approximately fifty pages left. They will have to wait until the morning."

❧

Around 10:30a.m., when Ivan finished the last page, he looked over at me. "The way it is written will be very understandable to those who are not academics. For example, how the fertilizer spill had to be treated as a hazardous waste cleanup. Yet Naintosa thinks it is acceptable to spray these toxins on the food people consume."

"So, you think our interpretations are correct?" I felt pleased with my work.

"Most are. I will help you amend the ones that are not."

Morgan came over with fresh coffee and we gathered around her laptop.

Ivan pointed out the areas that needed changes. Even though Morgan had taken notes, I took my own to make sure we didn't miss a detail. There was a lot of revision.

In the second to last chapter Ivan stopped and re-read two pages. "Is this all the information on the patented seeds?"

I shrugged. "That's all the documentation the notes contained."

Ivan scrolled up to take another look. "There is not sufficient proof."

"Why not?" I asked. "Naintosa's able to patent the seeds; the farmers have to buy new seeds from them every year; Naintosa controls the seed supply and makes a ton of money. Simple."

"He who controls the food supply, controls the world." Morgan sounded very serious.

Ivan and I looked over at her.

We were all silent for a moment. The information was sinking in to an even deeper level.

In a barely audible tone, as if speaking to himself, Ivan said, "That is how they are able to sue a farmer if the genetically engineered seed accidentally migrates into his traditional crops."

Morgan blinked. "What do you mean?"

"Leave this with me," Ivan said. "I need to gather more information."

⁑

It was late afternoon by the time we finished reviewing Ivan's edit.

He walked over to his briefcase and pulled out some papers. "There is another cover-up to add. I think it would best be added to chapter seven."

Morgan sat up straight. "What happened?"

"Experimental corn, not for human consumption, was suspiciously mixed with traditional corn in grain elevators. Over a million bags of taco chips were made from the corn. Many people became ill. The genetic alteration gave the corn a similar composition to methanol when digested. Methanol is very toxic. People developed blindness and/or flu like symptoms, with vomiting and diarrhea, as their bodies tried to flush the poison. Six people died."

I was still amazed at Naintosa. Every cover-up was a sign telling them that what they were doing was wrong. Yet they kept pushing forward. "So what happened then?"

"The manufacturer destroyed the bags in the warehouses and stores. They recalled the ones that had been sold."

Morgan looked horrified. "What did they tell the public?"

"There was a problem with the binding agent in the manufacturing process; nothing to worry about. They knew they could not be prosecuted, because no one could prove the actual chips had caused the damage." Ivan gave a wry smile of disgust. "If people returned the chips, they would get a new bag of good ones, twice as big. It showed they were good corporate citizens."

"Did they find out how it happened?" I asked.

"They said they suspected sabotage by a militant environmental group."

"How could they do that?" Morgan asked.

"By altering shipping forms."

"Why would the environmentalists do such a thing?" People had died!

"So they could expose how dangerous the genetically altered corn was and how easily it could get into people's stomachs. Even Naintosa did not want that corn on the market."

"I guess the environmentalists almost achieved their goal," Morgan said. "Too bad it was covered up so quickly."

Ivan sighed. "I do not always agree with some environmentalist's tactics, but they are effective at times. Yet, deaths of innocent people can never be justified."

"I agree." Morgan nodded.

I made a note for the future. We had to get the finished

book to as many environmental groups as possible. It could help with their causes in a more productive way.

"Nick, how much time do you need to make these changes and additions?"

"A week or so, I figure."

"Very well, I will return in a week. I have an editor I trust who is waiting for the manuscript. I will tell her to expect it in two weeks."

CHAPTER 25

Morgan was set on teaching me some yoga moves. I wasn't flexible at all and kept falling on the floor or cramping up. After twenty minutes and many laughs at my expense, she gave up on me.

"Let's eat." Morgan stood up, a smirk still on her face.

I hobbled to the kitchen after her.

"We barely have any food left." She scanned the contents of the fridge. "After breakfast, you go get your Blazer and I'll make a shopping list."

✧

Over two feet of snow blanketed the ground. Ice crystals shimmered, glinting blue, red and yellow in the direct sunlight.

I found a snow shovel in the storage room and dug my way up the stairs. It felt therapeutic to be out, breathing in the cold, crisp air.

When I finally reached the top of the steps, the shirt under my jacket was damp with sweat.

I slung the shovel over my shoulder and headed down the road. It hadn't been plowed from last night's five fresh inches, so I walked in a set of tire tracks.

The Blazer hadn't been moved since the snow started. If I couldn't get it out in four-wheel drive, I'd have to shovel a pathway a hundred yards long through the snow. That'd take me half the day. Just shoveling the three foot bank the snow-plow created would take at least an hour.

My first step onto the snow bank only sank in about six

inches. I took a second step. As I put my full weight onto my left leg, it broke through the crust. "Shit." My leg was half way buried and my hiking boot was filling with icy cold. There was powder under the crust.

I pulled my leg out and jumped from the bank to the virgin crystals beyond. It was up to my knees, but easy to wade through. My feet and legs soaked quickly as my body heat melted the snow that got into my boots and up my jeans.

The vehicle was covered. I cleared around the driver's side door with a few swipes of my jacket sleeve and opened it. The ice scraper/brush that I'd only used once was wedged under the seat. I yanked it free and began to clear the roof.

The squeak of brakes being applied made me stop. I heard the quiet throb of a large vehicle idling.

I slunk over to an evergreen bush, hunched down and peered through the branches. Right in front of the entryway was a late model black Suburban with tinted windows. It looked identical to the one that had followed us to the border.

The passenger door opened. Out stepped a tall man in a long, black coat and white canvas boots. I recognized him immediately. Holy fuck, the Lieutenant. I felt the trees and sky close in on me. My heart pounded so hard I was afraid he'd hear it.

He raised his sunglasses, bent over and touched an indentation in the snow bank. Then he looked up and followed my footprints with his eyes.

I crouched lower, even though I knew he couldn't see me.

The passenger window descended. The Lieutenant turned to face the driver. Whatever was said made the Lieutenant get back in.

I was shivering hard. Not from cold, but from panic. If I made contact with the tree in front of me, the vibration would send all the snow from the branches down on my head.

Right now, those tracks could have been made by anyone. There was no reason for them to think I'd made them. I hoped that Morgan wouldn't decide to stick her head out of the cabin and come look for me.

The vehicle moved slowly down the road.

If the thugs were in Christina Lake, it was only a matter of time before they found us. "Okay think, think, what do I do?" I said, out loud. The road reached a dead end half a mile away, so they'd be coming back in a few minutes. If they saw a second set of foot prints coming from this driveway they'd investigate and find the Blazer for sure. I had to stay put.

As I waited, I wondered how they suspected or knew we were in Christina Lake.

It was a good fifteen minutes before I heard a vehicle approaching. I crouched back behind the tree, with a clear view of the road.

The Suburban drove by at a snail's pace, but didn't stop.

After the sound of the vehicle had faded, I slid the snow shovel under the Blazer. Then with as much accuracy as possible and as quickly as I could, I retraced my footsteps back to the road.

When I reached the snow bank I couldn't see the black SUV, so I maneuvered awkwardly over the mound and sprinted toward the cabin. As I came around the bend in the road I saw the Suburban disappear around the far end of the cove.

I raced down the stairs, managing to stay upright by hanging onto the handrails and letting my feet slide over the individual icy steps.

When I burst through the door Morgan was coming from the back of the cabin.

"What happened? What's wrong? It sounded like you fell down the stairs."

I bent over, gasping for air. "I...just...saw...the...thugs."

"Are you sure it was them?"

"Positive."

Her eyes went wide. "Did they see you? Where are they now?"

I told her what happened.

"Now what do we do?" Morgan walked to the dining room, then paced back to me. "They obviously don't know exactly where we are, but if they keep looking around here, they're bound to find us."

"That's what I was thinking." I looked directly into her big blue eyes, "We need to make a run for it."

"Make a run for it to where?" Morgan turned toward the window. "We should go back to Vancouver and get lost in the crowd. From there, if we need to, we can fly somewhere."

That plan felt good. "Okay...Vancouver."

"Let's pack and get out of here." By the time Morgan had said the words, she was already on the stairs leading to the bedrooms.

"Hold on. I think we should wait until dark. It'll be safer."

Morgan stopped. "You're right. But while we wait we should keep a look out. In case they come back."

"Can you go on the first watch?" I asked. "I'll back up the manuscript and pack up the computers."

"Perfect." Morgan backtracked to put on her coat and boots.

I went to the front door and looked outside. "Where're you going to watch from?"

She came up beside me and we surveyed the embankment between the road and the cabin.

Morgan pointed up to the right. "How about beside that tree? From there I can see if they come around the cove." Morgan carefully climbed over the thick wooden railing. The bank was steep. Every time she took a step, she slid down a foot before gaining traction. She held onto a bush's branches as she made her way the couple yards to the young spruce that would provide her camouflage.

"Okay, I won't be long." I left the door slightly ajar in case she needed to get my attention.

I made copies of the manuscript and placed one disk with my papers and one with Morgan's. I inserted the phone line from the computer into the wall jack. As the slow connection was being made, I wrote a note to Sue asking her to put the attached manuscript in a safe place. Once the hissing of the internet connection was complete I sent the e-mail. Then I packed up the computers and all the papers.

Once everything was sitting beside the door I felt less anxious. The most important stuff was ready to go.

Morgan was probably getting cold, so I put on my jacket and soggy hiking boots and went outside.

"Any sign of them?" I asked, straddling the railing.

"Not a single car's come around the cove."

"Why don't you go inside to warm up and pack the supplies?"

"Gladly." She slid down the bank and I helped her over the railing.

I climbed over to the watch spot.

It was silent except for small gusts of breeze through the trees. Big snowflakes began to fall. I didn't welcome them; they'd slow our drive. Then I realized that fresh snow was to our advantage. It would cover our tracks, both physically and metaphorically.

❦

At dusk we went to dig out the Blazer.

I started the engine so it warmed up while we cleaned the vehicle off. An inch of fresh snow had already accumulated on the parts I'd cleared a few hours ago. I really hoped we could make it out without having to shovel the hundred yards to the road.

"Here we go," I said, as we got inside.

Morgan slammed her door and crossed her fingers.

I put it into 4LOW and then reverse. The tires gripped immediately and we slowly began to move.

Just before the road there was a crunching sound, as the back end lifted onto the bank left by the snowplow. We stopped.

I opened my door to survey the situation. The bank reached about eight inches above the bumper. "Hmm."

"I guess we have no choice but to shovel," Morgan said.

"Hold on," I said, with all the arrogance that only a male about to bash something could have.

Morgan put on her seat belt.

I drove forward about fifteen feet. Morgan reached for the brace above her door and gave me a reassuring nod. I put the truck into reverse and gave it gas. All four wheels spun and then caught. We hit the bank with an impact that lurched us forward in our seats. Snow flew in every direction. Then we broke through.

I didn't let go of the gas soon enough and we skidded right across the road.

Morgan shrieked.

We hit the other bank with a thud. Luckily that stopped us. Beyond it was a thirty foot drop.

"Oops." I tried to sound casual, all my male arrogance gone.

"Perfect." Morgan shook her head, as she looked out the window at the lake below. "You could've saved the thugs some trouble and killed us yourself."

I put it into drive and gently touched the gas. We easily pulled out of the snow bank and onto the road.

It took us three loads each to clear our stuff out of the cabin.

"I'm going to miss this place," Morgan said. "It was cozy."

"Uhuh, it's peaceful here." I locked the door behind us.

Morgan put her hand on my shoulder. "We accomplished a lot together."

Her sincere moment caught me off guard. "Yeah...we did."

"Now for the next chapter in our adventure." Morgan gave me an optimistic smile and a quick pat.

We both took a last look out at the lake.

❧

As we drove into town we spotted the black Suburban outside the Totem Motel.

"We made the right decision to leave tonight," Morgan said.

We left Naintosa's thugs behind and headed back to Vancouver in the dark, snow falling to cover our tracks.

CHAPTER 26

By the time we reached the hill leading down to Osoyoos, we were in near white-out conditions. Traveling at twenty miles per hour, the visibility was only about thirty feet.

"Maybe we should spend the night here." I strained to see, my chest right up against the steering wheel and forehead touching the windshield.

"That only puts them an hour and a half behind us." Morgan sat sideways on the seat, watching the road behind us. "Can't we go farther?"

"Okay, but let's at least stop and get gas so I can rest my eyes."

We stopped at the first gas station we saw.

I felt better after the short break and the snow seemed to have let up slightly. I could now see forty feet in front of us.

"Just a while longer," Morgan said. "We can spend the night in Princeton."

❧

We arrived in Princeton after two more hours and checked into a roadside motel, parking the Blazer at the back.

I collapsed on a bed. It'd been a long day.

Morgan went straight for the phone and called Ivan's friend. She relayed a message for him to contact us.

With effort, I rolled onto my side to face her. "How long before he calls?"

"Not too long, I hope."

I gave into the weight of my eyelids and closed them.

"Are you going to call Sue?" Morgan yawned.

"In the morning."

The ring of the phone startled me. I must've dozed off.

"Hi Ivan." Morgan paused and then continued, "We had to leave. Naintosa's men were in Christina Lake. We got out just in time." She listened for a moment then nodded. "Yeah, Nick recognized the one who shot at us. And no they didn't know where we were staying. We're on our way back to Vancouver, to get lost in the city." Another pause, then, "I'll call you when we get a place there."

She hung up and lay down.

"What'd he say?" I had one eye open.

"Ivan said it was a good decision to leave and to e-mail the manuscript to Sue. He also gave me the name of a hotel on Burrard Street. Do you know where that is?"

"It's close to where we stayed last time.

ﯦ

It'd stopped snowing, but I had to clean a good three inches off the truck. We left Princeton before first light.

Travel was slow over the pass on compact snow, but at least the road had been plowed and sanded.

After three and a half hours we exited the freeway onto the outer streets of Vancouver. Morgan navigated with the map. It wasn't long before we were downtown and found the hotel Ivan had recommended.

"It's a busy area." Morgan leaned forward and looked up from the street to the beige tower in front of us.

Once we were checked in and the Blazer stored in the underground parkade, we went up to our room.

It was classy, finished in a pale gray with green and burgundy accents. All the furniture was of a traditional style; dark stained wood with rounded corners. The floor to ceiling window showed a view to the West. We could see past the park to the harbor and the mountains of Vancouver Island in the distance.

"I could write in this place," I said, as I positioned the computers onto a table next to the window.

After lunch, we found a bank of pay phones in the lobby. I called the familiar work number.

"Sue speaking."

"Hey Sue."

Morgan had her back to me as if standing guard.

"Nick, how are you?"

"Good. Did you get the e-mail I sent?"

"I stayed up half the night reading it. Some parts blew me away."

"Can you copy it onto a disk and put it in a safe place?"

"Already done."

"Excellent. Did you get any information on Naintosa and Dr. Schmidt?"

"Just superficial stuff so far, but I'm still working on it."

"What've you got?" I tapped Morgan on the shoulder and motioned for her to place her head next to the receiver.

She moved up close and brushed my hand as she touched the top of the receiver. Our eyes met. I looked into those brilliant blue pools for a second, before she looked away. Focus, I told myself. This wasn't the time to have thoughts about her beauty. I could smell the familiar lavender scent of her hair. Focus, focus, focus.

"Are you okay?" Morgan asked me.

"Yeah...no problem."

"What's going on over there?" Sue asked, from the other end of the line.

"I've got Morgan listening in."

"Oh, hi, Morgan."

"Hi Sue. So what did you find out?"

"So far I found out that Naintosa is owned by Pharmalin, a pharmaceutical manufacturer. Pharmalin was founded in 1910 by Dr. Hendrick Schmidt, a doctor and chemist, in Cologne Germany. Their head office is still there today. Their main focus is on pain killers and cancer drugs. Oh, and they recently branched out into nutritional products. Remember that story we heard on the news at McMynn's, Nick?"

"Yeah, when all this started, right?"

Morgan asked, "How could Dr. Schmidt have founded the company in 1910?"

"Hendrick Schmidt the first started the company." Sue's tone was short. "Hendrick Schmidt the fourth now runs it."

I tried not to laugh.

"Oh sorry, strawberry blonde moment." Morgan rolled her eyes and elbowed me in the ribs. "Go on."

"It's a family business. Our current Dr. Hendrick Schmidt, number four, just like the others, is very reclusive."

"Of course," I said. "I would've guessed that's how they operate."

"I was able to find one picture of number four," Sue said. "He's a short, chubby, bald, Arian dude, in his fifties, with intense eyes that look as if they could see through steel walls. I haven't been able to find out more yet. He doesn't do charity work, doesn't schmooze."

"It's a start," I said.

"Then there's Naintosa. It was founded as a subsidiary of Pharmalin in 1948, by Dr. Hendrick Schmidt the third. Originally it was just a fertilizer manufacturer, but then expanded into pesticides and more recently, of course, genetic engineering."

"The background helps." She'd been thorough.

"More detailed information to follow," Sue said. "I've also started compiling a list of people and companies that'd be interested in the book."

Morgan glanced at me and raised an eyebrow. "Great idea."

"Just trying to do my part."

"Oh." I'd almost forgotten. "See if you can find out anything about a pharmaceutical company called DKKR. All initials, D-K-K-R."

"Okay. They're tied into this?"

"Dr. Elles did some work for them."

"They sound shady," Morgan added.

"Call me in a week for an update."

I pressed the button to disconnect the call and handed the receiver over. "I might as well meet you upstairs."

"I'll be up right after I check in with Ivan." Morgan looked over my shoulder at a clock on the wall. "He should be at the pay phone I'm to call any minute."

*

Once in our hotel room I started re-editing where I'd left off in Christina Lake.

Morgan's call didn't take long. "Ivan will be here in nine days to look at the second draft."

"Great. Anything else?"

"His home is still being watched, so there are more than two men looking for us."

"That's not very comforting. The sooner we get this thing ready to go to the editor, the better."

"I agree." Morgan sat down on the edge of her bed. "These people have a lot of resources. It's only a matter of time before they find us again."

I wondered if we'd be safe even after the manuscript was out of our hands. "Hopefully when this is done we can get some kind of protection."

"Yeah, hopefully." Morgan looked worried. After a moment she shrugged it off. "Ivan gave me the name of a good organic market. We should move to a place with a kitchenette in it. Also, he gave me the name of a restaurant that's really strict about where they get their ingredients and how they prepare the food. We can have dinner there tonight."

"But is the food any good?"

"He said it was." She smiled. "We can even trust the meat."

"Great. I'll admit my body is having trouble being vegetarian. Vegetables just don't fill me up like meat does."

"I'm with you." Morgan rubbed the sweater over her flat stomach.

She could be the poster girl for clean vegetarian living, I thought.

♨

We went for an early dinner.

The atmosphere at the restaurant was that of a casual new age place, which we expected. Lots of plants, green walls, wooden tables and chairs, somewhat cluttered.

The food turned out to be superb. We shared an olive tapenade. For the main course, I had a pork and potato dish, while Morgan ate salmon with rice. We stuffed ourselves.

♨

In the morning we decided to get back to our routine. The meditation started off rough. Both of us squirmed around on our beds trying to get comfortable. Finally we settled into silence.

Morgan's gasp brought me out of my relaxed state. It was as if she had just emerged from being under water for too long. "Are you okay?"

She was breathing heavy and her face was as white as the sheets on her bed. "Fine, perfect...no problem."

"Are you sure? Did you see or feel something bad?"

"No, just lost track of my breathing." Color began to return to her cheeks. "Don't worry about it. I'm fine."

I had to leave it alone. I couldn't force it out of her. She'd tell me in her own time if it was important.

♨

Morgan had spent the afternoon looking for a place with a kitchenette. "How's the writing?" she asked, when she returned. "Were you productive?"

"I edited twenty seven pages." I was proud of my progress. "How about you? Did you find us a new home?"

"Yep. It's a bit more than I want to spend, but whatever. It's a suite hotel across the street from the library, which might come in handy."

"When do we move?"

"Tomorrow."

CHAPTER 27

The red numbers of the bedside clock read 4:37am. I sat up when I heard another moan. It was coming from Morgan. She was weeping.

I slid over closer to her bed and turned on a lamp. "Morgan, wake up," I whispered. "You're having a bad dream."

Her body shuddered and she opened her tear-swollen eyes.

"You were having a bad dream," I repeated. "What was it about?"

She looked confused.

"It must've been sad."

She stared past me for a moment. "I'm sure it wasn't anything important."

"Remember, dreams can sometimes be premonitions."

"I can't remember." She looked uneasy. "Can't we just go back to sleep?"

Something was definitely up with her. I wished she would tell me what it was.

❧

The new place was basically a modern, furnished apartment. We each had our own bedroom and ensuite. There was a small kitchen off the entrance with lots of stainless steel. The main room contained a lightly stained dining room table for four, a taupe couch, matching chair, pine desk and armoire that hid the television. The walls were a soft, yellowy cream and the carpet off white. We had everything we needed, except for a view. Views were expensive.

It was a clear, crisp day. After we'd moved in it wasn't hard to convince Morgan to take a walk.

We made our way a few blocks north to an area called Gastown.

As we waited at an intersection for the light to change, I observed two fast food restaurants across the street from each other. A steady stream of people passed in and out.

The light changed and we crossed the intersection. As we walked past one of the restaurants I could see the people inside through the window. Most heads were down, stuffing their faces with food served in a bun. There wasn't much conversation or laughter, just getting down to the business of eating. Interesting, I thought. I'd never paid attention to that before. I used to be one of them. I put the image in the back of my mind for later use.

Morgan stopped to browse through a rack of clothes displayed outside a trendy little shop, but found nothing that interested her.

The sunshine brought out an eclectic group of people. All shapes, sizes and styles milled about. There was the overweight tourist with a safari hat on top, socks and sandals on the bottom. We passed two women whose hair was going everywhere, wearing baggy, flowery pants. Then there were regular jeans clad folk like us and a few suits in the mix.

Gastown was one of the oldest parts of Vancouver. There were about four blocks of restored brick buildings, with gas lamps and trees lining cobblestone streets. It was alive with activity around galleries, restaurants and souvenir shops.

We wandered block after block until we reached the end.

"What a contrast," Morgan said.

Behind us were clean, lively streets, vibrant with color. Ahead was grungy and dilapidated. Litter was scattered everywhere. The people looked disheveled. It felt and smelt sad and dirty.

"Let's stop here," Morgan said, with a sour look.

"What? Not into an adventure?" I sounded cavalier, but didn't want to continue either.

"I think we both have enough adventure in our lives right now."

As we turned around we heard an elderly voice. "Spare some change?" There stood a short, round, weathered looking lady. On her head was a straw hat decorated with multi-colored plastic flowers and dangling fruit. She wore a tattered, but somehow still bright, red and yellow flowered dress. It was covered by an open, gray wool jacket that was frayed at the hem. She was pushing a shopping cart filled with empty bottles and clothes. The lady's skin was fleshy, yet still had some pink life to it.

As she focused on Morgan, I looked into her eyes. They were a haunting, faded blue. There was a crazy look to them and she didn't blink often, but they had a sparkle.

Just then she turned her gaze on me and a faint smile crossed her thick lips. "Sir, please?" She held out a callused, dirt imbedded hand.

"Sorry, I don't have any change." I wasn't sure what to make of this woman. From a distance you'd think she was a typical bag lady, but close up, there was something intriguing about her.

"Wait." Morgan was fumbling around in her purse. "Here you go." She pulled out five dollars.

"Thank you, sweetie." She looked down at the three coins in her hand.

"You're welcome." Morgan gave her a faint smile.

Suddenly, with the other hand, the old lady reached out and gripped Morgan's arm. "Your mother needs your help. She wants you to meet Alice."

Morgan gasped and stepped back, pulling away from the woman.

"Do you understand dear?" The old woman's eyes had turned a brilliant, depthless blue.

"No." Morgan's own eyes were wide in shock.

"You will sweetie." Her voice was sympathetic. "You will."

She looked over at me. "Good luck to you and be careful. Follow your intuition."

I just stood there, not knowing what to say.

The old woman turned her cart to go around us, took three steps, and looked back. "Don't forget your dreams." Then with deliberate, slow steps, she pushed her cart across the street and disappeared into an alley.

Morgan's eyes welled with tears.

"Let's sit down for a minute." I pointed to a bench on the touristy side of the block. Morgan's arm trembled when I took it to guide her.

She sat down and dried her eyes with her jacket sleeve. "I can't believe that just happened. How did the old lady know? How could she get into my head?"

"What do you mean?"

"In the last few days I've dreamt about my mother and she's shown up in my meditations."

I sat closer. "That's what's been happening?" Now I understood.

"I didn't want to make a big deal about it. But..." She took a deep breath and sniffled. "Each time it was the same scene."

"Really? Dreams *and* meditations? That's important."

She stared out into the street. "What's the reason for this? What does it mean? I'm blown away..."

"Why don't we start by going over the dream? Can you describe it to me?"

Morgan gave me a troubled look.

"It'll help to say it out loud."

She absently rubbed her hands together. "Each time, I'd be sitting in the passenger seat of an old car. It was dark and cold. There was no traffic. We passed a set of signal lights, turned right and drove down along a river ravine; the city disappearing on either side of us."

"Who was *we*? Did you know the driver?"

"She was middle aged. It seemed like she'd had a hard life and was poor. Her face was pasty and puffy. She was dressed in an old denim dress, with a thick brown winter coat over it. There was a red kerchief over her thick, graying brown hair."

I tried to imagine what the woman looked like. Morgan had seen a lot of detail, for a dream.

"I knew where we were, because it was the way from our house in Boston to my parent's lab on the city's outskirts. We drove down and along the deep ravine. I felt a familiar park on the right and steep embankment that lead down to the river, on the left. The road wound for about two miles, before coming out at an industrial area where Naintosa's building was."

"Why was the park familiar? Did something significant happen there in the past?" I felt like I was interrogating her, but I needed to know as much as possible.

Morgan thought about it for a second and shrugged. "No, not really. My mother and I had a picnic there once, while my father was working on a Saturday. He joined us when he was done."

"Okay, sorry, go on."

"As we came around a corner, we saw two sets of headlights facing us. One car was stopped in the middle of the road." Morgan's voice faltered and she began to cry.

"It's okay." I reached over and gently squeezed her shoulder. "Do you want to stop for a minute?"

"No, I have to…" She took a deep breath. "I'm fine, I can do this. Okay." She inhaled quickly and exhaled slowly. "It was my mother's car. There was a man leaning into the driver's side window. As we passed he took a step back. I saw my mother's head slump forward against the steering wheel." Tears ran down Morgan's cheeks. "I couldn't do or say anything, only watch."

I squeezed her shoulder and felt her stiffen.

"No, I have to do this. You have to know my dream, so you can help me." She wiped away the tears. "The lady I was with drove half way around the next bend and pulled over. I turned around in my seat to see what was going on."

"Could the man see you?"

"Probably. We could see what he was doing."

"Yeah, most likely." Not a smart move for the lady, I thought.

"The man walked back to a big, dark pickup. The truck moved up until its bumper touched my mother's. Then it pushed my mother's car over the edge of the embankment." Morgan's voice went up an octave. "As the car went over, the front end clipped a tree, which caused it to roll. It flipped three times before it hit the riverbank."

Morgan had to stop. She was sobbing.

I sat patiently by her side until she could continue.

"I was frozen in my seat, screaming inside, watching without the ability to help. The lady beside me had intense fear in her eyes. She'd put the car in reverse, but didn't move. My mother's car was on its roof. Then there was a quick flash of light and a loud bang from where the pickup was." Morgan took a quick breath. "My mother's car exploded into flames."

She slumped back on the bench, putting her hands over her face. "That's where it always ended."

What a terrible reoccurring nightmare to have. I felt awful for her.

Morgan reached into her handbag, pulled out a tissue and wiped her face.

I watched until she looked pulled together enough before I asked, "Was your mother's car found in that spot for real and had it been on fire?"

She nodded and sniffled. "Yes."

A shiver ran up my spine. I'd heard of people having dreams like Morgan's about past events. By meditating she could've tapped into her psychic ability. "That means the lady driving the car you were in is most likely real and actually witnessed it."

"Don't you think they would've found her and killed her, too?"

"Probably." Then it came to me. "What if you meditate with the intention of finding out if this lady's still alive and where she is?"

"You want me to intentionally have these horrible visions?" Morgan sat up straight.

"It's worth a try. If she actually did witness the accident...I mean murder...and by some chance is still alive, we need to find her. And what about the old woman we just talked to?"

Morgan nodded, her expression thoughtful.

I went over the exchange on the street. "The old woman said your mother needs your help and wants you to meet Alice."

"You think Alice is the lady who witnessed the murder?"

"Yeah and I have a feeling she's alive."

"Me too."

We looked at each other.

"Let's go find the old woman." Morgan stood and put her used tissue in the garbage can next to the bench. "She couldn't have gotten too far."

We crossed the street and entered the alley into which we'd seen the woman push her cart. We were definitely out of our element. In doorways and beside almost every dumpster, homeless people and drug addicts, stood, crouched or lay. Some stared as we passed. This was the underbelly of Vancouver; the part they never talked about in travel brochures.

We walked quickly out onto the next street. No sign of her.

A tall man, with matted long hair and unkempt beard watched us with an intense stare. After we passed, he picked up a back pack and began to follow.

Morgan strained to whisper, "We gotta get out of here."

We sped up around the block, back toward Gastown. He kept pace with us, about twenty yards behind. As soon as we crossed into the touristy section, he stopped.

We turned and looked. The fury in his dark features was penetrating. An invisible line separated his world from ours and he couldn't or didn't want to cross over.

"I guess we'll see the old lady again, if we're meant to." I was breathing hard.

"Hopefully." Morgan looked at the man, looking at her from the other side.

CHAPTER 28

I *watched from the doorway, smelling grease and feeling my stomach churn. Inside was a rotation of people, wait-ing in line, ordering and paying. They'd carry their plastic red trays of wrapped food to red metal tables and eat quickly, not stopping to breathe. All had the same features – pasty, doughy skin, sweaty faces, lifeless eyes, globs of ketchup and sauce around their lips. Cheeks ballooned as they chewed. They struggled to waddle back out into the street; as if the extra layers of fat made their bones ache from the load.*

I opened my eyes and pulled the sheets back to cool off. I'd been well on my way to becoming one of those people.

It was early. My thoughts moved from the dream to the future. After we finished the manuscript, whether we got protection or not, we'd have to get on with our lives. Where should I live? Seattle didn't appeal to me anymore. Maybe I'd go back to Christina Lake? That had a better feel, but wasn't realistic; maybe someday.

Would Morgan and I stick together? That would make a dif-ference. Was that important to me? At that point I wasn't sure.

Should I change my name? What should it be...Dirk Long-man? I snickered.

What would I do with my life? I didn't want to go back to the newspaper business. That life was so distant to me now. Maybe this book would open doors? I'd always wanted to write novels. I could write thrillers using my current experi-ences to get me started. Nothing like hands on experience.

"Nick, are you awake?" Morgan's voice came from the main room.

I propped my head up on the pillow and saw Morgan's silhouette in the doorway. "Uhuh. Just doing some thinking. How are you feeling? Any dreams?"

"No. Your snoring kept waking me up."

"From your bedroom?"

"Unfortunately."

"Oops, sorry."

"Come out into the living room and let's meditate."

We reviewed what we'd discussed on the wharf at Christina Lake. Morgan needed to ask a question when she began and be open to receiving the answer.

This morning, during my meditation I went into the gap. My mind shut down and for however long, there was nothing. No thoughts, no sounds, no time; just sweet nothing.

At the end, I asked a question: What do I do when this is all over?

I opened my eyes and saw Morgan with her arms and legs crossed. "Anything?"

"Nothing." She pushed herself up to sit on the sofa. "I think I'm trying too hard."

⚘

The next five days were productive. It rained the whole time, so there weren't any distractions from the editing.

Morgan's inner work wasn't going quite as well. She had stopped dreaming of her mother's accident and her meditations were blank. She knew it might take time, but she wanted the answers *now* and was discouraged.

⚘

"Here are a few more changes you missed." Morgan handed me some loose papers.

"I'll fix them after I finish these last pages."

There was a knock at the door.

"Ivan's here." Morgan jumped off the chair.

She was always so excited to see Ivan. With her dad gone it seemed like Ivan was becoming the father figure in her life.

"Nick, good to see you safe and working hard," Ivan came in with Morgan at his side.

"Nice to see you too." I stood to shake his hand.

"How is the progress on the second draft?"

"Only nine pages to go."

He put his suitcase down beside the worktable. "How about I take you two out for dinner tonight? We can get started on the work in the morning?"

"Perfect." Morgan put her arm through Ivan's. "We've been cooped up in here forever."

Ivan smiled and patted her hand. "Have you been to the restaurant I told you about?"

"Five times," Morgan replied. "It's really good."

Ivan nodded. "I have a room two floors above. Let me go change and then we can go."

After escorting Ivan out, Morgan went to her bedroom to change as well.

I made some detailed notes, so I wouldn't forget the alterations I wanted to make in the morning.

"Nick, you'd better get ready," Morgan said. "Ivan will be back any minute."

I looked up at her. "Wow," I blurted out. She was beautiful no matter what she wore, but tonight she looked stunning.

"Do you like it?"

"You look fantastic." And I wasn't saying that just to be nice. Her makeup gently accentuated her big blue eyes, high cheekbones and full lips. Her strawberry blond hair was straight and silky. She had on a long black evening dress that clung to her every curve. The neckline was low, giving a good peek at her cleavage. A slit up one side reached half way up her thigh, making her legs look even longer. Did she ever look sexy.

"I felt like dressing up." She frowned only for a second, before turning it into a soft smile. "Do you have anything nice you could wear?"

I realized I was staring with my mouth open. "Oh, uh yeah, I do. Give me a second."

I rushed to my bedroom and put on my only suit. I had to

cinch the belt two notches tighter than before. As I looked
in the mirror to knot my tie, I thought I looked pretty dash-
ing myself. But if I kept up this clean living lifestyle, the suit
would need to be taken in around the middle.

"How does this look?" I asked, as I walked into the living
room.

"You look really nice." She gave me the once over. "I keep
forgetting to comment on the fact that you've lost your, uh...
little belly."

"Yeah, all my stuff fits loose."

"I've noticed that. We're going to have to go shopping."

"I'd appreciate your help. I don't like getting clothes on my
own. Sue usually goes with me."

Ivan returned, dressed in a dark suit as well. "I have a surprise. After dinner I am taking you to see the Moscow ballet.
They are performing in Vancouver. I thought it would be a
nice treat."

"Oh, thank you," Morgan chirped.

I'd never been to the ballet and frankly didn't care if I ever
went to watch a bunch of people in tights flutter around. Oh
well. "Great." I tried to sound enthusiastic.

The restaurant was busy that night with the usual earthy
crowd.

As soon as we sat down Ivan ordered a bottle of Bordeaux.
He said it was the perfect wine for a cold winter night.

I scanned the menu, trying to decide if I should try something new or go with the beef medallions I'd had the last two
times. It came with an awesome mushroom sauce that was
borderline addictive.

"I take it that everything has gone smoothly since you returned to Vancouver?" Ivan asked.

"We got a lot of work done," I said. "And I hope Morgan
makes some progress on figuring out her mother's accident."

Ivan looked at Morgan. "What do you mean?"

We couldn't see Morgan's face, because of the menu in

front of it. Her reaction was hidden from us. I thought for sure she would've told Ivan about her dreams and encounter with the old woman in Gastown. It was obvious she hadn't.

"Well..." She finally lowered the menu and shifted in her seat. "I sort of had a premonition and then we met someone who reinforced it for me."

Ivan's eyebrows rose. "Why don't you start from the beginning dear?"

Morgan was tentative. She stuttered and shrugged as she spoke, avoiding eye contact.

I wanted to jump in and help her, but didn't feel right interfering with her experience.

After she'd finished, Ivan sat quietly, just sipping his wine.

I had to ask. "Did you know a lady fitting the description who may have been named Alice?"

Morgan shook her head. "Of course he didn't. It's stupid."

Ivan finally set his wine down. "I do not give much credibility to such things as dreams and premonitions. However, I did know a lady by the name of Alice. She worked as a night custodian at Naintosa."

Morgan and I looked at each other. "Really?"

"She cleaned our lab. Since we worked very late at times, we would speak with her on occasion. Your description matched her perfectly."

"Did she disappear?" I sat forward in my chair.

"I do not know. Claudia's accident was three years ago. I had left Naintosa by then."

Morgan asked, "Could you talk to your contact there?"

"I will call him in the morning."

Optimism sparked in Morgan's eyes.

❧

Morgan and I were late getting up and had to rush to get ready.

"You look nice this morning," I said, as we got into the elevator. She always looked good, which distracted me more and more. I needed to focus on the task at hand and quit ogling her. Her form fitting jeans and tight pink sweater didn't help.

"I look terrible." She looked into the reflection of the mirrored wall and touched the skin below her eyes. "I'm puffy."

The elevator reached the ground floor and we proceeded through the clean, beige, sparse lobby. Two people stood at the front desk, either checking in or out. The hotel was geared toward longer stays, so there was never a lot of activity around the entrance.

We had to go outside to get to the restaurant, even though it was in the same building. The air was brisk.

"Thanks," Morgan said, as I opened the glass door for her.

It was a local chain eatery that advertised using free range eggs. The walls were pale yellow and had historic black and white pictures of Vancouver hanging from them. Dark brown booths lined the sides and one row down the middle. It smelled of maple and bacon.

"We really need to go shopping," she said, as we were about to sit down. She gave the bottom of my striped shirt a tug to straighten it. "It's just hanging off you. Most of your clothes are old anyway."

Ivan came in right behind us. "I spoke with my contact at Naintosa."

"How could you've talked to him already?" I asked. "It's only eight o'clock."

Morgan rolled her eyes. "There's a three hour time difference between Vancouver and Boston."

"Oh yeah." My face must've turned the same color as the strawberry jam on the table. "I must still be half asleep."

Ivan ignored us both. "He remembered Alice as well."

Morgan looked encouraged. "Really?"

"He does not know what happened to her. However, he has access to employment records and is going to find out what he can."

"How long do you think it'll take?" she asked.

"I hope to know later today."

After breakfast we went up to our suite and got to work.

"Nick, I have some additional information I want you to add toward the end." Ivan placed some papers on the dining table in between the laptops.

"What's it about?"

"Bill sent it from London. A colleague of his intercepted an internal report from Cologne. It is regarding the long-term consumption of a specific strain of genetically engineered wheat."

Morgan asked, "What's it say?"

"After two years of consuming food made from this strain of wheat, eighty-seven of the hundred people used in the study developed severe allergies. Out of that group, twenty-seven percent had developed polyps in the glands in the lining of the colon."

"What could those polyps be?" I asked.

"An early stage of colon cancer."

Morgan's voice raised an octave, "In only two years?"

Ivan shrugged. "Bear in mind it was a very small test group."

"But still," I said.

"There has to be an isolated toxin in the wheat."

"I'll add it to the part where Naintosa's own testing proves that what they're doing is hazardous."

Morgan raised a finger. "What if they *wanted* those results? What if that moves them to their end goal? Is that too far-fetched?"

I thought about it for a second. "Like, Naintosa makes the public sick and Pharmalin cures them? We already know they don't care about making people ill. It's just the cost of doing business to them. But giving people life threatening colon cancer on purpose might be pushing it."

"It is appalling, but the thought has crossed my mind on more than one occasion," said Ivan. "If allergies, immune failure and colon cancer rise dramatically, Pharmalin could be the first on the market with drugs that control the epidemic. They would stand to make billions of dollars."

Morgan shook her head in anger. "They won't be able to cure everyone. They're murderers!"

"Capitalists in the most negative sense." The sad look on Ivan's face made me think he felt somewhat responsible for all of this.

I felt so frustrated. How was this little book going to stop them? If only we had concrete proof of their real intentions.

CHAPTER 29

Ivan and Morgan sat in front of her computer reading the second draft, making notes as they went.

I added the facts from Ivan's latest report to the manuscript. Chills ran through me the whole time. I felt anxious, as if we were in more immediate, serious danger.

Morgan looked over at me. "Your face is as white as a sheet."

I didn't answer. I just finished typing.

I saved the manuscript onto two disks and then hesitated. What was wrong? Why was I feeling this way? My finger trembled as I clicked on the e-mail icon.

The squelch of the phone line made Ivan and Morgan notice what I was doing.

Morgan asked, "Why are you connecting to the Internet?"

"I'm sending the second draft to Sue."

Ivan frowned. "Why not wait until we have made the corrections?"

"I'll send that as well once we've finished."

Morgan looked quizzical. "Is something wrong, Nick?"

I was afraid they'd think I'd lost it, but an excuse didn't come to mind. "I've had a strange feeling since Ivan gave us the information on the wheat causing cancer. It's probably nothing, but I don't want to take any chances."

"All right," Morgan said. "Go with your gut."

Ivan looked at Morgan with his eyebrows raised, but didn't say anything.

I added a brief note to Sue and pressed the send button. I felt some relief, but couldn't totally shake the uneasy feeling.

My mind took me back to the dark days when I was depressed. The possibility of going back to that state of being unnerved me as much as the sense that we were in immediate danger from the forces we'd chosen to battle.

After I was off-line, Ivan went to the phone and dialed.

It wasn't a good idea to call from the room, but I decided not to say anything. It would be awkward to question his actions.

Morgan and I waited as Ivan spoke with his contact at Naintosa.

"So, what did he say?" Morgan asked, the second he put down the receiver.

"Just as we suspected: Alice worked as a night custodian at Naintosa until Claudia's accident. She never came to work on that date and was never heard from again. No report was filed with the police. She had a history of instability and depression. It was not the only time she had missed work for a period of time. Whoever wrote the report recommended they terminate her employment if she returned."

"Wow..." Amazement shone in Morgan's eyes. "She's really a real person."

"Morgan's premonition is validated," Ivan said.

"We don't know if she's dead or alive." I thought back to the conversation with the old woman. Alice couldn't be in Vancouver...could she?

"We could hire a private detective to try find out what happened to her," Morgan said.

Ivan wrote on his pad. "I know who to ask about hiring an investigator."

Morgan looked anxious. "I really need to know what happened to her."

"We could do some of our own investigating." I looked from Ivan to Morgan. "You know, while we wait for the manuscript to come back from the publisher."

Morgan turned to me. "Yeah, good idea."

"We have about a third of the manuscript to read," Ivan said. "We should finish proofing tomorrow afternoon. Nick, if you continue to make the changes as we find them, the draft can be complete by the day after tomorrow."

I nodded. "That sounds about right."

"I will take a flight to see to the publisher on Thursday."

I picked up one of the disks I'd just copied and handed it to Ivan. "Keep this as a backup."

❧

It was hard for me to fall asleep that night. I still had the uneasy feeling of danger close by. Worse, now it was mixed with the knowledge that Alice was a real person. The clock read 1:26am when I looked at it last.

CHAPTER 30

My head felt as if it were being squeezed between clamps at my temples. This was the worst hangover I ever had. Wait a minute. I didn't drink anything last night.

I opened my eyes. Pitch black. I couldn't see. Arms and legs didn't work. I couldn't move. Panic overrode the pain in my head and engulfed my whole body. What was happening? It was hard to breathe. I gasped for air.

✤

I opened my eyes. I must've passed out. The sharp pain in my head had subsided somewhat, but a dull ache persisted. I tried to move. I was tied up, I realized, and some sort of dark fabric covered my eyes. I was on my back.

I *was* awake. I wasn't dreaming. This *was* real. Stay calm.

Think. What was going on? Think. Why didn't I pay attention to my sense of danger yesterday? Why didn't I move us to a different hotel...or something?

I tried to move again. The surface I was lying on was hard, like a table. It was slippery, but whatever bound me was anchored to it.

I heard a gasp and panicked moan beside me. I recognized who it was.

"Morgan," I whispered, "Are you all right?"

"What's happening?" she whispered back. "Where are..."

"They're awake," said a deep male voice.

"Sit them up," a second male voice said.

Footsteps like hard leather soles on concrete came toward us.

Hands reached under my arms and pulled me upwards into a seated position. The back of my head bounced against a wall. The throbbing in my head intensified. I gritted my teeth.

"Why are you doing this to us?" Morgan cried out.

"I admire your effort," said the second, familiar voice, through the darkness. "It's usually easy to find amateurs like you. I have to give you credit for staying one step ahead of us, until now."

Morgan growled. I could feel her thrashing near me.

Recognizing the Lieutenant's voice calmed me down. We'd been running from him for so long I felt like I knew him. How crazy was that? But being calm was to my advantage. I could think clearer.

"Nick, you're being awfully quiet," said the Lieutenant. "Why aren't you hysterical, like Morgan?"

"Fuck you, asshole!" Morgan's tone wasn't hysterical, it was menacing.

My voice cracked when I started talking. "What are you going to do with us?" I didn't sound calm. I had to be if there was any chance of figuring out a way through this.

"We'll see. It's not for me to decide."

"I have to go to the bathroom," said Morgan.

"Then go."

"Right here, in my pants?"

"What do I care? Sitting in your own piss and shit should be the least of your concerns."

From the sounds and surface vibration, Morgan was struggling with her restraints. "You can't get away with this."

"Nick, did you give any copies of your essay to anyone yet?"

"What essay?"

He laughed.

There was a harsh, sudden pain. A knuckle felt like it bore through my cheek into my upper gum. My head bounced off the wall. I saw stars against my closed eyelids.

"The one we found on your computers."

My mouth filled with blood. I swallowed the thick, copper tasting liquid and gagged. "No."

I strained for a deep breath. The place smelled industrial, somehow. I thought of dust on concrete. There was grease, too; lots of grease.

"What do you plan to do with this information?"

Without thought, I said, "Sell it to the highest bidder."

"So you're just in this to make a buck?"

"What do you think?" Morgan said. "It's pretty obvious why we're doing it."

There was a hard slap and Morgan gasped.

"Don't be cheeky with us. You want to cooperate, sweetheart. You don't want to have a sudden heart attack, do you?"

Morgan let out a growl and pulled so hard I could actually feel the surface we were on shift.

"Don't be mad at us, sweetheart. We're just doing our jobs."

It took everything I had not to freak out. "You don't have to hit her."

The other man snickered. "How else do we shut her up?"

The Lieutenant said, "Do you have a buyer for your essay yet?"

Using the word *essay* made the project sound smaller than it was. "We haven't finished it."

"Have you talked to anyone about it yet?"

"No."

Another sharp pain. It felt like my eye was being pushed into my brain. "Quit hitting me." I choked. "We're telling you the truth."

"Sure you are."

The other man laughed.

"Where is Dr. Ivan Popov? How much is he helping you?"

Where was Ivan? It sounded like they weren't sure how involved he was. Or that he was at the hotel. "Who?"

"Do you want me to hit you again? This time it won't be a gentle love tap."

I could feel his breath against my bleeding face. It smelled like peppermint. I twisted my hands, but the binds didn't give.

"Remember, Nick? You met him at my father's funeral."
It was clear Morgan was trying something. "We haven't seen
him since."

"I bet."

I did my best to sound sincere. "No, honestly."

"Wrong answer."

A fist hit just above my jaw. More pain. More blood. One
of my teeth was loose.

A second punch hit just below my eye. It glanced off the
blindfold. It still hurt like hell. The right side of my face
swelled almost instantly. Now I couldn't open my eye even if
I wanted to. I felt woozy.

"Let's go get something to eat, before we get the final orders," said the man who was doing all the hitting.

"Sure," said the Lieutenant. "You two want anything?"

They both laughed.

"Don't go anywhere. We haven't finished playing with you
yet," the Lieutenant said, as they walked away on the hard
echoing floor.

They kept talking from a distance, but it was hard to dis-
tinguish which one was speaking when.

"You stay here," one said. "I'll get the food. What do you
want?"

"Cheese burger, fries, and a diet cola."

That must've been the other guy. Somehow I didn't picture
the Lieutenant eating that kind of food.

As I heard the door close I began to try think of any way out
of this. It was hard. My brain felt scrambled. Any sense of composure I had was beaten out of me. They were going to kill us.

Morgan was silent.

A moment later, the man who stayed behind belched and
then grunted. It had to be the other guy. Not the Lieutenant.

He took a few steps and then a door slammed.

I waited a few moments, before I whispered, "Are you
okay? Any idea what to do?"

"Hold on a second," Morgan whispered back.

The man guarding us had obviously gone to the bathroom.
I could hear his grunting and smell the outcome of his efforts.

Whatever we were positioned on jiggled as Morgan moved around beside me. I waited, hoping she'd figured something out.

A hand pulled my head forward and untied the blindfold.

I opened the eye that still worked. It was hard to focus.

Morgan untied the faded yellow rope around my hands and feet.

Without a word, we got off the wheeled work bench that had been pushed up against a wall. Morgan held my arm to steady me. We moved quietly across the concrete storage room. Empty racks lined the other walls.

Once through the door, we found ourselves in a vacant warehouse. There was a set of larger doors all the way on the other side.

We ran, trying not to make noise. Morgan grabbed a hold of my arm to steady me as my knees wobbled and I veered off track. I couldn't stiffen my legs. Morgan pulled at me. She was on my left, but my body wanted to go right.

I cringed as the door creaked opened.

Before us was a loading bay leading into an alley. We bolted out into the pouring rain.

CHAPTER 31

The cut still bled. The warm blood mixed with the cold rain over my swollen shut eye. It affected my balance. Morgan held on and pulled me along. I rolled my ankle and caught it just before it could have sprained. I felt painfully intoxicated...impaired.

She dragged me through alleys until I couldn't go any further.

"Stop...please." I had to concentrate to keep from vomiting.

Morgan slowed and guided me to a doorway. A dumpster blocked part of the entrance. We could squeeze in behind it to hide if we had to.

I bent over and tried not to retch.

"You probably swallowed a lot of blood," she said.

The alley was quiet except for the sound of the rain bouncing off metal and the pavement. The only human resonance was our heavy breathing.

Once I caught my breath and the nausea subsided, I managed to ask, "How did you untie yourself?"

"I felt the rope around my hands suddenly slacken. My wrists, like my elbows, are double jointed, so then it was easy enough to get free." She bent her right arm back twice as far as most people could. "See?"

"Wow." The woman constantly surprised me.

"I don't know if they didn't tie the rope tight enough or if I had some help."

"What do you mean?"

"I may have felt a tug at the rope just before it loosened and something brushed against my wrist." Morgan looked down at her hands as if searching for a clue. "It happened real fast."

"How could that be? The Lieutenant went to get food. The other guy went to take a dump. I didn't hear anyone else." It hurt to concentrate.

"Neither did I, but something happened...I think."

Could there have been someone else there? Maybe hiding until the thugs were out of the room? Did we have an unknown ally? Or was Morgan not telling me everything? My thoughts were making me even dizzier.

I took a close look at her, trying to judge if she was really being honest with me. She looked perplexed.

Morgan wiped her face with the sleeve of her drenched blue sweatshirt. "If there was someone who helped me, who could it be?"

"No idea." I leaned against the door for balance. "What do we do now?"

"We can't go back to the hotel. We need some place warm where we can hide and fix your face. How do you feel?"

I touched my eye and flinched. My mouth was numb, but my teeth were all still intact. "I think I'll survive."

Morgan rubbed her cheek. "He hit me pretty hard too."

With my functioning eye I examined her face. "It doesn't look bad. A little bruised, maybe." All I could see was a small red mark.

"It hurts." She pouted, as if she wanted sympathy. Yet I was the one who got pounded. Was this a way of her coping with stress that I hadn't seen before?

My finger tips were damp, so I wiped them on my sweatshirt. Then it dawned on me. "Who dressed us? We didn't go to bed in jeans and these shirts last night."

Morgan had a disgusted look on her face. "I don't even want to think about it."

I felt around my pockets. "I don't have my wallet. We're screwed."

"Hopefully they didn't find them," Morgan said. "I hid them last night."

"What do you mean? Why?"

"You were all nervous and uncomfortable, making copies of the manuscript. It made me nervous too. So I put the backup disk, our wallets and passports, in a safe place. Just in case."

Was I being paranoid or was something not right? Morgan hid our stuff, because I was acting nervous. She barely got touched in the abduction. Someone, maybe, had helped her get untied. What the hell was going on? It didn't add up.

I didn't want to let on that I was suspicious. I'd play her game, whatever it was, until I could figure things out. "Okay, so how do we get them?"

"I did tell Ivan where I left them." Morgan tensed and frowned. "I hope he's okay."

"Remember, the Naintosa thugs didn't know how much he was helping us. That means they don't have him." My clouded mind cleared for a split second. How had Ivan escaped the thugs? Was he the true mastermind of all this? A sharp jolt shot through my temple, breaking my thought.

Morgan nodded. "It's obvious he got away somehow."

"Let's not panic," I said. While at the same time thinking: we were sitting in an alley, in the cold winter rain, no jackets, all banged up, no money, all of our possessions gone, in a foreign country two hundred miles from where we lived. And just when I thought it couldn't get worse, I was having serious doubts about the two people I had to rely on for my survival.

Another bolt of pain came and went.

I looked down. There was garbage strewn everywhere around the dumpster. Wet fast-food wrappers and chicken bones were ankle deep beside me. Something was sticking to my runner. A sudden stench of grease and rotting meat hit my nostrils. I wanted to puke and pushed past Morgan out into the open. The cold shower of rain stopped me from losing whatever could've been in my stomach.

Morgan placed her hand on my shoulder. "Are you going to be okay?"

Some deep breaths helped the gross feeling subside and help me regain control. "Maybe it's finally time we went to the police?"

"Do you think that's safe?"

"I don't have any other ideas."

"We better keep moving," Morgan said. "Are you okay to go again?"

"Yeah, let's go."

We walked to the end of the alley, putting more distance between ourselves and the warehouse.

"Let's go this way." Morgan pointed to the right.

"No, I think the other way is better."

"I have a feeling this is the way we need to go." She turned right and quickened her pace.

I'd regained my balance for the most part, but had to concentrate on my feet to keep up. Looking down didn't help my head throbbing.

As I followed my doubts grew stronger. Where was she leading me? Was I justified in my paranoia or was it a result of my head being pummeled?

We were in the part of town we'd avoided before. The buildings were grungy and street people huddled in doorways or under overhangs, trying to stay dry. Most ignored us, but some watched us pass. I tried to not make eye contact, yet was on guard for any sudden movements.

I fought back another wave of nausea and began to shiver from the cold.

After two blocks we turned left and then a few blocks later, right.

"I don't recognize any of the street names," I said.

"I have a strong feeling this is where we need to go," she repeated, as we turned down an alley.

This alley was cleaner and wider, with a long loading bay on the left.

A lone figure walked toward us. It was a woman. She was bundled up in a brown winter coat and grey knit hat.

When we came close, she stopped. It was obvious we looked out of place.

"Are the two ah you all right?" she asked, with a definite Bostonian accent. That was unexpected from someone walking in a Vancouver back alley.

"No ma'am." Morgan's voice cracked and her eyes were wide.

The woman took two steps toward us. "Are you lost?" She looked closer at me. "Son, you got beat something awful. My God..."

"I'll be fine." A warm, dry place to fix my face and figure out what to do would've been much appreciated. But, I couldn't trust anyone.

The lady turned her gaze onto Morgan. "What's wrong, dear?"

All the blood had drained from Morgan's face and her mouth was open. "Is your name Alice?"

The lady tensed and took a step back. A look of unease came over her, as if she was considering running away. "Who are you?"

"Morgan Elles. Carl and Claudia Elles' daughter."

Now it was the woman's turn to look shocked. Her eyes began to blink twice every second. "I know your parents."

Morgan exhaled. "We've been looking for you."

I couldn't believe it. Morgan's intuition was definitely at a heightened state. Or...were they just acting? Could this be part of Morgan and Ivan's plan – whatever that was? Was Alice really real?

"This is Nick Barnes. He's writing my father's memoir."

Alice's face was pale. "Good to meet you...sir."

"The pleasure's all mine."

"How is your father, Morgan?"

She looked down. Wet and stringy strawberry blonde hair fell forward. "He passed away a few months ago."

"Oh, I'm so sorry to hear that. He was such a smart man and always polite to me." Alice's look turned quizzical and she stopped blinking so much. "Why would you be looking for me?"

Morgan looked up. "This may sound weird, but I've had dreams about you witnessing my mother's death. That's how I knew who you were and what you looked like."

"Dreams?"

Morgan shrugged. "More like premonitions, I guess."

Alice stared at Morgan. She wouldn't blink for about ten seconds and then she'd blink many times in rapid succession. For some reason I associated her with a slow computer trying to process data.

"It's not safe here," Alice finally said. "Come with me."

We followed her through another alley, down three blocks busy with traffic and then onto a residential avenue. Alice walked ahead. Morgan stayed close to me.

My nausea had subsided and was replaced with a steady headache. I was getting more and more nervous. Was I being led on? What was my *real* role in all of this? Were Ivan and Morgan going to dispose of me when I finished the manuscript? Was I their patsy? Should I make a run for it?

"Are you holding up okay?" Morgan was watching me. "You're scowling."

I decided to sit tight until I could get a better read of what was going on. "My head just hurts."

Finally we arrived at an older, wood framed apartment building. It had probably been pretty fancy in its day. However those days were long since gone. The exterior was a dirty white stucco with peeling brown trim. My guess was that we were deep in East Vancouver.

"Hello, Alice. Hello, children."

As we came out of the rain, into the entry way, I looked up and saw the old beggar lady we'd met in Gastown.

Alice nodded. "Hello, Polly."

"I see you children have found Alice." She was wearing the same silly hat covered with plastic fruit.

Morgan was wide eyed. "Yes ma'am." Her voice was an octave higher than usual. "Thank you for your help."

I wasn't falling for it. She had to be a paid actress, like Alice. Who wears a fruit hat? That was over the top.

Polly smiled at me as we passed.

Alice led us up a flight of creaky stairs covered in dirty mustard colored carpet. The white wall had smears and dirty finger prints at waist level. The air smelled of mold.

Her apartment was halfway down the hall.

"Let's get you cleaned up, Nick." Alice took off her soaked

coat. She draped it over one of the chairs surrounding a seventies style dining room set. The four chairs were framed
with gold colored metal tubes with light brown vinyl cush-
ions screwed to them. The dark brown table had a strip of
arborite missing from the edge, exposing the particleboard
underneath.

"You two get out of those wet clothes." She turned her
back to us and walked into what was probably the bedroom.

The living and dining area were all in one room. The furniture was mismatched and well worn, but clean. Everything
was a shade of brown, except for the thin red fleece blanket
draped over one end of the couch. A lingering scent of burnt
toast hung in the air.

"I can't believe we found her." Morgan gave me a relieved
smile. "Thanks for continuing to push me."

"It was your intuition," I said, playing along. "I had nothing to do with it."

Alice came back, changed into a faded pair of pink cotton
sweatpants and a purple sweatshirt with sparkly kittens em-
broidered on it. It was the first time we got a good look at her.
She was as Morgan had described: in her fifties, simple, small
in stature, but thick around the middle. Her wavy, brown,
shoulder length hair was peppered with gray and unruly.

She held out two large white towels. They had to have originally been from a hotel, because of the large "S" woven into
each one's pattern.

After we took the towels, Alice went into the bathroom
and closed the door.

We removed our clothes with our backs to each other. My
wet sweatshirt was sticking to my skin. I stumbled and had to
reach for the support of a chair. I could hear Morgan having
similar difficulties.

The apartment was warm, but we both shivered and had
goose bumps even after we were wrapped in the towels.

Morgan ran her hands through her hair to untangle and
straighten it. I palmed mine in hopes it was in place and dried
flat.

Alice emerged from the bathroom holding a roll of toilet

paper, a bottle of alcohol and a box of bandages. "Here, Morgan. Sit here and help Nick while I put your clothes in the dryer."

I looked around for a washer and dryer, but Alice walked out the door with our wet clothes. These types of buildings probably had communal laundry in the basement; like mine at home.

A sudden a wave of melancholy swept through me. I missed my apartment in Seattle.

"Ouch, shit that hurts." I winced away from Morgan's hand. She'd just dabbed the alcohol soaked toilet paper above my right eyelid.

"I'm trying to be as gentle as I can." She grabbed my arm to keep me from squirming. "Hold still."

"How bad is it?"

"You've got a bruise and cut on your cheek and mouth and your eye's pretty swollen." She pulled back and surveyed my face. "You could probably do with a couple stitches on the cheek." Morgan cupped her hand under my chin. "I feel bad. I got you into this."

I looked at her face, within kissing distance from mine. My mind cleared. Had the blows to the head caused some internal damage to my brain? Her expression was authentic. She couldn't be setting me up. What'd I been thinking? I gave my head a shake. "Don't feel guilty. I'll be fine."

"Maybe they gave you a concussion." She looked and sounded cautious. "You've been acting strange since we got away, with a far out, angry look on your face."

"That's what I was just thinking." It must have been a concussion that was causing me to have negative doubts about Morgan. I had to dismiss future thoughts like that.

I endured the pain until she was finished, cursing every time she touched me. The alcohol stung! In the end I was disinfected and had a bandage on my cheek and above my eye. On the inside I was embarrassed for doubting her.

"Now, how do I look?" Morgan asked.

I closed the eye that didn't work anyway and studied Morgan's statuesque face. "Your cheek's bruised, but you're not cut."

"Oh, you look much better Nick," Alice said, as she hurried

back into the apartment. "Let me get you some tea. I'll be right back."

Morgan sat down at the table and crossed her legs at her ankles.

My towel slid up as I sat down, exposing my bare ass to the vinyl. As I stood back up, there was a tearing sound, as my butt briefly stuck to the chair. I pulled the towel under me and sat back down.

Morgan wrinkled her nose. "Ouch."

We heard a kettle boil in the kitchen. Within a moment Alice returned with tea and cookies.

She sat down and faced us. "Now what are you two actually doing?"

"My father kept notes of all his experiments on genetically engineered food and wanted to publish them." Morgan took the mug of tea Alice had passed to her and blew on it. "He asked Nick to help him."

Alice looked at me. "Did you know Dr. Elles long?"

"No, I was a reporter for the *Seattle News* and he liked my work." With one eye shut I had no depth perception and had to concentrate to grab the cup Alice passed me without spilling. "He contacted me to help him."

"When my father died, we decided to continue his work." Morgan reached for a cookie. "However, Naintosa doesn't want us to get the book published." She inhaled the cookie in two big bites.

"Yes, I'm sure they don't." Alice frowned as she took a sip of her tea. "Morgan, tell me about your dream."

I watched Alice's expression as Morgan went into detail. Her thick brow furrowed, eyes squinted and mouth hung ajar as she paid attention. Something wasn't quite right with her. It was as if her brain synapses weren't firing properly.

Suddenly Alice flinched and her concentration turned to tears.

"Do you want me to stop?" Morgan asked, emotional herself, describing the part where her mother was slumped over the steering wheel.

Alice covered her face with her hands. "Yes, please." Her voice was muffled. "I know the outcome."

We sat in silence, allowing her to regain composure.

After a few minutes Alice wiped the tears from her eyes and took a deep breath.

"What happened to you?" I asked. "Tell us how you got here."

"Without thinking, I drove away as fast as I could." Alice sniffled and a saliva bubble popped as she opened her mouth. "I knew who the man was. He was a high up security guy at Naintosa. I was so scared."

Morgan bit her lip. "Did he chase after you?"

"I was sure someone would. So, I went home, packed some things I couldn't live without and left." Alice's eyes looked haunted. "I got on the Interstate and just drove."

"Where did you go?" I asked.

"South to Carolina and then West until I reached Arizona. I used my mother's maiden name and traded my car for another one. I think most people think I'm dead."

It felt uncomfortable to say it, but I did, "They do."

"Better that way, I guess." Alice looked sad and sipped more tea. "I stayed in Arizona for a few months, but it was too hot and I was almost out of money."

Morgan sat forward. "Then what?"

"I went north, where it's cooler. I stayed in Spokane, Washington for over a year. I got a job as a cleaning lady and rented a small place."

Morgan asked, "So, how did you end up in Vancouver?"

"I have an aunt here and I thought Canada would be safer. One day I just packed up and drove to a small border crossing. It was called Christine on a Lake or something. Really pretty. I got across without any problems and headed to Vancouver."

Morgan and I looked at each other.

Christina Lake, another coincidence. She was right; if you wanted to get to British Columbia from Spokane, the Christina Lake border crossing was the nearest one.

Morgan asked, "Is your aunt around?"

"She's the lady you met downstairs. She has an apartment on the first floor."

This was getting more intertwined by the minute.

"Oh." Morgan nodded. "We originally met her a few days ago."

"Yeah, she told me about meeting a couple that were important for me to talk to. She said it'd help me deal with my past. She says I have some serious issues. She thinks she's psychic."

"I would agree with her," I said.

Morgan's eyes went wide open.

I realized Alice might take my comment the wrong way. "I mean about being psychic." And maybe some serious issues, I said, in my mind.

Alice shook her head in a kind of figure eight. "I don't believe in that nonsense; premonitions…psychics. It's the devil's work."

"So how do you think we found each other?" Morgan asked.

Alice scrunched up her face in a way that folded her skin into wrinkles around her eyes and on her forehead. It made her look dim upstairs. Then she smiled, appearing as if she'd gotten her answer. "It was either chance or the Lord wanted us to find each other."

"Who?" I asked, without thinking.

In that instant Alice's expression turned threatening and she started that rapid blinking again. "Our savior, Jesus Christ."

Morgan gave me a look that meant *leave it alone.*

"The Lord works in mysterious ways." Alice stared right at me, teeth clenched. "You don't believe? You're a heathen. I can tell." She rose to her feet, turned and walked into her bedroom, slamming the door behind her.

"What the hell was that?" I whispered.

Morgan had the same shocked look that I must've had. "It's obvious she's really religious."

"Or possessed."

CHAPTER 32

Twenty minutes had passed and Alice was still in the bedroom. At one point it sounded like she made a phone call. We could hear her muffled voice. Then there was silence.

I decided to sneak over to her door to see if I could hear what she was doing. Morgan shook her head, frowning, as I stood up. Just as I got out of the chair the phone rang. I must've jumped a foot and quickly sat back down.

Alice answered on the first ring. Then the whispered conversation started again.

I got tired of straining to hear what was going on. "Should we leave? We need our clothes."

"I want to hear the rest of the story." Morgan had a stubborn look on her face. "Apologize to her when she comes out."

"I didn't know I did anything wrong."

"I don't think you did either, but something triggered her." Morgan looked down at the plate in front of her. All that was left on it were crumbs. "Do you think she'd mind if we had some more food?"

I pointed towards the kitchen. "There's a cookie jar on the counter."

Morgan tip-toed to the kitchen. She took the top off the brown and cream ceramic jar that was shaped like a dog, glanced inside, and quickly put the head back on.

She tried to restrain a smile as she slunk back to her seat.

"No cookies?"

"No cookies, just money," she whispered, trying to keep a straight face.

"What? I can't believe anyone would actually keep their money in a cookie jar."

"I know." Morgan giggled.

Alice emerged from the bedroom. She'd changed into a too tight, red, velour sweat suit and black rain boots.

Trying not to stare at her hips, where dimples of cellulite were accentuated by her unfortunate choice of clothing, I cleared my throat. "Alice, I'm sorry if I..."

Ignoring me, she fixed her eyes on Morgan. "You two wait here. I'll be right back." Her eyelids were fluttering non-stop and her cheeks twitched. "Don't move." She took a dark green, puffy looking jacket off a hook by the door and left.

"She looks ready to snap." Morgan looked worried.

"Something's not right with her." The crazy look on Alice's face had been almost threatening. "I think it's time for us to go."

Morgan got up. "I'll go get our clothes. It shouldn't be hard to find the laundry room."

"It'll be in the basement."

"You watch at the window to see where she's gone." Morgan re-secured her towel as she walked toward the door.

I felt guilty about upsetting Alice, but I didn't mean it. She was overly sensitive. Besides, what about all we'd been through?

I went over to the apartment's single window. The rain had stopped. The clouds were a contrast of dark gray, with bright orange and red edges. Beams of setting sunlight snuck through.

I had to squint with my undamaged eye as Alice appeared outside the building. She sat down on a bus bench at the curb. Pulling what looked like about a six inch cross from her pocket, she rested it on her lap, but held onto the base with both hands. Her lips began to move, as though she was saying a prayer.

Morgan returned, her clothes already on and handed me mine. "Did you see where she went?"

"That was quick." I pointed down to the street. "It looks like she's waiting for a bus."

I stepped back to get my clothes on, as Morgan came to the window. I put a small tear at a seam in my boxers when I pulled them up too quickly. My jeans and sweatshirt were still damp.

A bus pulled up, but Alice didn't get on.

"This is too weird," Morgan said. "Let's get out of here."

As the bus pulled away, we saw them across the street. The two men who'd been following us for months, tied us up and beat us. They were walking directly toward Alice.

Morgan panicked. "We have to warn her."

"Hold on." I put my hand on her shoulder. Morgan was shaking.

I knew we couldn't expose ourselves. At that moment all we could do was watch.

They walked right up to Alice. We couldn't make out her facial expression.

The one we didn't know stood directly in front of her, at the curb. He was a tall imposing figure, with darker skin and hair. All of his features were big and masculine.

The Lieutenant sat down right beside Alice.

"What's she doing?" Morgan said. "It's as if she was waiting for them."

I put my head right up against the glass. What the hell was going on? Was she working with them? Or was she beyond crazy?

The Lieutenant reached inside his right pocket and pulled out a white envelope.

Alice opened the flap and looked inside.

"That's money in there," Morgan said. "Is she selling us out?"

As Alice thumbed the bills, the man standing looked around and nodded. The Lieutenant placed his left hand in his pocket and pulled something small out, holding it against his body.

"What's he doing?" I asked. Then I caught a small glint from a ray of sunlight hitting chrome. "He's got a syringe."

In a quick, fluid movement he wrapped his right arm around Alice's shoulder. His left hand pressed the needle into Alice's neck. She jerked and her head came up. After a few seconds she went limp. The envelope fell on her lap and her head dropped forward. The man on the curb retrieved the envelope and put the contents into his coat pocket.

"Oh my God, Nick."

"Holy fuck, Morgan." A sudden flash of Dr. Elles dying at the hand of a needle whipped through my mind.

The Lieutenant put Alice's head against the back of the bench. It looked as if she was napping. He then reached inside her pocket and pulled out her keys.

Getting to his feet, he turned and looked directly at our window.

"We gotta get the hell out of here!" I jerked back from the glass. If they caught us this time, we'd suffer the same fate as Alice.

"Wait." Morgan ran to the kitchen and stuck her hand in the cookie jar.

"Just take the whole thing."

She grabbed the dog, leaving the lid.

Once in the hallway, we hesitated.

The sound of creaking steps came from the direction of the main stairwell.

"There." Morgan pointed to the end of the hall on the right.

We bolted toward the exit sign, down the back stairs and out into the alley.

We ran for blocks.

Finally we found a hidden spot at the rear entrance of a second hand furniture store.

I doubled over, head and heart pounding.

Morgan was breathing hard and tears streamed down her face.

When I could finally speak, I asked, "How much money is in the dog?"

Morgan fished inside and took out three handfuls of colorful Canadian bills. She bent down and turned it over. About two dozen coins fell to the concrete.

I picked up the coins and counted while she added up the bills.

"I have $8.56."

She finished counting. "I have $175."

"We can live on that for a few days."

Morgan looked so sad. "This was probably her life savings. Poor lady."

"What?" I was angry. "She tried to sell us out. She's an idiot!"

"I guess those phone calls were with Naintosa," Morgan said.

"I can't believe how stupid she was to think that she could turn us in for money."

"And not get hurt herself."

We heard a siren in the distance.

"That's probably for her," Morgan said.

I looked around. It was almost dark.

This had gotten so out of hand. Another sharp pain split my temples. It felt as if a noose were being tightened around our necks. What the fuck had Alice been thinking?

"Do you have any idea where we are?" Morgan poked her head out into the alley. "I sure don't."

"Somewhere in East Vancouver, I figure." I put the coins into my pocket. "Let's get moving."

We walked and walked. At least the rain had let up.

We entered a residential area. The houses were older, smaller in size and most were boxy. Dispersed amongst them were three storey walk up apartments similar to the one Alice had lived in. The streets were tree lined, with leaves strewn on the ground. Concrete sidewalks buckled from the roots growing underneath.

CHAPTER 33

Alice's change was put to good use in the pay phone at a corner beside a small convenience store.

"Hi Sue. It's Nick."

"Holy crap! I knew it. I could just feel that you were still alive. Where are you? Are you hurt?"

"Other than scrapes and bruises…"

"Morgan's okay? You're still together?"

"Yes, but we're stuck in Vancouver with barely any money and no I.D.'s. We need help."

Sue's voice sparkled with excitement. "I'm so glad to hear you're both in one piece."

I suddenly became suspicious, again. "Wait a minute. How'd you know something happened to us?"

"Ivan called me a few hours ago."

Of course. I turned to Morgan, who was looking anxious, waiting for information. "Ivan called Sue."

"Fantastic." Morgan leaned back against the edge of the booth and gave a sharp exhale. "Where is he?"

I talked back into the receiver. "He's okay, isn't he?"

"He's fine, but he was really worried about you."

"Tell me what he told you."

"He said that when he came to your room this morning, the door was propped open and you and the computers were gone. Everything else was still there. So, what happened to you guys?"

I gave Sue a brief overview of our abduction. I didn't feel the need to tell her about Alice.

"He got your wallets and passports," Sue said. "Lucky Morgan told him where she hid them."

Morgan had leaned in closer to hear and gave me a quick glance. I tilted the receiver toward her. "Where's Ivan now?"

"On his way to Chicago with the manuscript. He left instructions. Do you have a pen and anything to write on?"

"No, we'll have to remember."

Morgan was right up against me. Her body heat felt good.

"Go to the men's restroom at the south corner of domestic arrivals at the airport. In the last stall, behind the toilet bowl, he taped a locker key. He put your wallets and passports in a locker near that restroom."

"Then what?" I asked.

"You get to Seattle somehow. You're gonna have to figure that one out."

"What about my Blazer?"

"He thought of that too."

"Ivan seems to have thought of everything."

"He did." Sue sounded thoughtful. "It's obvious that this isn't the first time he's been involved in something like this."

"Huh." Maybe there were important things we didn't know about Ivan. I glanced at Morgan, but she was looking straight ahead. I'd have to ask her more about his background, later.

"He didn't check you out of the hotel," Sue continued. "You're supposed to be staying there for another few weeks. So when it cools down, someone will have to go back and get your stuff."

"We'll worry about that later," I said. "What time's it now?"

"Just after seven," Sue said.

"Okay, wish us luck."

"Call me when you get here, no matter what time it is."

It was getting colder and began to rain again. We walked a few more blocks until we arrived at a main thoroughfare – Cambie Street.

There it was easy to get a dry, warm cab.

The driver was wearing small headphones, so we felt safe to talk.

"So, how do you think we should get back to Seattle?" Morgan asked.

"We could fly."

"We'd have to use our credit cards and passports. They could be traced."

I shrugged. "We're going to have to show our passports at the border anyway."

"Do you think they can get into the government computers? Besides, when we cross the border we'll disappear again. If we fly they'll know exactly where we're going."

"We can't get my Blazer because we'd have to go through the lobby to get to the secure parking. I'm sure someone's watching there."

"Let's use that as the last resort. Can we take a rental car across the border?"

"We'd have to use the credit card."

Morgan frowned. "I guess we take a bus."

"We should have enough cash on us." I tried to sound positive. I wasn't looking forward to sitting on a bus for hours either.

Within twenty minutes we were at the airport.

The pain in my head was dull and steady, but manageable.

Once inside, we followed the signs while keeping an eye out for anyone who looked as if they might work for the Naintosa security force.

"I understand Ivan's logic," I said, as we walked. "If they're watching for us, they'd be at International Departures, not Domestic Arrivals."

"Oh yeah." Morgan nodded. "We're at opposite ends of the terminal."

I spotted the washroom, just past the last baggage carousel. The lockers were on the wall beyond.

"See you in a minute." I quickened my pace.

The room had toilet stalls on the left, urinals and sinks on the right. It looked deserted, but I couldn't tell for sure. Someone could be in a stall. I walked the length of the room bent over, peering into the spaces under each door for feet. None.

I opened the last metal door. It was relatively clean. Only a few squares of discarded toilet paper lay on the floor. I crouched beside the white porcelain bowl.

A sudden sound of heavy footsteps on tile echoed off the walls. I froze. They were coming toward me.

The door opened to the stall next to me. The thin wall vibrated like a drum. A belt buckle clanked. A zipper scraped. Then came the thud of a heavy ass plopping onto the seat. This guy had diarrhea...bad. The sound of the toilet filling, the stench and the grunts of relief, were disgusting. I was at bowl level and all that separated us was a flimsy wall. I could see his brown loafers with tassels.

I felt around the contoured porcelain, holding my breath. There it was. I ripped the tape loose and took the key.

I had an urge to wash my hands, but didn't. I couldn't get out of there fast enough. I'd heard and smelled two guys crap in *one* day.

"What number is it?" Morgan asked, as I came out of the washroom. "You look upset."

"Never mind." I was just happy to breathe non-toxic air again and headed straight for the lockers. "636."

Morgan was right behind me.

The key fit easily into the slot.

Before I could even finish pulling out the two large envelopes inside, Morgan said, "Let's get out of here. We'll go through them later."

"Maybe we should take a chance and fly?" We were so close to getting home, from here.

"No. I have a bad feeling here."

With the way her intuition was working today, I wasn't going to question her.

We retraced our route back outside. As we walked down a moving escalator, to our right was a beautiful wooden carving of a killer whale, with indigenous symbols painted onto it in black and red. I hadn't noticed it on our way in, but we didn't have time to linger and admire it.

A row of cabs waited right outside the main doors.

"To the Greyhound bus terminal, please," I said, to the driver of the first cab in line.

He took a long look at us through his rear view mirror. "Sure." I knew he was looking at the bandages on my face and our damp, disheveled clothes.

I ripped open the top of one of the envelopes, tipped it over and dumped the contents onto the seat between us. Morgan took her wallet and passport, along with a once folded piece of paper. I flipped open my wallet and found everything intact.

All that was left was a sealed, letter-size envelope. I tore it open and found about a thousand dollars in cash. "You're in charge of the money." I passed it over to Morgan.

She looked up from the note she was reading, took the small envelope and glanced inside. "Perfect."

Morgan passed me the note. It said: *Nick and Morgan, if you are reading this, you are safe and have spoken with Sue. I am going to see the publisher. Here is some money to help you get back to Seattle. Please be careful and find a place to hide. I will contact Sue again when I can. Ivan.*

I passed the paper back to Morgan and turned to watch the city pass by. Beads of moisture on the cab's window refracted the many lights. The street looked slick and deceptive. Small store fronts lined the way, most closed for the night.

This was the first time during the most traumatic day of my life that I had a quiet moment. Was my probable concussion the root of my suspicions of Ivan, like they were about Morgan? Or were they justified? How come the Naintosa thugs didn't know he had been staying at the hotel? That would be sloppy on their part. How had he gotten away with such ease?

"What's in the other envelope?" Morgan asked. "It's pretty full."

I decided I wasn't going to let Morgan know I was questioning the man who helped guide us.

I broke the glued seam of the second manila envelope and pulled out a series of eight by ten photos; about twenty of them. Also, there was a stack of papers, maybe fifty pages.

"Oh, prints." Morgan was leaning toward me. "What're they of?"

I thumbed through the pictures. They were all of sick looking people. Everyone looked sad. Some were outside and the others in what looked like a hospital ward. These people clearly hadn't known they were being photographed. It was as if they had been taken by a spy.

I passed the photos to Morgan and shuffled through the papers. They were all some sort of scans. The type on many of them was crooked and the resolution low. However, all the pages were legible.

We stopped at a red light. I looked up and saw the cab driver watching us in the rear view mirror. His gaze was narrowed in suspicion. He looked away as soon as we made eye contact. The light turned green.

I nudged Morgan with my elbow. As soon as she looked at me I darted my eyes to the left twice. Then I took the papers and slid them back into the envelope. She handed me the pictures to do the same.

Within a few more minutes we were at the bus terminal.

"What was with the driver?" Morgan asked the second we got out of the cab.

"He was just looking at us funny. I didn't want to take any more chances."

Morgan nodded. "We'll take a better look at what's in that envelope when we're on our way out of here."

A set of large glass entry doors slid open in front of us.

"Do you think they'd be staking out this place too?" Morgan's eyes darted from side to side, as we stepped into the big, old, rock faced, three story building.

"I doubt they have enough men to watch every way out of the city." Or so I'd hoped.

Just in case, we walked to the corner of the entry hall and peered around the corner. It was a big room with back to back, sturdy wooden benches down the center. There was a bus kiosk on one side of the room and a train kiosk on the other. A chemical scent of pine hung in the air, as a janitor wiped down a bank of pay phones near us. Laughter from a group of teenagers echoed above the sound of hard soled shoes clicking on the concrete floor. Quite a few people milled about. I tried to study faces for something that would trigger suspicion. Most looked uninterested or tired.

"What do you think?" I asked.

"Let's do it," Morgan replied.

We walked over to a large board that listed departure times.

"We missed the last train," Morgan said. "But a bus leaves in twenty minutes."

CHAPTER 34

No one approached us while we bought our tickets. After ten minutes that felt like an hour the bus pulled into the loading area and we boarded.

The bus was half empty. We went right to the back and sat across the aisle from each other, so we could stretch out.

Lilac air freshener tried and failed to cover up an undertone of foot odor. Behind Morgan was a bathroom. I hoped I wouldn't have to hear anyone else take a dump.

Morgan and I leaned toward the middle so we wouldn't have to raise our voices.

"You know, I've never been on one of these before," she said.

"You mean you've never been on a bus?"

"Downtown a few times, but never on one that traveled longer distances."

"Really?" I shouldn't have been surprised. People with money didn't travel by Greyhound.

She looked embarrassed, so I changed the subject to something that'd been gnawing at me. "Do you know much about Ivan's past?"

"Some, why?"

"He seems to have more street smarts than the average scientist."

"My dad did mention that Ivan was in the Soviet military when he was younger. I don't know what he did. And I don't know how he got out of the Soviet Union."

"That could explain things." Actually, it made me even more suspicious.

"Also, Bill worked for British Intelligence before he went to Naintosa."

"Do you know what he did there?"

"No, neither of them talked about their pasts much; not around me anyway."

"I guess that's where they learned how to deal with these situations."

I leaned back and looked out the window. The wet road reflected the glare of oncoming car lights. The bus swayed and the engine rasped in acceleration. We were entering onto highway 99 that would take us to the border.

I could worry *more* about Ivan and now Bill, because of this new information or I could see their past experiences as an asset. I really didn't know much about Bill. Could they be working together, against us? Could they be using us? I watched raindrops streak against the glass. No. We had to trust them. It was too late not to believe they were on our side. But I would keep it in the back of my mind and be more watchful.

Another jolt of pain stabbed at my temples. It came and went. That reminded me that I most likely had a concussion. Instead of doubting Morgan like before, I was having negative thoughts about Ivan and Bill now.

"Let's look at what's in that envelope." Morgan had turned on her overhead reading light.

"Okay." I turned mine on and picked up the envelope I'd placed on the seat beside me.

We looked at the pictures first. I'd take a good look at one and then pass it to Morgan.

The photos had been taken only three months ago; they each had a date in red on the bottom right. The first few were of people outside in what looked like a clearing. One showed a wire fence and thick jungle beyond. Everyone was in a white t-shirt and knee length brown shorts. In two shots people a short distance away wore white lab coats.

"Is this a prison?" Morgan cringed.

"It could be. It's definitely a compound of some sort."

Next were some close up pictures. They had been taken

at odd angles, looking upward. It was as if the camera was located around the operator's chest area. The people in them all had dull, lifeless eyes. They looked Latino, yet their skin, even though tanned, was pasty. Their posture was weak. Two had lumps where the glands under their chins would be. All but one wore bandaged dressings at the base of their necks.

The shots were disturbing. "They look like zombies."

Morgan nodded, studying each photograph.

The next ones had been taken in what looked like a hospital ward. The first one showed a long white room with a row of metal framed single beds on each side. Each bed had a standing portable fan at the foot, aimed at the occupant. Thin white sheets were pulled down to reveal the same white t-shirts and brown shorts.

The remaining photos were all close-ups of individuals. Three were lying on their stomachs. Their shirts and shorts had been pulled back to show from the middle of their backs down to their buttocks. Two had dressings just above their butt cheeks, along their spine. One had no dressing, revealing a large purple bump, about six inches in diameter, with a red incision line running vertically through the center.

"Are those tumors?" Morgan asked.

"It looks like it," I said, even though I had no medical experience to go on.

The last pictures showed people on their backs. One was a middle aged woman. Her eyes were closed, with dark puffy circles around them. The glands on her neck were swollen. Her black hair looked like it was blowing, so a fan must've been pointed at her head. There was a small red stain on the collar of her shirt. Finally, there was a photo of a middle aged man with graying black hair and thick moustache. His pupils were dilated and he was grimacing in pain. There was no dressing. At the base of his neck was a bump or tumor with an incision line.

These people were definitely Latino. They were being cared for in a place with a warm climate. A picture I'd seen of a Hawaiian leper colony came into my mind.

I was about to reach for the documents in the envelope when bright lights outside the bus drew my attention.

"Those poor people," Morgan said. "Let's go through the papers to find out what it's about."

"We're pulling into customs." I returned the photos to the envelope.

The twenty or so of us passengers departed the bus. We walked inside the sanitized, white building and got in line. There weren't any other people waiting, so it didn't take long. Four agents were stationed at the counter to process us.

We'd decided to separate. Morgan went first to the agent on the far left. Next, I walked over to the officer on the far right.

"Citizenship?" asked the clean cut customs agent, holding out his hand. He had an intense stare that seemed to look straight through my eyes, into my brain.

"American." I handed him my passport.

He opened it, looked at the picture, then back at me. "Were you in some sort of altercation, sir?"

"I was robbed in Vancouver. They took my luggage."

"Did you report it to the authorities there?"

"Yes, sir."

He scanned the bar code on my passport, looked at the computer screen and keyed in a few numbers.

I looked over at Morgan. She was smiling and looked like she was flirting with her customs agent. She didn't look like she'd been put through the ringer, she looked natural.

"Were you in Canada on business or pleasure?" my agent asked.

"Pleasure."

"Duration of stay?"

"Two weeks."

"Are you bringing across any fruit, produce, meat or valuables?"

"No, sir."

Morgan passed behind me and went out the door.

"Anything to declare?"

"No, sir."

He handed me back my passport.

As I walked to the bus I noticed that my legs were sore

from all the walking and running we'd done that day. Combined with my still throbbing face, I needed rest.

Cigarette smoke wafted in the still night air as a couple of the passengers got in a few needed drags before we got underway again.

Everyone was spread out on the bus. It only looked like four people were travelling together. There were three rows separating Morgan and me from anyone else.

"Go okay?" Morgan asked, as I sat down.

"Yeah, fine and you?"

"No problems."

"Flirting didn't work with my agent," I said.

She shrugged. "It comes in handy when I need it. I sure had to act though. Today hasn't been the happiest of days."

Within a few minutes the bus was back on the way to Portland, with stops in Bellingham, Everett, Seattle, and Tacoma.

"Let's see what this is all about." I pulled out the papers.

"I wonder where Ivan got this from?" Morgan peered from the other side of the isle.

"And why didn't he tell us about it yesterday?"

On the top was a ten page summary. I turned right to the end and saw no documentation or signature to show who had written it.

"Do you want to read the summary first or shall I?" I asked.

"You go ahead. Give me the other papers."

The document explained that since 1949 Pharmalin had maintained a ten thousand acre property in a remote area of the Beni region of Bolivia. Even though people knew of its existence, the perimeter was fenced and heavily guarded. It contained a hospital compound, large lab and small village. Since Naintosa started genetic engineering, they had taken over the crops of the indigenous people who had come with the property. These people grew Naintosa's seed and ate what the plants produced. They were also subject to Pharmalin's pharmaceutical testing. They were not allowed to leave and had, over the years, become inbred generations of guinea pigs.

"It says here..." Morgan pointed at the document in front

of her. "There's a breakdown of the immune system, followed by a build-up of toxicity in the glands. Side effects included inflammation and tumors around the neck and lower spine. They haven't been able to solve that problem yet. It states that long term consumption of their genetically engineered soy and wheat causes colon cancer." Her voice went up an octave, "Do you know how many things we eat contain soy and wheat?"

"Yeah, I'm just reading about how they think they've found a way to control the cancer. The obvious cure would be to not eat their tainted food. But their goal is to have a drug people would need to take continually to manage the disease." I looked over at Morgan. "This is the proof we were looking for."

"This gives total credibility to that earlier small test group information that Bill intercepted. They really are giving people cancer and then curing them."

"Managing it, not curing it; there's a big difference." I had mixed emotions. I felt sad for the indigenous people used in the experiments, even more disgusted at Naintosa and Pharmalin, but excited that this information would really nail them.

"Oh my God." Morgan raised her voice to a loud whisper. "Here's an internal memo from four years ago. It's asking some guy named Manny to go find more people. It suggested going to Santa Cruz and asking the Christian missionaries for more help to round up some homeless. He was to offer them food and a place to live. It says the birth rate in the *camp...* they call it a camp, continues to slow, even with their encouragement to procreate."

"No. Can I see that?" I held out my hand and she passed me the page. I had to read that for myself to believe it.

"Holy shit." I had to absorb all of this. I looked out the window and only saw black, with one faint light in the distance.

I took a deep breath. "Is there anything else there?"

"Just copies of formulas that I can't decipher. My guess is they have to do with how the cancer develops and how to manage it."

I read the last page of the summary. It stated that the

information was incomplete and more could not be obtained at this time. There was no mention of who had infiltrated the camp.

"I'm not sure this is enough proof to make it conclusive for the book." I sighed. "Not without knowing who got the information and how they did it."

"We need to talk to Ivan." Morgan passed back her pages and gestured for me to give her the summary.

I placed the papers she'd looked at back in the envelope. I'd read all I could handle for right now.

In the past day we had been captured, beaten, met Alice, witnessed her murder, almost got recaptured, escaped and finally gotten out of Canada. Then we got this information; the most sinister of all. Yet it still might not be enough.

The gentle rocking of the bus, combined with my fatigue and a dull headache, made it hard to keep my eyes open.

CHAPTER 35

We'd decided to get off in Everett even though our tickets were for Seattle, just to throw off any possible pursuit. It was after midnight. We backtracked from the bus station to a motel within walking distance, just off Interstate 5. We hoped no one would think of looking for us there.

I called Sue to let her know we'd arrived and agreed to meet for breakfast.

❧

"The last time they remodeled this place was in the early seventies," Morgan commented, as she got out of bed. "And they didn't do a good job then."

The room we shared had a worn and stained caramel beige shag carpet. The colors were all dark, including the wood paneled walls. The brown drapes were so thick we had to turn on the lights even though it was daytime outside. The bathroom was an almost comical pale pink.

The bathroom had the usual complementary shampoo and soap. I walked to a nearby store for toothbrushes, toothpaste, and fresh bandages.

We were clean, now, but needed new clothes. My shirt was torn under my right arm and permanently stained. Nobody would be able to tell what caused the stains, but I knew it was my own blood. Morgan had a two inch rip in her jeans at the back of her thigh. Neither of us could remember how or when that happened.

We were meeting Sue at the greasy spoon connected to the motel. It had also been in business for a long time and never updated. There were booths against the walls and a long counter with dark red swivel stools. Customers faced an opening into the kitchen. A big old cook with huge forearms, wearing a stained white t-shirt, cooked eggs and bacon on the grill. All the smells of breakfast mingled together in the warm room.

We sat down at a window side booth. I tried to avoid the tear in the brown vinyl of the seat.

Sue hadn't arrived yet, so we ordered coffee.

"Let's go shopping after this." Morgan fidgeted. She looked sour. "Every time I move, I feel these clothes and think of all the horrible things we went through yesterday. I'm gonna burn them."

"Do you think it'd be safe for us to go to our places for more things?" I asked, already knowing the answer.

"Don't be silly."

"I don't have money for a new wardrobe."

"I said I'd pay for your expenses and this is an expense. You wouldn't have lost your clothes if you weren't working on the manuscript." Morgan looked down into the coffee, holding the mug with both hands. "I feel guilty enough as it is. None of this would've happened to you if you hadn't been helping me. Thank you. I don't know if I'd have stuck it out if I were in your shoes."

I took one of her hands away from the cup and held it. She looked so vulnerable. "The reason I'm sticking to this is because I believe in you, your father, and this project."

Tears welled in her blue eyes and she squeezed my hand. "I could never have made it this far without you."

I really wanted to kiss her. I leaned in. Her eyes locked on mine.

"Hi guys." Sue slid into the booth beside me, thumping a big oxblood colored handbag on the linoleum floor at her feet. She looked straight across the table. "Are you okay, Morgan?"

I dropped Morgan's hand.

She wiped her eyes. "It's been a rough couple of days...or months."

"Yeah, spending so much time with Nick would make me cry too."

That got a smile from her.

Sue nudged me with her elbow, but her smile faded when she saw my face. "They sure nailed you, didn't they?"

"I'm fine." I was beginning to feel self-conscious. At least I'd only had one bolt of pain pass between my temples that morning.

Sue hugged me. "It's so good to see you again."

Now we were all teary eyed. I realized how much I'd missed her.

She pressed harder. "You're getting so skinny. Other than your face, you look good." Sue let go and pulled her bag up onto her knees. She withdrew Morgan's purse and two sets of keys. "Here you go. Ivan over-nighted these to me; back up, you know."

Morgan reached across the table for her belongings. "That's fantastic. Thanks."

Sue asked, "How do you plan on getting more money?"

"I have money in an account I opened with a friend, in her name." Morgan looked smug. "Nick knows about it. That's where I've been getting the money all along. I have a bank card."

"Pretty smart," Sue said. "I'm running out of money for Nick's bills."

"I'll give you more next time we meet."

It felt weird having them look after my finances, but I had no choice. "Thanks, you two."

It was great to see Morgan and Sue warm up to each other.

"Notice anyone watching you since we last talked?" I asked Sue.

"I haven't seen anyone in the last month. I've checked my phones for bugs and couldn't find any. However, I'm not sure you need actual bugs anymore, for surveillance."

I shrugged. "Yeah, I don't know."

A nervous look came over Sue. "Dan keeps asking about you."

"He never paid that much attention to me when I was there."

"He told me that if I ever talk to you to get you to call him."

"He probably just wants to know when I'm coming back."

"Except whenever he asks about you I get an uncomfortable feeling. The hair on the back of my neck stands up."

"I wouldn't worry about it." Sue still had to work with Dan. I didn't want her to be even more nervous by admitting that I now had my own concerns about him. Sue's *feelings* were usually right. "He's a little prick."

"It's his tone and the look on his face; like he knows something."

"Just be extra careful not to give away anything about us to Dan. I'll call him when it's safe and quit."

The waitress came over with coffee for Sue and took our orders.

"So, now what do we do?" Morgan looked from Sue to me.

"You've done all you can for now," Sue said. "You just have to wait for re-write requests from Ivan's editor. Do you feel safe chilling in the place you're in now?"

Morgan shrugged. "It's the worst example of retro, but it'll do."

"I need to write out the Bolivia part to include in the manuscript."

"Maybe we should get Ivan's thoughts on it first?"

"There's a missing part?" Sue asked.

"The most damning part," Morgan said. "If Ivan agrees with us that there's enough proof to include it."

"There's an even more damning part?"

I explained to Sue about the camp, the abuse of the indigenous people, the cancer and the drug to control it.

Sue sat frozen, her mouth open, until I was done.

Morgan said to Sue, "Isn't that beyond pathetic?"

"Just when you think they're the most bottom feeding slime, they sink lower." Sue stopped talking as the waitress placed her toast on the table. As soon as we were alone again, she pushed it away as if it was poison. "I read they have a huge lab in Bolivia, but nowhere did it say what they did there."

Morgan said, "Now we know."

"How'd you get the information?"

"Ivan left it with our wallets and passports yesterday," I told her.

"He did?" Sue furrowed her brow. "Interesting."

"What's wrong?" I asked.

"Nothing. He just never mentioned it." She reached into her bag and pulled out two pieces of paper. "I have more stuff on the Hendrick Schmidts. It fits with what you just told me."

"What?" Morgan and I said, in unison.

"Apparently Dr. Schmidt number two received many German medals and awards during the Second World War for his company's research. German drug companies were using people from concentration camps like lab mice. They often killed them with their experiments."

I looked from Morgan to Sue. "Just like in Bolivia, now."

"I saw a documentary on it," Sue continued. "They showed letters from a pharmaceutical company stating that the latest people that were sent had all expired. Then they asked if the camps could send a hundred more. Only one company was exposed. It wasn't Pharmalin."

"I bet you they were involved," I said.

Sue was wide eyed in agreement. "With some digging I learned Pharmalin had many dealings with the company implicated."

Morgan shook her head. "I still can't believe that ever happened *and* is still going on in this day and age."

"There's so much happening out there that regular people have no idea about." My words hung in the air.

There was a period of silence. Nobody touched the food the waitress brought.

In time, Sue looked down at her papers. "Have you guys seen those commercials on TV for the Society For Biotechnology? Healthy, happy people living better lives because the scientists are making better food?"

"Oh yeah," Morgan said. "Quite a while ago."

I didn't remember the commercials, but understood what Sue was getting at. "It's genetic engineered food propaganda."

Sue's eyes gleamed. "Guess who the chairman of the Society is?"

We all said together: "Dr. Hendrick Schmidt."

"It's funded by Naintosa."

"Have you had a chance to check out the legal records on Naintosa?" It was so obvious how bad Dr. Schmidt and Naintosa were. Why hadn't anyone else put the pieces together before?

"There have been lots of filings. Mainly patent infringement and always settled out of court, so I couldn't get any details. They really know how to work the system."

"What about DKKR?" I asked.

"More of the same. Corporate bullies. They're headquartered in Venezuela."

We all sighed.

Sue pulled a large envelope from her bag. "Here's the list of people and organizations we should send the manuscript to. You can go over it to make sure I didn't miss anyone."

I looked inside. "There are quite a few pages here. Did you include any environmental groups?"

"Yeah, and it was a lot of work."

"We really appreciate it," Morgan said.

"How're the two of you going to get around?"

That was a good question. "We need a car, but can't use a credit card."

"Do you want to use my grandmother's? She doesn't use it, but it's still insured."

INTERLOGUE 2

"Mr. Thompson is on line three," his secretary's voice came over the intercom.

"Thanks, Sherry." Peter Bail was wearing a blue and red pinstriped shirt and black slacks. He ran his hand through his close cut, thick brown hair. After a deep breath, he picked up the receiver. "What the hell's going on up there, Sigmund?" Peter called him by his full name when he wanted Sig's full attention.

"We still haven't located them, sir."

"It's been a full day. You're better than that or supposed to be. Do you have any leads?"

"No sir. We don't have enough support to cover all the bases."

Peter took another deep breath, letting it out slow and loud. "Okay, brief me."

"We took care of Alice," Sig Thompson said. "It was simple, no hitches. I can't believe she was stupid enough to call your office and ask for a reward to turn them in."

"We all make our beds," said Peter. "We would've caught up to her eventually. What happened next?"

"We went up to Alice's apartment, but they were gone."

"Are you sure they were there in the first place?"

"Sure enough. There were three teacups on the dining room table and a bunch of blood stained tissues. We'd messed Barnes up pretty good."

"Then what?" Peter rubbed the wrinkles that formed on his forehead when he was frustrated.

"We searched the area. Skeels and Hall watched the hotel."

"Any movement there?"

"By the time they found out Ivan Popov was there he'd already gotten on a plane to Chicago."

"Yeah, we now know the extent of his involvement. I've dispatched an agent in Chicago." Peter let out an angry breath. "Anything else?"

"They still haven't checked out. Their vehicle and clothes are still there. Skeels is watching the hotel. Hall is monitoring the border and airport. Matt and I are searching the city."

"This should've been a simple exercise." Peter enunciated each syllable.

"They're more resourceful than we anticipated, sir." Sig's defensive tone revealed his discomfort with the lack of results. "We'll find them again."

"You should've never lost them, Sigmund. If you don't want to find yourself a night watchman at the Bolivia lab, deliver them to me."

"Yes, sir."

Peter swiveled his chair toward the window, but didn't register the harbor view. What would he do if he were Nick and Morgan? "Any chance of them getting back to Seattle undetected? What if they got across the border before you set up surveillance?"

"They would've had to move pretty fast and have had some help, but it's possible."

"Okay, leave Hall and Skeels in Vancouver. You and Matt go back to Seattle. My hunch is that's where they are or where they're heading."

"You got it, sir."

Peter hung up the phone and said to himself aloud, "If it'd been me out there it would've been over months ago."

"I should hope so."

Peter turned his chair around.

Dr. Hendrick Schmidt the Fourth stood in the doorway.

Peter almost choked. "Oh, I didn't see you there, sir." He stumbled over his words. "What brings you to Boston?"

Schmidt was immaculate as always and clearly not fooled by Peter's attempt at nonchalance. He wore a black suit, crisp white shirt, and purple patterned tie. What little hair he had left was combed back. "I have business to attend to." He closed the door behind him and sat down in a burgundy leather chair opposite the mahogany desk. "This is a very nice office you have, Mr. Bail." His formal German accent vibrated in the air.

"You've been here before, Dr. Schmidt."

His dark brown eyes scanned the room as if taking inventory. "Yes, once, but I never appreciated how well we provide for you here."

Peter picked up the small dagger-shaped letter opener that lay on the blotter in front of him and squeezed the handle. He would never tolerate such a condescending tone from anyone else.

A brief sneer appeared across Dr. Schmidt's lips and the glint in his eyes confirmed that he enjoyed the power. "I've read the computer disk they found on Mr. Barnes and I'm very concerned. It's propaganda. I don't want it made public. There is *no way* it can be published. Do you understand?"

"I understand, sir."

"Do you really?" Dr. Schmidt rose from the chair and put his hands on the polished wood desk. "I think that if you really understood the gravity of this situation, you'd have them by now."

"Dr. Schmidt, we're doing the best we can. It's only a matter of time."

"How many times do I have to say this? These are not professionals. They are young innocents who don't know who they're dealing with. Your operatives' incompetence is only fueling their fantasy that they can damage us. If you want to keep your office and not become a night watchman in Bolivia," his lips shaped a cold smile, "you'll put all of your attention on finding these two thorns in my side."

Peter caught himself leaning forward aggressively and felt his forehead wrinkle in anger. He swallowed deliberately and hard, pushing down what he really wanted to say. "Yes sir, I will." Peter had the sense not to mess with his boss. Even he wasn't safe from Hendrick Schmidt's personal *Gestapo*. They were quick and brutal. And permanent.

"Now..." Dr. Schmidt sat back down. "I overheard you say that you suspect Mr. Barnes and Ms. Elles have returned to Seattle. I would concur. What are you doing that is extraordinary to hasten the resolution of this issue?"

"I've secured an informant at the *Seattle News*," Peter said. "If Mr. Barnes and Ms. Elles surface in Seattle, he'll know about it."

Dr. Schmidt nodded in approval. "I will congratulate you on one accomplishment. You successfully disposed of the Alice Turnbury woman; even though she placed herself right into your hands."

"Thank you, sir." Peter forced a smile, even though Schmidt's mocking tone stung like salt in a wound.

Dr. Schmidt pointed his finger at Peter. "Mr. Bail, I think it's time you became personally involved. Didn't I overhear you say you could take care of the situation faster than your operatives?"

"Yes, I may have to, sir."

"Then do so. Now!" Dr. Schmidt rose. "And bring in Dr. Popov, as well. His scent is all over the manuscript."

"Yes sir, I will."

Watching Dr. Schmidt leave, Peter resigned himself to putting everything else aside and going to Seattle or Vancouver.

After a few moments of contemplation, Peter focused on his computer screen. It was time to put them on the W.I.R.E. He hadn't done it until now because he thought his people could handle it. He typed an Internet address. The WIRE was a service to find people of interest. The site was used by secret services of countries, private companies with deep pockets and others of questionable morals and intentions. It relied on people wanting to profit by exposing others.

He keyed in his password and went to the insertion template. Peter filled out everything he knew about Nick and inserted a picture from his file. Then he did the same for Morgan and Ivan. For each one he added that they were to be taken alive and that he be informed immediately upon contact with them.

CHAPTER 36

We had to buy clothes, shoes, underwear and toiletries, a suitcase each, a laptop, and a printer/scanner. We kept a brisk pace moving from store to store making our cash purchases. It didn't feel wise to be in public for longer than needed. The only thing that slowed us down was Morgan's insistence on advising me on my clothing choices. I didn't mind, because Sue had always helped in the past. Morgan managed a few poses in front of mirrors and asked my opinion on her outfits. Of course she looked great in all of them.

It was lucky one mall had all the stores we needed, because after a while my head began to pound.

🕉

I had to lie down when we got back to the motel. That evening, after I recovered, we read through Sue's list of whom she thought we should send the finished book to.

A sudden light burst through the crack in the dark curtains and we heard a car pull up, right in front of our room.

We looked at each other and froze. Within seconds there was a knock on the door.

I went to look through the peep hole. "It's Sue."

Morgan came to my side as I opened the door. Her thigh pressed up against my hip. I wasn't sure what to do. If I let my arm fall to my side it would be on Morgan's leg. So I wedged my thumb under my belt buckle to hold my hand in front of me.

Sue gave us a questioning look. "I brought you your chariot." She handed me a key.

"Nice." Morgan peered around me.

I followed her gaze toward a cream colored 1994 Cadillac CTS in pristine condition. "Sweet ride."

"Take good care of it," Sue said. "Grandma would kill me if you did anything to it."

"We promise," I said.

"Come on in," Morgan said. "We're just going over the list you made."

"No, I gotta go. My ride's waiting for me."

I hadn't noticed the dark Ford F150 with oversized tires wrapped around chrome five spoke wheels parked sideways behind the Caddy. In the driver's seat was a guy with blond shoulder length hair. Black sunglasses were clipped to the v-neck of his tight white sweater. His big muscular arm was resting on the sill of the door window. He looked like a barely twenty year old surfer dude. "Who's that?"

"Sue's got a boyfriend?" Morgan smiled. "Or a boy toy?"

Sue blushed. "I met Glen at the gym. He has the potential to entertain me for a while, but that's about it. He's a little dim, but cute."

Morgan laughed.

"You didn't tell him anything, did you?" I felt protective, but tried not to show it.

"Don't be stupid," Sue said. "Of course not."

I could tell by Sue's sneer that she was trying to push my buttons.

"Just be careful," I said.

"I always am." She fluttered her fingers at us. "See you later."

"Good on Sue," Morgan said, after we closed the door.

"Whatever."

"Are you jealous?" Morgan's eyes narrowed.

"No." I went back to the bed and picked up the list. Why was it that every time Sue dated someone I felt protective or jealous or something? And why was Morgan brushing up against me? Was that for Sue's benefit or mine? Or was Morgan unaware that she had even done that?

Morgan didn't say anything more and went back to checking her list. Every once in a while, out of the corner of my eye, I could see her glance over at me.

⁂

We had one thousand and sixty six people, companies, organizations, universities, and media on the list. Eight hundred and eighty six of them had e-mail addresses. We made three copies, so we each had one.

It was late.

I reached for the remote and turned on the television. As I flicked through the channels, a commercial caught my eye. A man in a chair on a patio was speaking about needing to lower his cholesterol. His doctor prescribed a new medication. That part of the commercial took about thirty seconds. For the next thirty seconds a rapid voice listed the side effects while they showed fun lifestyle pictures. The side effects included liver damage, rash, flu like symptoms, abnormal sweating and internal bleeding. At the end Pharmalin's logo flashed on the screen.

I looked over at Morgan, shaking my head.

She rolled her eyes.

A few months ago I wouldn't have second guessed that commercial. I would have believed that it would be good for me, just like the millions of others watching it.

"Me too," she said.

I didn't make that realization out loud. She had read my mind. I opened my mouth to say something about it, but the phone rang.

Morgan reached over for the receiver. "Hello."

"It's so great to hear your voice." She looked up at me, a large smile on her face and a tear in her eye. "Go pickup the other line. It's Ivan."

I went to the bathroom. There was a phone on the wall beside the toilet. I put the lid down and sat on it as I picked up the phone. "Hello, Ivan."

"Hello, Nick. I am relieved that both of you are all right."

"Other than a few bruises," I said. "Are you calling from a safe line or should we call you back from a pay phone?"

"I am at a pay phone, so we are fine. I just spoke to Sue and she told me what happened to you."

Morgan said, "Thanks for taking care of everything at the hotel, Ivan."

"I wish I could have done more. I was afraid for your lives."

"How did you get away from the Naintosa guys?" I asked.

"I didn't. I assume they did not know I was there. It wasn't until I went to your room that I discovered something had happened."

I decided to leave it at that. The more I thought about Ivan not being on our side, the more absurd it seemed. "How's it going with the publisher?"

"An editor is working on it, but the publisher I was counting on is too scared to print the book. I went to a second house and they will not take the project on either."

"What are you going to do?" I asked.

"I do not know." Concern thickened Ivan's accent. "I do not want to shop the manuscript around too much. Every time I show it to someone, there is the possibility that they will contact Naintosa."

"Maybe you need to find a small independent publisher?" I said.

"There is one in New York that I know. They may be able to help us. I am flying there in the morning."

Morgan's tone was encouraging, "That sounds promising."

"Yeah," I said. "And we'll just wait here."

"I want to discuss that," Ivan said. "This is going to take more time than we thought. Naintosa's men are not going to stop looking for you. Seattle is not a safe place for you to wait for long."

Morgan asked, "Where should we go?"

"You need to decide. As well, think of new names for yourselves. You should get new identification and passports. Do you know anyone who can make forged ID's?"

Morgan said, "We'll try to find someone."

"Ivan, do you want me to type out the Bolivia camp

information and send it to you?" I asked. "I'll need a new email address, since the old ones are compromised by Naintosa taking our computers."

There was a pause on the line before Ivan asked, "Bolivia information? What Bolivia information?"

Morgan said, "The stuff you left in the locker at the Vancouver airport."

"Yeah, in the envelope," I added.

"I only left money and your identification. What exactly was in that envelope?"

He didn't know about it? How could that be? A cold chill ran down my spine as I gave him a brief explanation of the pictures and documents.

"I have heard of a lab there, but did not know about what you just described."

Morgan said, "Then how did it get there?"

Good question. A shiver ran *up* my spine that time.

"I have no idea," Ivan said. "But the information is staggering. It is proof of what we suspected."

"Exactly," Morgan said.

Silence filled the line.

The question of who the hell could've put it there raced through my mind. We really did have an outside ally. Someone must have watched Ivan hide the key, retrieved it, and hidden the Bolivia information in the locker for us.

"Send it to me," Ivan said. "We can figure out who gave us the gift later. Take down this email address."

"Go ahead," Morgan said.

Ivan gave the new address. "I will call you at 9pm in two days to discuss our progress."

I placed the receiver back on the wall, rose from the toilet and absentmindedly flushed. I didn't realize what I'd done until I was walking out of the bathroom.

"What're you smiling about? This is serious."

"I'm sorry." I pointed toward the bathroom. You could hear the old pipes squealing as the tank filled back up. "I was sitting on the toilet and without thinking flushed it when I got up."

Morgan shook her head and I caught a glimpse of a smile.

We discussed the phone call. We agreed that we trusted Ivan to do his job of getting the book published. It was the placement of the new information that freaked us out. Who was helping us? Morgan reminded me that someone may have helped her get untied at the warehouse. It could've very well been the same person.

"I'm still not a hundred percent sure there really was someone there," she said.

"We've considered all the angles we could think of," I said. "Regardless, whoever got the Bolivia information has a lot of power and resources."

"And knows how to spy."

"Well it's out of our control. Let's hope they reveal themselves." I sat back onto my bed. "So, what should our new names be?"

"It might be easier if we were married," Morgan said.

CHAPTER 37

That was good. I opened my eyes.

"Are you finished?" Morgan asked.

"Yeah." I raised my arms and stretched. "I got some answers."

"Me too." She swung her legs over the side of her bed and looked intently at me. "I finally had one of those meditations you've talked about. It felt great."

"Excellent. Tell me about it."

"I did the usual stuff and about half way through, I went into total silence. There was nothing. I felt totally free. Then all of a sudden answers popped into my head."

"That's great. What were they?"

"They weren't monumental, but we should use our real first names. That way we remember them and it'd be easier not to screw up. Also, we should definitely have the same new last name. It'd seem more natural if we looked like a married couple."

"Okay." I'd decided last night that if she pushed the acting like being married thing I'd go along with it.

Her eyes had narrowed and she looked like she was ready to debate the issue. "Really?"

"Yeah. Let's just choose a simple last name. One that's easy to pronounce and remember. Oh, do you have a ring you could use?"

"I'll just switch the one I wear on my right hand. It was my mother's wedding band." She had to twist the ring around her knuckle to get it off and give it an extra push to get it on her opposite finger. Morgan held out her left hand. "There."

Seeing the ring there jarred me. I really liked Morgan, was maybe even falling for her, definitely was attracted to her. But even being pretend-married was freaky. I gave my head a shake on the inside.

"There's that weird look you get sometimes," she said. "What're you thinking about?"

I wasn't about to tell her. I was happy her intuition hadn't developed to the point that she could read my mind all the time. I rolled my legs over the side of my bed to face her. She looked beautiful in just a long t-shirt with her hair messy. "I want to tell you about my meditation."

"Oh yeah. Sorry, I was all caught up in mine."

"I saw us in a tropical place, a secluded hut near a beach at the far end of an island. Fiji popped into my head."

"Fiji, huh." Morgan tilted her head back, as if imagining what it would be like there. "Well...it's remote."

"I doubt they'd ever look for us there, especially with new identities."

"I could handle Fiji." She reached for the list on the night-stand of names we'd thought of last night. "Now, what about our names."

"Do any of those resonate today?"

A big smile brightened her face. "I thought of the perfect one. Jagger...Nick Jagger."

"Yeah, like that'd be inconspicuous."

She laughed and read on. "What about Hansen?"

"Hansen?" I let it roll off my tongue. "Hansen."

"You could pass for having Scandinavian ancestry." She tilted her head. "It doesn't matter if it suits me."

"You look more Scandinavian than I do." I got up and walked over to the only window in our motel room and part-ed the heavy curtains. It was a rare sunny day in a Pacific Northwest winter. A coating of frost sparkled on the parking lot pavement. "It's beautiful out there."

"Perfect." Morgan turned to see out the window. "We have a lot to do today and it's more fun in the sun, than the rain."

"Like in Fiji?" I smiled.

"As the Hansens." She smiled back.

The decision was made.

"I'm going to have a shower." She sauntered to the bathroom. "You get that. It's probably Sue." The phone rang just as she finished speaking.

The flashes of synchronicity that Morgan seemed to be unaware of were getting scary. I went to the phone on the nightstand between the beds. "Hello."

"Morning Nick, what're you guys up to?"

"Hey Sue, we're deciding on new names and where to lie low. Ivan doesn't think Seattle is safe and it's going to take longer than he thought to get a publisher."

"Yeah, he mentioned that. I hope he can find someone."

"He will." I wanted to be optimistic. "Do you know anyone who can make fake ID's?"

"Yeah, I talked to a guy about a year ago for a story."

"Do you know how we can find him?"

"I'm one step ahead of you," she said. "I already dug out his contact information."

I copied down the guy's name, phone number and address.

"He's a slimy skid, but he can do the job for you," Sue said. "I'll call him first and jog his memory. He owes me. I protected his identity in the story."

"Great," I said. "You know Ivan didn't give us the envelope on Bolivia. Someone else did."

"What? Who?"

"We don't know. It's obvious someone else knows what we're doing and wants to help. And was following Ivan."

"Holy shit."

⚓

I typed the Bolivia notes into the new computer in the way I'd want it in the manuscript.

Our motel didn't have an internet connection, so Morgan and I found a coffee shop a few blocks away that did. From there we e-mailed the most incriminating information we had to Ivan.

CHAPTER 38

"Are you sure this is the address Sue gave you?" Morgan squirmed in her seat.

"Yep. Where else do you think a criminal who forges ID's would live?" I looked around the grungy street. "In a neat little pink house, with daisies growing on the front lawn?"

"Shut up." Morgan gave me an evil look. "I've never been in this area of Seattle."

I was still getting used to the changed Morgan. A few hours ago she had gone into the bathroom as a strawberry blonde and come out a brunette. Her hair was six inches shorter. She had bangs. With her fair complexion all of her features stood out more; especially her striking blue eyes.

We both leaned over the dash of the Cadillac and looked up at the building. It was a dirty, old, brown, three floor walk up. All the buildings on the block looked the same, but this one had the address we were looking for.

"What if he doesn't want to help us?" Morgan bit her lip. "What if he wants to cut us into small pieces and stick us into a freezer?"

I wondered if the hair dye had screwed with her brain, creating melodrama. "Remember, Sue called ahead. He owes her a favor. It'll be fine."

"I'm not sure if I like the people Sue knows." Morgan managed a smirk.

I couldn't help but smile. "It's all in a day's work. Now get out of the car."

We walked across the street, glued to each other's sides. No people were out. Only a ratty looking dog sniffed around some crumpled fast food wrappers at the edge of the sidewalk.

I looked at the dented intercom and buzzed 305.

After a few seconds we heard, "Heh."

I leaned closer to the speaker. "Hi, it's Nick and Morgan. Sue Clark from the *News* sent us."

"Yea, come up. The fron der's bus hed."

Morgan looked at me, wide eyed. "Did you get that?"

"I think so."

The hinge creaked as I pulled on the unlocked door and the handle was sticky. There wasn't a foyer, just a hallway on the left and stairs on the right. The linoleum was worn right through to the plywood in places. The walls were stained and peeling at the edges. The air had a rank undertone, like piss mixed with skunk weed.

As we were climbing the stairs, I looked back at Morgan. She was trying to avoid touching the railing.

I gave apartment 305 a knock. We heard shuffling on the other side before the door opened. In front of us stood a short, skinny guy, with shoulder length, sand colored, straight hair. He looked like a twelve year old with wrinkles. I guessed he was really in his mid thirties. He wore a black Judas Priest t-shirt that he probably bought at a concert in the Eighties and faded Levis.

"Heh, I'm Max." He didn't make eye contact, just looked past us.

"I'm Nick and this is Morgan."

He took a good look at Morgan. I could tell by his expression that he was impressed, but intimidated. Her brown leather jacket was open, exposing a form fitting white sweater.

Morgan attempted a smile as Max stepped to the side to let us in.

The smell of stale cigarette smoke overpowered the air. The small apartment had clutter everywhere, except for one clean white wall. I imagined the other walls had been white originally, but were now off yellow.

He motioned for us to sit on an old brown couch. He sat down in a worn rust colored chair across from us.

"So, whah da yah wan?" He had a prominent lisp.

"We need ID's and passports," I said.

"Ha'll cos yuh. You goh cash? I onie hake cash."

Morgan hesitated, squinting to understand him. "We have money."

"Up fron. I goha have the cash up fron." Not only did he have a lisp, but he couldn't pronounce the letter T. It came out sounding like a lazy H.

Morgan had a stubborn look. "How about we pay you half now and half on delivery?"

Max scratched his head, exposing a skull tattoo on his forearm. "I guess."

There was a rustling noise in the other room.

He said, "Never mind, that's just my old lady."

Morgan pulled the wallet from her black leather handbag. "How much will it cost?"

"Hold on." I placed my hand over her wallet. "How do we know they'll look authentic?"

He looked down his crooked nose at me. "Where's your driver's license?"

I pulled it out to show him.

Max reached into a well worn box beside his chair and picked up a stack held together by a red rubber band. At random he pulled one out. "Here's Washington State."

Morgan and I looked closely at it, comparing for accuracy against mine.

"They look identical," I said. "I can't see any difference."

"Me neither," she added.

"It'll be fifteen hundred for *each* of you for licenses, passports, and social security numbers."

"Fine." Morgan counted out hundred dollar bills and passed them to him. "Here's half."

Max tried to conceal a smirk. He must've been charging us way more than usual.

We needed them and I didn't feel that haggling was an option. "Now what?"

"Did you bring pictures or do you want me to take one with your black eye?"

My eye was still dark around one side and I had a small blood spot near my pupil. "We'll need pictures."

Max got up and went over to a beat up cupboard with its doors barely hanging onto their hinges. He pulled out a fancy looking camera. "Up against there." He pointed to the clean white wall.

Morgan went first. He took a dozen pictures of her and only two of me.

"Let me get your details." He reached for a pad of paper from the box, as we all sat back down. "You first." He pointed at me. "What name you want?"

"Nick Hansen. H-a-n-s-e-n."

"Address?"

"Shit, we never thought of that." I looked over at Morgan, who shrugged.

Max said, "Make one up."

"Okay." I thought for a second. "How about 590 Carson Road, Everett." I looked at Morgan for approval.

"Think that's a real address?" she asked.

"Yeah, I had an uncle who used to live on that block. There was a little park beside his house which was 588. I think if we're going to be married, we should live in the suburbs."

Morgan nodded. "Good thinking."

Max scribbled. "Birthday?"

"August 4, 1970."

"Eyes?"

"Green," I said. "My hair's brown, I weigh one hundred and eighty pounds and I'm six feet tall."

"Right, now you." Max pointed his pen at Morgan. "Name?"

"Morgan Hansen, same address. My birthday is March 19, 1973. My eyes are blue, hair is..." Morgan reached back and pulled a fist full of hair forward to look. "Brown."

That made me smile. It was cute the way she wasn't sure.

Max didn't notice. He was slowly writing out each letter. "Weight?"

Morgan pondered for a second. "I'm one hundred and twenty seven pounds and five feet seven inches tall."

It was painful to watch Max's deliberate penmanship. When he was finally done, he said, "Right, come back in three weeks."

"What?" I sat straight up. "We need them in three days, not weeks."

"I can get the ID's ready in three days, but not the passports."

Morgan stood up. "Okay, we'll come back in three days for the ID's."

We left Max sitting in his chair and showed ourselves out.

As we walked down the stairs, I asked, "What are you thinking?"

"Why don't we fly to Hawaii and get Sue to send our passports when they're ready?" She flashed me a smile. "Then we can fly to Fiji."

"So we get out of here fast and lay low in one paradise before moving on to another paradise." I pondered for a millisecond. "Sweet."

CHAPTER 39

For the next two days we got ready. We bought warm weather clothes and purchased tickets to Maui. Sue agreed to forward our passports. We were all set.

⋙

"Good evening."

"Hi Ivan," Morgan's voice went up a few decibels, "Nick, grab the other line."

I was already in the bathroom. "Hey, Ivan. Did you get the material on the Bolivia camp I e-mailed?"

"Yes, and you articulated it very well. It filled in many blanks about Naintosa's procedures and what happened with some of our research. Their level of inhumanity still shocks me."

"Is there enough proof to include it in the manuscript?" Morgan asked.

"Well...we would benefit from having more documentation. Yet now that we have this information, the book would feel incomplete without it. It would be nice to know who our generous ally is and find out if they are able to get more proof."

I said, "Since that may not happen, you'll have to make a judgment call."

"I've decided to consult a lawyer. We should have done it from the beginning."

"Good call." Of course; why hadn't I thought of that?

Morgan broke in. "How's your progress otherwise?"

"I am in New York, but have not had any luck here either. Publishers are not willing to take the risk."

I said, "Have you tried to sell them on the fact that it could be a big seller?"

"That is not their objection." The frustration in Ivan's voice was clear. "They like the way it is written. Everyone has commented on how understandable it is and they are sure they could sell many copies. Their concern is about the power of Naintosa. They are afraid of spending money to prepare the book only to have it stopped by a law suit before it makes it to print."

"Naintosa already knows what's going on," I said. "I'm sure they've read the disk they got from us in Vancouver."

"They just don't know we're shopping it already," Morgan said.

"I have decided to fly to London. Bill has been quietly looking for publishers and one is willing to meet with me. Bill also has law connections."

"It might be easier there." I hoped so anyway.

"What about your plans?" Ivan asked. "Have you decided on your next destination?"

I let Morgan tell him. I was racking my brain about how to get the book published. Even though Sue and I were in print media, neither of us knew any book publishers personally. Was self-publishing an option?

"Nick? Nick are you still on the line?" Morgan's voice cut through my thoughts.

"Sorry, I was just thinking about publishers."

"Any conclusions?" Ivan sounded weary.

"No, but I'll keep considering possibilities."

"Let me worry about that," Ivan said. "You two just get to Maui and Fiji safely."

Good plan. "We'll communicate through Sue until we get settled."

CHAPTER 40

We arrived at Max's apartment just after noon. He looked the same, except this time he had on an old black Led Zeppelin t-shirt. At least he had good taste in music.

"Hey's ready."

"Who's ready?" I asked, without thinking.

Max had two envelopes in his hands. "Yeah ID's."

"Oh yes, the ID's." The guy really needed speech therapy. "Great."

Morgan snickered beside me. She was wearing form fitting jeans and a tight blue button up shirt under an open white jacket. Max eyed her with lust.

Trying not to pay attention to his leer, I took the envelopes and opened one. It was Morgan's so I passed it over and then opened mine.

Morgan stepped over to an old lamp that was on and surveyed her ID. "Brilliant," she said, after a good look.

I pulled my real driver's license from my wallet and compared the two. "Great job, Max. You really know your stuff."

"I know. Now give me the rest of my money."

Morgan looked at him, annoyed. "What about the passports and Social Security Numbers?"

Max squirmed. "They'll take a few more weeks. I told you that before."

"And I told you you'll get the rest when the job is done. But, in good faith..." Morgan reached into her black shoulder bag and pulled out her wallet. "Here's two hundred more."

"Here's Sue's number in case you don't have it." I passed

him a piece of paper I pulled from my jean pocket. "Call her when they're ready. She'll pick them up and pay you the rest."

"Remember." Morgan narrowed her eyes. "Don't tell anyone about us."

Max's body twitched. "What do you think, I'm an amateur?" He looked insulted. "I wouldn't be in business if I told."

"We trust you Max." Morgan grabbed my arm and pulled me toward the way out. "We've got to go. Thanks for everything."

Just as we reached the door it opened.

In front of us was a short, very skinny woman. She was trying not to drop a case of beer as she fumbled with her keys. She had on tight, tight jeans and an old red Mac jacket. Her long, thin, dry hair was bleached blonde. She was probably in her mid-thirties, but from the looks of her, she'd been partying hard since her early teens.

"Hi," Morgan said, as she pushed me past her.

"Hi." The woman looked up, startled.

Descending the stairs, Morgan glanced back at me. "They make a cute couple."

"Both stuck in the Eighties." I kept close behind her.

We walked out the door onto the street and stopped.

A guy got up from behind Sue's grandmother's car across the street. He was wearing a black hoody and baseball cap, had a crowbar in one hand and the Cadillac emblem from the trunk in the other. He walked around to the driver's side window and raised the crowbar.

"Hey!" I yelled.

"Don't you dare, asshole!" Morgan yelled.

I raced toward the car.

"Don't fuck with me." He raised the menacing metal tool.

"Don't fuck with you? Don't fuck with me!" I stopped just out of range.

We stood there. Staring. Sizing each other up. We were about the same height and build, but the crow bar gave him the advantage. Looking into his dark eyes I could see he wasn't going to take it further. They weren't mean enough.

"Fuck this." The Cadillac emblem hit the pavement with a rattle. He backed off. When he was twenty feet away he turned and jogged off.

I hadn't noticed that Morgan was standing right by my side with her hands clenched.

When the robber disappeared around the corner, I picked up the emblem and we got in the car.

"I can't believe you just did that." Morgan's voice sounded shaky.

I didn't know I had it in me either.

CHAPTER 41

It was 7:00am when we met Sue. The plan was for her to take the Cadillac back to her grandmother after we went to the airport.

Morgan passed an inch thick stack of $100 bills to Sue in the back seat. "Here's money for the passports, Nick's rent and bills. Also, there's some extra for all your help and to get the emblem put back on the car."

Sue's eyebrows rose as she flipped through the bills. "This is more than just a little extra."

"You've helped us so much and you're putting your own life at risk. It's the least I could do."

Sue placed the money in her bag. "Thanks, Morgan."

I looked in the rearview mirror as I drove. "Sorry about the car."

"Don't worry about it." Sue held the Cadillac emblem up. "Good thing you stopped the guy before he did more damage."

Morgan said, "I thought Nick was going to waste him."

"I wasn't. I just wanted to make him think I would." I felt like I'd toughened up, but I was out of my comfort zone with *everything* that was going on. "Besides, you were right next to me."

"I doubt it was me he was afraid of."

"Well, thank you both." Sue looked from me to Morgan. "Aren't you two overdressed for Maui? And what's with the matching turtlenecks?"

"I have a t-shirt on underneath," I said. "And mine's blue and loose, hers is white and tight. They're not matching."

Morgan shrugged. "They were on sale."

"There's the exit to Sea Tac." I changed lanes to leave the interstate.

"I think everything's in order?" Morgan turned back to Sue. "You have the address and phone number of our hotel. It's booked for a week."

"We'll find someplace more secluded after we settle in," I added. "We'll probably be there for over three weeks."

"I'll keep everything moving on this end." Sue squinted up as a departing jet roared overhead. "What did you decide to do with your job?"

"I'll call Dan from the airport and quit."

"Make sure you have a story, in case he backs you up against a wall. If he asks me, I'll tell him I haven't heard from you and look surprised."

"Forget the story. Who cares about what he thinks." I didn't. Not anymore.

"I like your attitude," Sue said. "What about you, Morgan?"

"I decided it's best I just disappear and not contact my PR firm. There're some really nosey people at the office."

Within minutes we'd arrived at the departure terminal drop off point. We got out, pulled the luggage from the trunk, and hugged Sue.

She looked worried. "See you later."

I felt exposed standing in the open. "Let's get going." I hurried Morgan inside.

In the terminal we scanned the area for anyone who might be watching for us. It was busy with line after line of people waiting to check in. I forced myself to be acutely aware of all the activity. Everyone seemed to be doing their own thing.

The lady at the counter didn't question our new identification. She just wanted to make sure the ID's matched the names on the tickets. I wondered how much information was supposed to come up on the screen.

We made our way through security, past a bookstore, two restaurants, a souvenir shop and along a corridor to our gate.

There was over an hour before we had to board.

"Go have a seat. I'd better finish things off at the paper." I pointed to a line of pay phones.

"Good luck," Morgan said.

"I'll make it quick." I gave her a grin as we separated.

Dan liked to have his calls go through the editorial receptionist so he could screen them. It was another one of his power quirks. So I dialed his direct line.

"Dan speaking."

"Nick Barnes calling."

"It's about time you checked in." He almost sounded welcoming. "Where are you and when're you coming back?"

I wanted to get straight to the point. "I won't be coming back."

"Why don't you come into the office and we'll discuss it?"

"I can't do that."

"Okay, I'll come to you. Where are you?"

"Why, Dan? I quit."

"I just want to talk to you. Are you in town?"

"I've got to go. I'm sure you've already replaced me."

"No I haven't. The other reporters have taken up your slack. I can meet you in an hour." He could be nice if he really wanted something.

I wasn't falling for it. "It's not going to happen. Sorry if I gave you false hope."

Suddenly loud words cut through the air, "This is the final boarding call for United Airlines flight 5106 departing for Salt Lake City." I looked up and saw a speaker ten feet from my head. Shit.

"You're at an airport," Dan said. "Are you flying to Salt Lake? Are you at Sea Tac? It wouldn't take me long to get there."

I had to think quick and throw him off. "No, I'm in Vancouver. So no matter what, we can't meet up."

There was a pause on the other end. "Who're you working for? I know you couldn't afford to be without an income for this long. Is Sue involved?"

"Sue? Absolutely not!" I think I was too quick with that. "Why do you all of a sudden give a shit about what I'm doing?"

"I care about all of my team and you don't sound like your old self."

That comment was so insincere he couldn't hide the fact that he was probing. I'd had enough. "Good bye, Dan. I've gotta go."

"But..."

I hung up.

I walked to where Morgan sat reading a brochure about Maui that the travel agent had given her.

She looked up. "How'd it go? Did you get your sweet revenge?"

I took the seat next to her. "The conversation gave me the creeps."

"What do you mean?"

"He faked being nice. Kept asking if we could meet."

Morgan put the brochure down. "Do you think the thugs from Naintosa got to him?"

"That's what I was thinking."

CHAPTER 42

Morgan slept through most of the five hour flight. She looked so peaceful. It was probably the first time she'd felt safe in a long time.

Flying over the ocean made me feel like we had washed our pursuers away. It'd been a couple of weeks since we had fled Vancouver, with no sign of the men from Naintosa since. My physical wounds had healed. I hoped time in Maui and Fiji would help my mental and emotional state. But they were still looking for us. I wondered if we'd ever be able to *truly* relax.

As the plane adjusted direction for its final descent, I could see Mount Haleakala on the right and Kihei below. Welcome to paradise, I said to myself.

A sudden jolt threw my heart into my throat. The plane abruptly dropped. It recovered, but kept shaking and pitching from side to side as if it wanted to come apart.

I tightened my seat belt and grabbed the arm rests.

"It's beautiful," Morgan's voice purred.

"You're awake." My voice trembled and my knuckles were turning white. "We're gonna crash."

"Don't be silly." Morgan's voice bounced around like the plane, but calm. "It's always turbulent coming in, because of the trade winds sweeping through the valley. We'll be fine."

I looked around and realized I was the only one in a panic. "I'll take your word for it." That relaxed me some. "I forgot to ask, how many times have you been here?"

"Three." Morgan smiled. "I'll be your tour guide."

The plane shuddered and dipped all the way in. I hadn't flown many times before, so it felt as if my heart repeatedly jumped between my groin and my tonsils. I had to close my eyes for the landing, but we made it.

We stepped out of the plane onto portable stairs and straight into a wall of humid heat. All the cold and wet of the Pacific Northwest evaporated out of me. And the smell was unique; a mix of sweet orchids, jet fuel, and dust. Waves of hot air rolled, distorting the look of the tarmac.

The baggage claim area was sparse with five carousels surrounded by three tan polished cinder block walls. I was surprised to see one side of the building open to the street, allowing a warm breeze to flow through. It didn't have the busy feel of most airports. Everyone was smiling, beginning their vacations.

It didn't take long to collect our luggage.

Outside a film of milk chocolate brown dirt covered the concrete. It was in the air and the earthy smell filled my nostrils as we walked to the shuttle that would take us to our rental car.

Morgan knew the way to Lahaina, so she drove.

I enjoyed the scenery along the winding highway. Rust colored rocky soil on the mountainside to our right contrasted with deep blue ocean on the left.

We passed through an uphill tunnel cut into lava rock.

"This place is beautiful, but I imagined it being more lush," I said.

Morgan smiled. "It will be where we're going."

I was looking in every direction, trying to soak it all in.

"You know, Maui's wind patterns are very predictable." Morgan began her tour guide role. "The mornings are calm, then around noon the wind picks up and blows until a few hours before sunset. I'd say that pattern repeated ninety percent of the days I've been here."

I half listened. I was more interested in watching the surfers to the left.

Further along, clusters of green bushes and short trees dotted the hillside and palms appeared along the beach. The ground had a dark, moist look. A few dilapidated small buildings appeared on the side of the road.

I read a sign out loud as we passed: "Welcome to Lahaina. Are we here?"

"It's pronounced *La hi nah*, not *La hyena* like the animal," Morgan snickered. "We're staying in a place further along, called Kaanipaali."

"Oh."

Beyond Lahaina the road wound inland. The topography had turned green and lush. The soil under all the plant life looked dark and rich. This was the Hawaii I had imagined.

After a few miles we turned off toward a resort area.

"This is it," Morgan said.

Wide, palm lined, manicured fairways spread out on each side of the road and large hotels stood along the shoreline.

The grand, circular entrance of our hotel was spectacular. Lights strategically placed on the grounds accented a variety of trees, ferns, flowers and plants. Jungle paradise met Christmas at dusk.

"You know Christmas is only two weeks away," Morgan reminded me.

"I hadn't thought of it until I saw these lights."

"Me too."

"I guess we'll be here for Christmas and probably ring in 2001 in Fiji."

"That'll be nice."

Outside the air conditioned car it was humid and warm. The mild breeze made it comfortable. The rich scent of orchids pleasurably assaulted my senses.

The main entrance was white marble, accented by plants in shining glazed clay pots beneath brass artwork hung on the walls. In the center of the foyer was a two-story lava rock waterfall. The cascading water cooled the air and provided the perfect background sound. A colorful bird flew over our heads right through the open-air structure.

I walked over to a railing overlooking a lounge. Beyond was a pool and the beach. "I don't think I've been in a more beautiful place."

"This is why I wanted to stay here a few days." Morgan

took a deep savoring breath. "Enjoy the scenery and I'll check us in."

"Sure." I was glad to wait there. I didn't want to know how much it was going to cost.

Our room was on the second floor, overlooking the Pacific. I went straight to the patio. The last sliver of the sun was sinking into the ocean. Wisps of clouds glowed in shades of brilliant orange, yellow, and red. The scent of salt and orchids mingled in the air.

Morgan joined me on the lanai. The hotel was horseshoe shaped and our suite was at the front inside corner. "This is fantastic." She bent and folded her arms on top of the railing to look down at the beach. Tiki lamps were being lit at the water's edge in front of an outdoor restaurant.

"What a place to lay low." I smiled. "Thank you."

"We deserve it," she said softly.

I felt compelled to put my arm around her, but at that moment Morgan straightened up.

"We should get unpacked," she said. "Then go have dinner."

I felt disappointment as I turned to watch her walk away. I had to remind myself that we were here to hide and not on a romantic vacation. I hadn't paid any attention to our room when we'd first walked through it, so I went inside.

The base color was white; the floor was a cream tile, the walls had a green tint and the furniture had brass accents. More vibrancy was added by the two green ferns in dark brown pots and vivid yet tasteful Hawaiian landscape paintings on the walls. It was classy.

I followed Morgan into the bedroom. The decor was the same, except for the king size bedspread, which was black with bright flower patterns.

"Only one bed, huh?"

"Since we're pretending to be married I couldn't ask for two beds." Morgan shrugged. "It'd look suspicious."

"So..."

"The couch is a pull out." She smiled.

I glanced back toward the living room. "I want a divorce."

INTERLOGUE 3

Peter Bail sat behind a small, gray metal desk at Naintosa's field office in Seattle. It was a nondescript warehouse near the port. He had rather enjoyed roughing it since he'd arrived three days ago. He felt more relaxed in jeans, boots and heavy shirts. Ties had always irritated him.

He was studying the latest set of Sue Clark's phone records, delivered this morning by the team's forensic computer analyst. He scrolled down the now familiar list of numbers on his laptop. He made note of a number with a New York area code, two in Seattle, and one in Everett. Those needed to be checked out.

He felt the vibration of the cell phone in his pocket and pulled it out. "What've you got?"

"I was just contacted by that informant," said Sig Thompson. "Nick Barnes quit his *News* job and might be at the Vancouver airport."

"Why would he think that?" Peter sat forward.

"There was a departure called over a loud speaker while they were talking. Then Barnes said he was in Vancouver."

Peter was skeptical. "How long ago did this call happen?"

"About an hour," Sig said.

"Why'd he take so fucking long to contact you?" Peter unconsciously crumpled the piece of paper he'd been writing on.

"No idea." Sig sounded irritated. "I asked him the same thing, but he jumped on a soap box about having lots on his plate."

"Anything about Morgan Elles being with him?" Peter asked.

"No, but I'm sure she is."

"Did you dispatch anyone to the Vancouver airport to check it out?"

"Hall's on his way."

"What about Sea Tac?" Peter asked. "In case Barnes wasn't telling the truth."

"On my way now," Sig said. "Any news about Popov?"

"Yes, we're closing in on him in New York."

"Good," Sig said. "Okay, I'll get back to you after I check out the airport."

Peter swiveled his chair and looked out the small, grimy window. Where would they be flying to? To meet up with Ivan Popov? That was a good possibility.

Peter turned back to his laptop and went to the WIRE, looking to see if there were any postings related to his request. He'd been checking almost every hour. This time, he got something. There was a message from a guy who was making passports for Nick Barnes and Morgan Elles. He wanted to be paid to reveal their new identities.

Peter drew conclusions. The passport guy was in Seattle. They'd been back from Vancouver for awhile. Therefore, it was most likely they'd be flying out of Sea Tac. Their passports weren't ready yet, so they'd be traveling somewhere within the country. However, they eventually wanted to go somewhere outside the US. They'd be either coming back to Seattle for the passports or they'd get someone to pick them up.

Peter dialed Sig's cell number. "I'm pretty sure that the call came from Sea Tac." Peter told Sig about the WIRE information.

"I'm almost there," Sig said.

"Chances are they're gone by now, but take a look anyway." Peter stared unseeing at the window. "If you don't find them at domestic departures, go see the guy that posted on the WIRE. Pay him off and get the information we need. With the new names I'll trace them. The passports, when they're ready, will lead us right to them."

Peter gave Sig the number Max had left on the message.

Within two hours, Sig called back.

"They both changed their last names to Hansen; h-a-n-s-e-n," Sig said. "They kept their first names. Rookie mistake."

"What about the passports?" Peter asked.

"They won't be ready for another week."

"Who's picking them up?"

"Sue Clark."

Peter thought for a second. "How slimy is the informant?"

"The sludge at the bottom of an oil barrel," Sig replied.

"Give him some extra money to speed up on the passports and to contact you when they're ready."

"Already done."

❧

It didn't take Peter long to find out where Nick and Morgan Hansen had gone. He was back on his cell to Sig within an hour.

"They're on their way to Maui."

"Do you want me to get on a plane?" Sig asked.

"No, you shadow Sue Clark," Peter said. "Send Matt. Tell him just to locate and tail for now. No showboating. You and I will escort the passports."

CHAPTER 43

For the next five days we looked for a place to lie low while enjoying the sights along the way. We drove to Hana, but decided a getaway was impossible from there. There was a house for rent past Big Beach, but it was really expensive. The gated community beside the Kapalua Plantation golf course was a possibility, but pricy too.

If you needed to hide out somewhere, Maui was a heck of a lot better than most places. Plus they had Mai Tai's.

⁂

"I'm going to that rental office in Lahaina we saw the other night," Morgan said. "Want to come?"

"No, I haven't meditated in a week and I have a strong urge to." I took another bite of papaya. The morning sun was already hot on our lanai. "I think I'll go down to the water to do it."

"I'll be back in an hour or so," she said, as she got up.

After I finished my breakfast, I grabbed a towel and walked down to the beach. There was a row of wooden lounge chairs toward the end of the property, where it was quiet. I draped my towel and shirt over the recliner, kicked off my flip flops and settled in. "Ouch." It took a moment for the sear of the hot recliner against my bare skin to ease as I stretched out. The shade of a palm tree only covered my face. A slight breeze moved the frond over me letting the sun come through, heating my head in an instant then providing relief as it moved back to its original position.

I closed my eyes. The sound of waves breaking and local birds chirping filled my ears. The sweet smell of the flowering bush behind me mingled with sea weed and salt. My senses felt in harmony.

Soon my mind faded into nothingness.

Just as I was coming out of the gap, I had a vision of Sue's face. She looked panicked. That brought me right out of the meditation. My first thought was to call her.

Morgan was entering the lobby when I got there. She was wearing a tight pink tank top and an almost see through white skirt. A bellman took a good peek as she walked by him. I instantly felt defensive, but brushed the feeling away. There was no time for such reactions.

"Why are you back so soon?" I asked, as soon as she was close.

The bellman looked at me, so I gave him a quick scowl. That made him turn away. Morgan didn't seem to have noticed.

"I think I've found the place." She was beaming. "I met a man who overheard me explaining what we need to the rental agent."

"Hmm...this sounds like either synchronicity or a trap."

"I'm thinking synchronicity." Morgan smirked. "He said he was there to advertise a place he has. He thinks it could be perfect for us. It's a camp, north of Kaanipaali. The property's secluded and has its own beach."

"That could have potential," I said.

"I knew you'd think so. We're going to meet him in an hour to see the place."

"Did the man make you uncomfortable in any way?"

"No, he was older, kind, and really nice. Oh yeah, the place used to be a bible camp."

"A bible camp?" I pondered that for a second. "I guess we need all the help we can get."

She laughed. "How was your meditation?"

"It was fine, but I need to call Sue." I pointed to the pay phones, tastefully hidden from view in an alcove. "I'll be right back."

"Wait..." Morgan rummaged through her white knit bag

and produced a cell phone. "It's pre-paid, so we don't have to register it. All we have to do is keep buying minutes." She handed it to me.

I stared at the basic object in my hand and shook my head. "Now why didn't we think of this sooner?"

We walked over to some comfy chairs overlooking the pool. I dialed her direct work line. "Sue Clark speaking."

"Hey, Sue..."

"About frickin time you called!" She went from loud, to a whisper, "A lot's happened that I need to talk to you about."

"What's going on?"

"It's not safe to talk in the office." Her voice became even quieter. "Give me a number I can reach you at in five minutes."

I looked up. "Morgan, what's the number of this phone?"

She reached into her bag and produced a small booklet with the number on it.

I read it to Sue.

"Okay, stay where you are." She hung up.

"What did she say?" Morgan asked.

"Lots happened and it wasn't safe in the office."

Morgan looked guilty. "We should never have left her there alone."

"We'll know what's going on in a few minutes."

It wasn't long before the cell rang. I answered right away, "What's happening?"

"I'm being followed again. I saw him. It's the Lieutenant guy. He's watching me from a distance."

"Oh shit."

"Oh shit is right. And whenever I'm on a call, Dan's close by, trying to listen. I feel he's involved somehow and not on our side."

"How could that be?"

"My guess is they wanted someone on the inside to watch us?" She sounded even more anxious. "He's the perfect one; weak and self serving."

"I don't know..."

"You know what Ivan told us," Sue said, "These guys control people in the media."

"Yeah and Dan's the perfect little stoolie. He'd do it just so he could feel like a big man." A thought popped into my head, "Maybe you should come to Maui?" I looked over at Morgan, who was nodding with vigor.

"I was hoping you'd say that." I could hear the angst drain from Sue's voice. "I'm already getting Max to make me fake ID. And he said he's been able to speed up the process."

"Great, it's time for you to get out of there," I said. "You're too involved now and I think it'd be safer if we stick together."

"I can always get another job." She sounded almost cheerful. "Helping you guys is more important. I need a change of scenery."

"Well, you'll love the scenery here."

"Also, three nights ago I had a bad dream about being captured and beaten." Caution returned to her voice. "The next morning the vision returned in my meditation. That was the first day I noticed I was being followed. I'm scared."

"Drop everything and come now. Don't go back to the office. Just pack a bag and head to the airport."

"No. I'll wait for the passports."

"Screw them. We'll figure something out."

"No. I just have to be extra vigilant for a couple more days."

"Are you sure?" I wanted her here with us right away, but couldn't think of who would get our passports to us.

"Ivan called and we talked about it. For a scientist, he seemed pretty open to that stuff."

That was because of Morgan's premonitions about Alice.

"We decided to e-mail the manuscript to everyone on the list I had an address for. I wrote a cover letter and sent it off. I hope that's okay?"

"Isn't that jumping the gun?" I looked at Morgan, who was frowning. She was trying to follow the conversation from just hearing my side.

"The rationale is that if anything should happen to us, these organizations will know who did it."

It made sense. "Maybe one of them could help us get it published."

"I even sent it to the World Health Organization."

My mouth dropped and my head spun. "What'd you do that for? We're screwed. You know it's controlled by the pharmaceutical companies and Hendrick Schmidt's on the board of directors."

"Oh shit, I forgot." Sue's voice sounded defeated. "I'm sorry, I've fucked everything up."

"Hold on," I told Sue. I put the phone on my lap and explained what happened to Morgan.

Without saying anything back to me Morgan took the phone. "Don't worry about it, Sue. Everything happens for a reason. You did what you thought was best. We just want you here."

Morgan was really showing her new strength. She anchored the situation.

Morgan paused for a second and then asked, "What else did Ivan say?"

Another pause before she said, "Okay, we'll talk to you tonight."

"What's happening with Ivan?" I asked as she touched the end button.

"He's in London with Bill," she said. "Still no luck."

I sighed. "That sucks."

"I have a feeling someone Sue sent the manuscript to will be able to help us," Morgan said.

"I hope the World Health Organization doesn't come after us."

"Schmidt already knows what's in the manuscript. Now, unfortunately, he'll know our strategy."

We sat in silence for a few moments, digesting the conversation.

Morgan got up. "What's done is done. We'd better get going to see the bible camp."

CHAPTER 44

We drove to the designated strip mall to meet the gentleman who owned the camp.

"There he is." Morgan pointed as we drove through the parking lot.

A mature man leaned against the tail end of a blue mid-nineties Ford pickup. The truck was coated in a rust colored film of dust, making it look pale. It really could do with a wash, I thought.

We parked in the open stall two spots away.

He looked scruffy in well worn jeans, plain green t-shirt, a red bandana around his neck and a sweat-stained green John Deere baseball cap. His tanned, leathery face was sprinkled with gray stubble. As we came up close, I looked down at his crossed ankles. He wore brand new black sandals with nylon straps and leather soles. They were out of place with the rest of his outfit. Not to mention his feet looked in better shape than the rest of him. Were his nails pedicured?

"How ya'll doin?" he said, in a distinct southern drawl. "Jack Carter at yer service." He reached out and shook my hand.

"Nick Barnes, err, I mean Hansen...Nick Hansen." I felt my face heat up. It must've turned the color of a beet.

He gave me a smile as he reached out to Morgan, "Howdy there, Miss Morgan. You ready to see my estate?"

We left our rental and packed into his pickup. Morgan sat in the middle of the bench seat.

After a couple of miles the road narrowed and snaked around the mountainside. The blue ocean was always to our left, peeking through gaps in the green curtain of vegetation.

I thought about the driver. Why did the name Jack Carter sound familiar?

Within ten minutes we turned left off the paved highway onto a dirt road. A few hundred yards in, Jack stopped to unlock a gate.

"Helps keep the riff raff out," he said.

Morgan and I nodded to each other. Every bit of security would help.

We continued slowly on what looked like an old, dried out riverbed. The soil was red, studded with black rocks. Tangled trees hung over us as if we were passing through a tunnel.

"This is secluded all right." I flinched as a branch smacked the side of the truck.

Jack nodded. "Complete privacy."

We broke free of the jungle into a clearing with a rustic wooden house at the far edge. It needed a coat of paint, but looked structurally sound and definitely livable. It stood high on stilts at least six feet off the ground, with a broad set of stairs in the middle that led up to a large wrap-around porch.

"That's nice," Morgan said.

"Thank you, that's my home. The cabin's are up a ways. You get your pick. Nobody else is stayin there at the moment."

The road led back into the jungle. After a couple hundred yards we reached another clearing. Eight old cabins were clustered around a central building.

"That middle one has a kitchen, toilets, and showers. Everything works and it's clean. Choose which cabin you want. I suggest the one closest to the ocean. It's got a view."

We all got out. The air was hot and smelled of orchids.

The central building was made of cinder blocks painted brown. The cabins were identical: green, one foot wood plank exterior, up on three foot stilts, with porches on the front and tin roofs.

The cabin he'd recommended was at the edge of the trees, only about forty feet from the ocean.

"Is that your private beach?" I asked.

"All beaches are public in Hawaii, but hardly anyone ever comes here."

Jack opened the cabin door for us. It was a basic camp bunk-house. The floors were unfinished planks and the walls were plywood. Two rows of built-in bunk beds lined the walls. A long dark wooden table etched with graffiti was in the middle.

"There's a bedroom back here where a counselor would stay." Jack pointed. "You can use that."

We proceeded into the small room with a closet, night-stand and a double bed, all constructed of plywood.

"I got bedding for yah," Jack said, in his deep southern accent.

Morgan stared at the small bed.

I stared at it, too. "At least it's clean."

Jack started back to the front door. "I gotta go up to the house. Look round and make your decision. I'll be back in a shake."

Morgan and I walked over to the rocks that bordered the beach.

I looked at the ocean, waves breaking out on the reef, then back to the camp. I was trying to feel how welcoming it was. I thought of Jack. There was something about him that I couldn't quite pin point, but it wasn't threatening.

"What do you think?" Morgan asked.

"I guess it'll be okay," I said. "For awhile."

"Agreed."

There was rustling in the underbrush on our right. I caught sight of the top of a fern moving. A hefty dog jumped out, closest to Morgan and leaped up to plant his front paws on her chest. It happened so fast, we didn't have time to react. Morgan hit the sand with a thud and grunted as the wind was knocked out of her.

The black and brown Rottweiler gave her a long sniff be-fore licking her face. After the initial shock, Morgan smiled. "What a nice puppy." She pet him, dodging slobber the best she could.

I was surprised by her light hearted reaction to being bowled over. She showed me yet another side.

The dog looked up and focused his big brown eyes on me. He jumped off Morgan and pressed up against my leg. The force almost knocked me over. I reached down to pet the beast, while looking at Morgan. "Are you okay?"

"I'm fine." She got up and brushed sand off her tank top and arms. "Looks like we have a watch dog."

"He looks like an over friendly baby buffalo to me." I gave his side a couple of firm slaps.

"Friendly is right." Morgan bent over and focused on a stain at the bottom of her skirt. "I hope this comes out." She scratched at it for a moment and gave up. "Let's take our protector and see what the kitchen and restrooms look like. Maybe some water will help this."

We walked over to the middle building, the dog at our side.

Inside, the concrete floor felt cool. The wooden tables were lined up in three rows and the chairs were stacked together in one corner. The walls were bare, except for a black velvet painting of a Hawaiian sunset and a cork message board at the head of the room.

The dog sniffed around while we continued into the kitchen. It was industrial and clean. The counters and appliances were stainless steel. White wooden cupboards held equipment, utensils and dishes.

"All we need is the food," Morgan said.

At the opposite side to the kitchen entrance was a short hallway with three doors. They were marked in a hand written script – boys, girls and janitorial.

"I've never been in a boys' bathroom." Morgan shrugged and pushed the door open.

"I don't think it's much different than a girls'," I said, as I followed.

It was clean and basic, like everything else. Eight urinals, six stalls, a handful of sinks and an open shower with a bunch of nozzles spaced along the walls.

Morgan turned on a tap at one of the sinks and dabbed some water on her skirt. After some scrubbing, she declared the stain removed.

Once back outside we saw Jack walking toward us. "I see you've met Moose."

The dog leapt forward and trotted to him.

I chuckled. "Moose, that's a good name."

"He ain't much of a guard dog, like I originally wanted, but he'll let us know when somebody's comin.'"

Morgan asked, "Do you get many visitors?"

"Nope. I just bought the place a few months back. I have future plans for it. But for now, you'd have your privacy."

"Okay, we'd like to stay then," she said. "If you could take us to our car we'll be back in the morning."

⋇

We'd been eating a lot of fresh fish. The dining room at the hotel specialized in local organic food. We ate well.

After a really early dinner we were in our room by 6pm. The cell phone rang right on time.

"I've got great news," Sue shrilled. "I got an e-mail not long after I talked to you this morning. It was from The Northern European Council for Ethical Farming, in Norway. Have you heard of them?"

"No." I turned to Morgan and asked if she knew of them. She shook her head. "Not that I can remember."

I asked, back into the phone, "What're they all about?"

"They were one of the organizations I e-mailed the manuscript to. They said they were very grateful to get the information. They've been monitoring Naintosa, Pharmalin and in particular Dr. Schmidt. They want to talk to you and verify the information."

"How do we go about that?" I asked. "What if Ivan goes to talk to them? He's already on the same continent."

"I talked to Ivan," Sue said. "He hadn't heard of them either. I gave him the contact information, so he can follow up. I'm sure they'd be fine with meeting him first."

"Does the Council have a website?"

"Yeah, I skimmed through it. They're only two years old. The Council was formed by Scandinavian farmers and scientists. Their goal is to protect the authenticity of their agricultural practices. They want to keep genetic engineering out of the food chain."

"Sounds like the people we need to be talking to." I looked over at Morgan. She was staring at me, trying to decipher the conversation.

"This could be the break we need."

"Oh I almost forgot," I said, to Sue. "We've found a secluded bible camp to stay at."

"Bible camp? That's a good one."

"It's very rustic. You'll like it."

"I'm sure I will. Ok, I'll call you as soon as I hear back from Ivan."

CHAPTER 45

My hand slid up, slow, under her shirt, over the soft skin, until I reached her breast. So firm and warm. How sensual, except for the irritating ringing sound every other second.

There was a sudden pain in my arm.

"Nick, get your hand off me and answer the phone."

I snapped awake. "What?" I opened my eyes and tried to focus in the dark. I was in bed. My hand was glued to Morgan's chest. The cell phone on the nightstand was ringing. I jerked my hand away. "Sorry."

Morgan sounded sleepy, yet annoyed, "Get the phone and I don't want to know what you were dreaming about."

The pull-out couch hadn't turned out to be comfortable. You'd think in such a fancy place that every detail would be looked after. But our pull-out was just like all the others; hard springs with a sheet over them. Morgan had taken pity on me last night and let me share the king-sized bed. I bet she had second thoughts about that decision now.

I fumbled for the phone, dropped it on the floor and fell out of bed retrieving it. Thud. "Ouch. Hello."

"Sorry to call so early," Sue said. "What time is it there anyway?"

I looked up at the alarm clock. "It's 4:36." I leaned back against the side of the mattress. "Did you hear from Ivan?"

"I just got off the phone with him."

Morgan slid over and sat at the edge of the bed next to me. As I looked at her bare legs, I decided it was lucky the phone rang, because who knows where my wandering hand would've gone next.

"Nick, are you there?"

"Sorry, Sue, what'd he say?" I purposely rolled to the side to avoid looking at Morgan and concentrated on Sue.

"He spoke to the Council for Ethical Farming. They want to meet with Ivan and Bill. They're flying to Oslo tonight."

"Great, but what about us?"

"Ivan said to hang tight until he can get a handle on things."

"Okay, after you get here and Ivan figures things out over there, we'll go to Norway." I looked up at Morgan who was nodding.

"I'll call Max and check on his progress," Sue said. "Talk to you later."

Morgan and I crawled back into bed and discussed the call. She'd caught the gist of it from listening to my end.

I expected a lecture about feeling her up, but it didn't happen.

"Let's try get some more sleep," she said. "Pleasant dreams."

I wasn't sure what she meant by that. I wedged my hands between my knees in hopes they didn't go on an adventure again after I fell asleep. She did have phenomenal breasts.

CHAPTER 46

"Here's the turn off." Morgan veered from the subject for a second. "I thought you'd be more excited. I've been doing all the talking."

"I'm excited about the Council for Ethical Farming helping us. Hopefully," I said. "I just think we should be even more careful now." I'd had a nervous feeling all morning. My mind jumped from what the Council could do for us, to hoping Sue got here safely, to my feelings for Morgan.

Morgan got out of the car and went to the gate. It was unlocked, as Jack had told us it would be.

She looked sexy in her denim shorts and green tank top. Her hair was in a pony tail. I liked her as a brunette. I reminded myself yet again that this wasn't a good time for romantic thoughts.

Morgan locked the gate as Jack had instructed her to do, after I drove through.

Jack was out front of his house with Moose. As soon as Morgan opened her door the Rottweiler came bounding up, put his front paws on her lap and gave her a sloppy lick on the face. "Down puppy." She wiped the slobber off and pushed him aside to get out of the car.

"Howdy," Jack said. "Moose, you get back here and give these nice people some space."

Morgan smiled at him. "How are you?"

"My sciatica's buggin me, but otherwise I'm just dandy."

"Jack, a friend of ours will be joining us in a few days," I said. "I hope that's okay?"

"Sure, that's fine. Nice to have the company." Jack leaned

the shovel in his hand against the side of the stairs and took the dog by his collar. "Go on, drive up to your cabin and get settled in. I'll be along in a bit to make sure everything's co-pasetic. I've given it a dust and made the bed."

We drove the short distance to the next clearing.

Indeed the cabin was cleaned up and more welcoming. We dumped off our suitcases and then took the food we'd bought that morning to the kitchen.

When everything was put away, we walked down to the beach. Jack had put two white plastic reclining chairs in the shade for us.

"It's tranquil here," Morgan said.

A tourist boat cruised by the mouth of the bay and a snor-keler popped to the surface near the reef.

"You know, while we're out here I'm going to start my next book," I said. "It's a perfect place to write."

Morgan perked up. "That's a great idea. What're you going to write about?"

"I'm thinking of using our experiences to write a thriller set in Christina Lake and Hawaii. I could create a P.I. kind of character as the protagonist."

"Sounds interesting." She sat down on one of the recliners and gave me a shy look. "I can help you...if you want."

"I was hoping you would."

"I'll get some paper." She jumped up and walked with a spring in her step towards the cabin.

"We don't have to start this second," I called after her.

She either ignored me or didn't hear and kept going.

Watching her, I thought about how much I enjoyed being with her. Even with all the danger. What was going to happen to us when all of this was over?

⚓

"I think that's the same snorkeler out there." Morgan was looking at the reef, not more than one hundred and fifty yards out.

"For the last two days?" I sat up in my lounger and put the

book outline notes on my lap. I could see distances clearer without my sunglasses, so I propped them up onto the top of my head.

"The mask looks the same and the tip of his snorkel has that thick yellow ring," she said.

"Every time I notice him, his mask is just above the water and pointed in this direction," I said.

"Like he's watching us." Morgan gave me a concerned look.

Slurp, lick.

"Oh, Moose." Morgan wiped the drool from her face. The dog had his front paws on the arm rest of her chair. She gave him a vigorous rub on the side of his neck, but her eyes were on the person in the water.

Moose was oblivious to what we were looking at. His left front paw waved in the air in ecstasy from the attention.

"Nick? Morgan? Come in, do you read me?" Jack had given us a scratched up blue walkie-talkie, so we could reach each other if we needed anything. It now crackled to life.

I pulled it out of Morgan's beach bag. "I hear you, Jack. What's up?"

"Have you seen my dog anywhere?"

I pressed the speak button. "He's right here."

"Moose, come home boy." Jack pitched his voice higher.

Moose's ears perked up and in an instant raced off into the jungle.

"He's on his way."

"Thank you kindly, over and out."

Just as I was putting the walkie-talkie back into the bag, the cell rang. I grabbed it and answered.

"Things are looking up," Sue said.

"Progress with the passports?"

"Yep, I've got them in my pretty little hands, as we speak."

"So Max came through, huh?"

"He did, but what a slime ball. He kept leering at me like a dirty stalker."

"Surprising, since he's got such a foxy babe for a girlfriend."

There was a snort of laughter on the other end.

Morgan rolled her eyes at me. "That's not nice."

I smiled at Morgan and asked Sue, "How do the passports look?"

"Just like the real thing."

"So when are you coming?"

"Tomorrow, Alaska Airlines flight 1606. It arrives at 2:36pm, your time."

"We'll be there to pick you up."

"I'm already packed."

"Did you quit your job?"

"I quit yesterday. It was like Dan knew it was coming. He was all smug and everything. Said I could leave right away; didn't need two weeks' notice. He didn't bother to ask why I was quitting, but did ask if I was going to meet you."

"Well, whether Naintosa got to him or not, you're out of there and away from him now."

"Thank Christ!"

I couldn't help but laugh at her emphatic reaction. "Seriously though, be extra careful. The guys from Naintosa will know you're on the move."

Morgan chimed in, "Tell her to be extra, extra careful."

"Gotcha. Oh, just so you know, my new last name is Pearce."

"Sue Pearce. Got it."

I looked out into the bay. The snorkeler had disappeared.

CHAPTER 47

In the morning we went down to our chairs at the edge of the beach. The air was still and the sand cool on our feet. A dive boat skipped over the water in the distance.

Morgan wore a long, loose white shirt over her shorts. Her freshly washed brown hair was still damp and hung down to her shoulder blades. She looked ready for a relaxing day, but her posture was tense.

We'd decided we were being paranoid about the snorkeler, but I took a quick scan of the reef anyway. I couldn't see anyone out there.

"Let's both ask the same question before we go into our meditations and see if anything comes up," I said.

"Good idea," Morgan said. "Like, will there be any danger involved in Sue coming to Maui."

Focusing, I mirrored Morgan's breathing in and out. That would help us go deeper and be in synch. The only things my senses picked up were the sound of breaking waves and the salty smell of the air. I pictured myself in the white room with one wall open to the cosmos I had created long ago in my mind. The white leather recliner was the only piece of furniture. Sitting in it triggered deeper relaxation.

Within a moment everything disappeared. I experienced all that the space between dimensions had to offer me. It was blurry and dark. Shadows moved in and out of the trees and plants around the cabins. It felt ominous. As soon as I judged the feeling the vision was lost.

I opened my eyes and looked at my watch. Twenty-six minutes had gone by, but it only felt like five.

"Well, what did you see?" Morgan asked, sitting up.

I told her what I experienced.

"Mine wasn't positive either." She rubbed her arms as if she was cold. "I saw Jack's house. It was like I was looking at it through red acetate. Everything was bloody."

"Oh." I mulled it over. We couldn't disregard what we got from our meditations. I didn't have the same feeling about this place I did half an hour ago. "Let's not ignore the signs this time."

"I agree." Morgan looked worried. "It's not safe here anymore."

I looked at my watch. "We should get going to the airport."

⚘

"I think we should go straight to a travel agent after we pick Sue up," Morgan said, from the passenger seat. "We may even be able to fly out tomorrow."

We were stuck behind a slow moving bus with nowhere to pass.

"Where should we go?" I asked. "Fiji seems too out of the way now."

"Maybe Tokyo or someplace that's more on the path to Oslo?" Morgan replied.

"Or just go straight to Oslo." Then it dawned on me. "Do we need visas?"

"The travel agent will help us figure it out."

It was hot and the trade winds hadn't picked up yet. Even with the air conditioning it was warm in the car.

⚘

At the airport we positioned ourselves across from the baggage claim, so we could watch for Sue and anyone suspicious. One of the five carousels was rolling and a crowd had gathered around it. A breeze flowed through the open-air terminal as the trade winds finally kicked up.

We checked the flight arrival monitor. Sue's plane had just landed.

In a rush all the tension of the past months came screaming back in. Everyone looked suspect and I was on full alert.
Why were those two middle aged men wearing sunglasses inside? Those bright flowered shirts were over the top, trying
too hard to fit into the environment. The guy by the pillar was
awfully serious for someone in paradise. That Mumu looked
too big on that lady; was she concealing something?

We watched people for almost ten minutes before Sue entered at the far end of the room.

"Hang back to see if anyone's tailing her," I said.

Sue had spotted us and was coming over. She was in jeans
and a loose fitting blue blouse. Her brown hair was shorter
than when we last saw her. It was just above her shoulders
and had blond highlights. She carried a light jacket in one
hand and a backpack over her shoulder. She looked good,
even after sitting on a plane for five hours.

"Hey sweetie." I wrapped her in a warm embrace.

"Hey Nicky." She kissed me on the cheek. "I missed you."

"How was the flight?" Morgan asked.

"Uneventful, thankfully." Sue let go of me and hugged
Morgan like an old friend. "How're you holding up?"

"Good." Morgan embraced Sue back.

"I can't wait to see the island," Sue said. "Even with this
breeze, the air sure is hot. It feels good."

"It's unfortunate you're not going to get to stay longer," I
said.

"What do you mean?" Sue stepped back to look at both of us.

"Let's get your bags before we fill you in," Morgan said.
"We have a decision to make."

Luggage began to roll out onto the conveyer with her flight
number on it.

I continued to judge everyone.

"How many bags do you have?" Morgan asked.

"Sue packs like a guy," I said. "Clean pair of underwear,
shorts, t-shirt, toothbrush and she's on her way. Not like some
people I know."

Morgan caught my verbal jab. "You're a guy and you don't
pack like that."

"I brought a little more than that." Sue watched Morgan. "You two still seem to be getting along well."

Morgan smiled. "Yeah we're getting along fine."

Something happened in that instant that I didn't quite understand. It was in their eyes as they looked at each other; like an unspoken conversation between them. I'm sure if I was a woman I would've gotten it. We had no time for territorial nonsense, if that's what it was.

I wanted to change the moment. "Did you see anyone suspicious in Seattle or on the plane?"

Sue turned to face me. "Nope, all clear."

An increased unease rose through me. I felt as if we were being watched. "Can you see your bag? We should get moving."

"What's wrong?" Morgan turned round in slow motion and scanned the room. "Did you see someone?"

"No," I said. "Just doesn't feel right. We shouldn't loiter around."

Sue looked anxious herself. "When Nick's got it together I trust his perceptions."

"Me too," Morgan said.

"Here it comes." Sue pointed to a medium, hard-shelled suitcase. "The dark blue one, there."

I pulled it off the conveyer in one quick motion. It was packed full and heavy.

We proceeded out of the terminal to the parking lot. We didn't see anyone that would raise suspicion, but my feeling was still nagging at me.

On the drive to Lahaina, we filled Sue in on our plan to leave as soon as possible.

Sue spoke up from the back seat, "I talked to Ivan last night and he said to wait in Maui until he's comfortable with the Council for Ethical Farming."

"Has he met with them yet?" I asked, focusing on the road ahead.

"Yep, he and Bill are confident that they'll help us, but they need a few more days."

"Why?" Morgan turned to face her.

"He didn't really explain." Sue shrugged. "He's going to call your cell as soon as he knows more."

My mind went off the main topic for a second and I looked back at Sue through the rearview mirror. "Why hasn't Ivan just been calling us on the cell all along? Why has he been relaying messages through you?"

Morgan frowned. "That's right. I hadn't thought of that."

Sue shrugged again. "I don't know? That's just the way we've been doing it. I'm sure it's nothing to worry about."

There were a lot of cars on the road. We were forced to stay below the speed limit.

Sue was right. Why worry about something trivial like which person Ivan was calling. I went back to the more important subject. "I still have an uneasy feeling about staying."

"So do I," Morgan said. "But it's only for a couple more days."

"Let's still see a travel agent today," I said. "We need to find out if we need visas."

Morgan nodded. "We'll get things rolling for either Tokyo or Oslo."

"Then take off as soon as Ivan gives us direction," Sue chimed in.

We drove into Lahaina and stopped at the first travel office we saw. It was in a green one-story strip mall, with white pillars at the front.

After describing our needs, the petite middle aged lady in a silk grey sleeveless top, searched on her computer.

After a few minutes, she looked up from the screen. "You don't need visas for either country."

We had her print off flight schedules that would get us to our potential destinations for the next week. We told her we'd be back to book our flights, most likely the next day.

※

After stopping at a restaurant for a quick salad and picking up some groceries we headed for the camp.

"It's beautiful here," Sue said, as we drove down to the cabins. "Uh...very rustic."

When Sue had finished unpacking in the bunk area, we changed and headed down to the beach.

Palm fronds rustled in the light breeze. The sunscreen Sue had brought overpowered the natural scents. Jack had delivered a third lawn chair. A panting Moose lay in the shade of a large bush.

Sue walked over to him. "Is he friendly?"

Morgan rolled her eyes. "Overly."

Moose rolled onto his back and drooled the second Sue rubbed his belly. "This is one happy dog."

The late afternoon sun was hotter than we'd experienced before. The trade winds hadn't been blowing as long that day.

I spent a long moment scanning the water around the reef. No snorkeler.

"Do you ladies want to go for a swim?" I asked, as I took off my shirt.

Morgan removed her white cover-up. "Yeah, it's hot." Standing there in her pink bikini, her darkened skin made her lean body look flawless.

Sue stood up, rubbing the drool and fur from her hands. "Hey Nick, your beer gut's totally gone. And it's been ages since you've had a tan."

I looked down at my flat stomach and ran my hand across it. "Clean living, I guess." It'd been a long time, maybe since I was a teenager, that I felt comfortable without a shirt on.

Sue slid out of her t-shirt and shorts and placed them on a lounger. Her bikini was a black and blue pattern.

"You'd better put more sunscreen on after you get out of the water," Morgan told her. "You can burn quickly out here."

She looked down at her pasty white skin, up at Morgan, then over at me. She seemed uncomfortable, which wasn't like Sue. I'd never seen her self-conscious before.

"Still hitting the gym I see." I felt a few well-placed compliments were in order. "Is that a new bikini? You look great in it."

"Yeah, it looks really good on you." Morgan must've caught onto what I was doing. "I wish I had your muscle tone."

"Thanks." Sue still looked sheepish. She slipped a foot out

of her flip flop and quickly put it back on. "Shit, the sand is hot."

The cell phone in Morgan's bag began to ring.

"It's Ivan," Morgan said, after answering. She stepped over to the shade under a palm near where Moose lay.

"We'll wait over there." I motioned toward the water.

Sue and I tossed off our flip flops, trying to keep them close to the chairs. We raced the short distance down the beach, trying to get to the water before our soles got scorched. The small, cool waves gave us instant relief.

I pointed off shore, "You can go out about twenty feet before it drops off."

Sue went out a little ways until the surf was up to her waist. She splashed some water over her shoulders. "It's too bad we can't stay a while. I could use a few beach days."

I waded up beside her. "You need to work on your tan."

"Ha...ha."

Morgan's call with Ivan didn't take long. She bounded to us in exaggerated leaps through the burning sand. "Ah!" She exclaimed in relief when she reached the water.

"So?" Sue asked. "What'd he say?"

"They're making progress. The Council for Ethical Farming hasn't been infiltrated by proponents of genetic engineering or pharmaceutical companies." She said it as if quoting Ivan. "They seem like the real thing."

I said, "Finally, this is the break we needed."

Morgan waded to us, her legs splashing water forward with every step. "The Council said the manuscript is the strongest proof they've received. They're going to request that the World Health Organization investigate."

Sue frowned. "But Dr. Schmidt is on the board of directors of the W.H.O."

"The Council thinks the W.H.O. will have no choice but to investigate after they read the manuscript. Ivan said they're even willing to help on the legal side. So the Bolivia evidence can be added in."

That was great. We had a proactive ally. A group that was willing to take risks and do what they could to right injustices. All the work we'd done would not be in vain. I sighed aloud.

"What about us?" Sue asked.

"Ivan said we should get to Oslo as soon as we can. We'll get protection there and can help the Council."

"It's too late today." I looked out at the setting sun. The wispy clouds were their usual brilliant shades of yellow and orange. "Let's go straight to the airport in the morning. We can catch a flight to Honolulu. From there we can fly to somewhere in Asia and then on to Oslo."

"That'll be the fastest way," Morgan said.

Sue cupped water in her hands and spread it over her shoulders. "Christmas in the Far East or Norway; I think Norway would be more authentic."

Morgan looked at her, confused. "What do you mean?"

"Christmas is in three days. Did you forget?"

"Wow. Yes."

I shook my head. "I can't believe that we were so absorbed in this that we forgot Christmas is coming *again*."

Sue shrugged. "It's understandable."

"I like the idea of spending it in Norway best," I said. "We should be able to get there in time."

The undertow from a wave pulled us all a step farther out from shore.

Sue stopped playing with the water and stood rigid. "You know Dr. Schmidt's going to be even *more* pissed when the W.H.O. starts to investigate his companies."

Tension rose in Morgan's voice. "I bet there are other powerful people involved in this, in one way or another, with Schmidt. They aren't going to be happy to be exposed by an investigation. They're going to try even harder to hunt us down."

"Now we have to worry about people we don't even know of." I began to move toward shore. "Let's hope the protection the Council is able to provide will be enough."

CHAPTER 48

Morgan picked up a plate. "There is no way I'm going to get any sleep tonight."

Sue took the dirty dishes from my hand. "Are we psyching ourselves out?"

Morgan and Sue loaded the dishwasher while I wiped down the stainless steel countertop.

"We'll be fine," Sue said. "Otherwise we would've seen someone at the airport."

"One more night and we'll be out of here." The whole discussion from the time we left the beach was about how easy it would have been for the Naintosa thugs to track us from Seattle. One more night, I repeated to myself.

"We need something to calm our nerves," Sue said.

I caught what Sue's eyes were focused on; the three bottles of organic Cabernet Sauvignon next to the sink.

"I could use a glass of wine right now." Morgan was looking at me.

I rummaged around in the drawer next to the cutlery and found a corkscrew.

Morgan held up three plastic tumblers. "I can't find any wine glasses, so these will have to do."

"Sue, can you bring the other bottles?"

Morgan's eyebrows rose. "We're going to drink all three?"

"We're leaving tomorrow," I said. "We can't take them with us."

We walked back to our cabin and settled on the porch. We were just out of range of the single light on the exterior of the main building. The full moon and stars were bright, giving the surroundings a shadowy visibility. The now familiar smell of orchids and ocean salt filled the air.

"It's still really warm out here." Sue touched the exposed part of her shoulder that wasn't covered by her tank top and cringed. "I can't believe how fast I burned."

The wine was great. It wasn't long before we opened the second bottle.

"Hey, Sue…" I adjusted the white plastic lawn chair I was sitting on. One leg had slipped into a crack between floorboards. "Does the name Jack Carter ring a bell?"

"It's a pretty common name," she said. "The only one that stands out is Jack Carter the oil and cattle tycoon. Remember, he sold everything last fall, donated a bunch to that Seattle charity and disappeared."

"That's right." It finally registered to me why the name rang a bell. "I edited a short piece on him just before I left the *News*."

"Have you ever seen pictures of him, Sue?" Morgan asked.

"Yeah, he's tall, grey hair, good shape for his age. He's in his late sixties. Why?"

Morgan said, "The guy who owns this camp is named Jack Carter. He fits the description."

"I wonder if it's the same guy?" I said.

Sue reached for the open wine bottle. "Why would a gazillionaire own this place?"

I held out my empty glass. "True enough."

Morgan turned her chair a few degrees to face Sue, who was sitting on the built in wooden bench. "So…what happened with that boy toy we saw you with in Seattle?"

"Oh nothing." Sue waved it off. "He lasted maybe a day after you left. Like I told you from the beginning, he was only meant for some short term fun."

Why did I even still get a pang in my heart whenever Sue talked about another guy? Was it the protective side of me? Or did I even now, in spite of everything, feel something *more*?

"You got to travel light in our situation." Sue smirked. "Can't have any attachments."

Morgan glanced my way and I wondered what she was thinking.

Sue drained her glass. "Let's open the last bottle?"

Morgan covered the top of her glass with her palm. "We shouldn't drink anymore. I'm feeling it."

"Just one more," Sue said. "Otherwise I won't be able to sleep at all."

Morgan stood up. "Well, I'll leave the last bottle to the two of you. See you bright and early." She swallowed the last sip of her wine and went inside.

"Goodnight," I said, while working the corkscrew into the bottle. "One more glass and that's it."

Sue nodded. "Yup."

I popped the cork and filled us up.

"So, what's happening with you and Morgan?" she asked, in her usual direct way.

"What do you mean?" I wasn't sure how much to divulge.

"I see the way you two look at each other. You *are* sleeping in the same bed."

"That's just for appearances. Nothing's going on."

"Do you want something to go on?"

I looked at Sue, assessing how honest I should be.

"You do. I can tell." Sue smiled. "I would, if I were in your shoes. She's cool and smart. Not to mention hot."

"But like you said, we shouldn't have any attachments in our situation."

"Yeah and I'm right about that." She took a gulp of wine. "But, what if circumstances were different?"

"You told me before that she was out of my league."

"You've changed. You have more confidence now than you've ever had before."

"That's good to hear." It was true. After all we'd been through, this respite in Hawaii had given me an extra inner strength. "Thanks for the compliment, but right now my only concern is to get to Oslo."

"You and me both."

I drank the last of my wine. "I'm done."

She swirled what was left in her glass and then swallowed it. "Okay, let's pack it in."

Sue hugged me goodnight and went to the bunk she'd made up.

The air was cooler and not so stagnant in the bedroom. Morgan must've opened the windows at either end of the room. A mild breeze wafted through.

I took off my t-shirt and crawled into bed, trying not to disturb her. As soon as I settled in on my side, she rolled over and spooned against me. It felt comforting and made sleep come easy.

CHAPTER 49

There was a sudden bright light.

My face hit something or something hit it. The impact was so violent my skull felt like it'd cracked.

Not again.

Someone grabbed my hair and held me face down on the bed. I tasted metallic tang and couldn't swallow. This wasn't happening again? I opened my mouth to let the blood escape.

Morgan thrashed beside me. She must've been flipped onto her face as well. Her cries were muffled.

My arms were pulled behind my back. Zip ties squeezed around my wrists. Then my ankles were bound. In one quick motion I was spun over and pulled into a sitting position. My vision was a blur. Something went around my neck and tightened. It was now impossible for me to move.

There was movement in the room, but I couldn't focus. Yet it was obvious who was there.

Why hadn't we caught the last flight out yesterday?

Blood mixed with saliva dribbled down my chin onto my bare chest. I slurred something even I didn't understand.

"Matt, bring the other one in here."

My eyes began to focus. A man dressed all in black stood at the foot of the bed, against the wall.

With great effort I turned my head to the left. Morgan stared back at me looking petrified.

A second man in black was standing beside her. I recognized the half moon scar under his right eye. The Lieutenant.

My voice was shaky. "It'll be okay."

Morgan looked into my eyes and some of the fear dissipated. It was replaced with determination. She managed a nod.

I surprised myself. This had to be the end for us, but I wasn't hysterical.

A third man dressed in black dragged Sue into the room. She had a brown fabric gag in her mouth. The man hauled her up onto a gray metal chair. Her hands were also tied behind her back.

The Lieutenant stepped over to tie Sue's legs. Her breathing was labored, so he removed the gag.

Sue's eyes turned wide and wild. She gritted her teeth, squirmed, struggled and almost knocked the chair over.

"This one's got spunk," said the man who'd brought her into the room. He was the Lieutenant's side kick. The man standing in front of us had called him Matt. Matt had black hair that was receding and a darker complexion than the other two. His nose was wide, eyes set far apart and he looked to be of mixed race. He jumped to grab the back of Sue's chair before she could tip it over.

All three were big guys, over six feet tall and in good shape. They were dressed the same, and in their late thirties or early forties. Each had a gun in a shoulder holster.

The Lieutenant had been the superior in our other encounters, but this time it was the man against the wall who gave the orders. He looked confident and in control, with intimidating, piercing, light eyes.

The pain in my head began to ease. The blood that had come from a cut on the inside of my cheek was clotting. My head began to clear. Don't give up. I sat up straighter.

"Asshole!" Sue yelled. "Untie me so I can kick your fucking head in!"

"Make sure it's tight, Sig." The man against the wall had a distinct east coast accent.

So the Lieutenant's name was Sig. That's not a name I would've pictured for him.

Sig leaned forward to tighten the zip tie around Sue's ankles. She jerked forward in a violent movement and bit into his ear. She clamped down so hard that blood came pouring out of her mouth and down the right side of his neck.

"You bitch!" Sig yanked away fast, tripped over her legs and hit the floor. He clutched his ear as dark red blood seeped through his fingers and trickled down his arm.

Sue spat the chunk of ear toward its owner. It fell just short. She spat again, hitting him square on the chest with his own blood.

Sig got to his feet. "You fucking..." He wound up and hit her full force on the left cheek.

Sue's head snapped back against the man behind her. In slow motion, it fell forward. Droplets of blood started to flow out of her mouth. They pooled onto her lap, staining the long shirt she had worn to bed. She hung forward, limp, not moving.

Oh Sue, why did you provoke them? I wished with all my might that I could rush over to her.

"You killed her." Morgan sobbed. "You asshole!"

"You're next." Sig, the Lieutenant, clutched what was left of his ear, with his bloody hand.

"Let me help her." I squirmed and tried to break free. "At least check if she's breathing."

The man leaning against the wall looked at us with a detached coldness. "You should be more worried about your own fate right now." He stepped toward Sig. "Go fix that up. You're no good this way." He pointed to the deep crimson spots on the floor. "Get something to clean that."

Sig kicked Sue's bare leg as he left the room.

Matt reached down and felt Sue's neck for a pulse. At that moment I had a flashback to when the Lieutenant had stuck a needle in Alice's neck. A foreboding shiver ran through me.

Matt moved around the chair, over to the man in charge and whispered something.

Morgan held back sobs. "Is she alive?"

"Like I said, Morgan, worry about yourself." The man in charge stared at us. He had close cut brown hair speckled with gray and a prominent nose.

I tried to keep my voice even. "Who are you?"

"I've met you somewhere before." Morgan drew a sniffled breath and I knew she was trying to gain composure as well. "At Naintosa, when I was visiting my father at work. It was maybe ten years ago."

He showed no emotion. "Surprised you remember."

"Yes, I remember...Peter something." Morgan looked hard at him. "My father said you were an up and coming thug and not to trust you."

"That was a long time ago," Peter said. "Maybe if your father trusted me more, he'd still be alive and you wouldn't be in this *situation*."

"*You* killed my father!" The look on her face was all out hatred.

Peter didn't blink. "Not personally."

Morgan's eyes pierced as if they could burn a hole through him.

"How can you justify being so cruel?" I said. "He was a good man. How can you live with yourself, with what you do?"

Peter scoffed. "How can you be so naive? Did you actually think you could get away with what you're trying to do?"

I met his stare. "The truth has to be told."

"Well my job is to protect the interests of the people I represent and *you* are not serving their best interests."

"The stuff Naintosa grows kills people." I matched his intensity. "You've got a pretty screwed up set of values."

"In your mind maybe. To me, you're a mere bump that must be flattened, so the people I protect can have a clear path to their goals."

I was surprised at how talkative he was and kept pushing. "Who exactly are your people?"

"I'm the one who asks the questions here. Or haven't you noticed? Do you want to end up like your rag doll friend over there?"

Morgan gave a guttural growl. She was pulling and twisting to free herself.

Matt took three long strides to reach Morgan. When he went to pull her back, his arm brushed her face. She strained forward to bite into him, but just missed.

"Bitch." He grabbed her hair and jerked her back. Morgan's head banged off the headboard.

I tried to take the attention away from her and focused on Peter. "I'm trying to talk sense into you."

Morgan's anger raged through tears. "You can't talk sense into cold blooded killers!"

"Matt, tighten the noose around her neck," Peter said. "You don't want her getting free on you."

Matt adjusted the rope from behind, pulling her tight to the headboard, while staying clear of her mouth.

"Now I need answers from you," Peter said. "Are Ivan Popov and Bill Clancy still in London?"

I was surprised. "You mean you don't know exactly where they are? You aren't as good as I thought you were."

"Oh we'll find them," Peter said. "You'd just make it easier on them if you told me where they are."

"You mean easier for you." Morgan spat the words at him. "We're not going to fall for that shit."

Peter's voice was calm, but heavy. "Listen, I can beat it out of you, then kill you or you can tell me and I may let you live."

Morgan and I both looked over at Sue's limp body. Blood had clotted on her lips.

A deterrent came to me and I didn't hesitate to share it. "Our blood and the Lieuten...Sig's is all over this place. If anything happens to us, it won't be hard to figure out who did it." I turned my head as far as I could and spat on the floor for emphasis.

"DNA," Morgan said.

Peter looked at us, unblinking for a moment. A sneer twisted his mouth.

There was a sudden noise outside. Moose's growl was recognizable. There was some rustling, followed by a dull thud.

Peter and Matt pulled out their weapons.

Moose gave out a yelp and there was running through the underbrush. I couldn't tell if it was a dog or person, maybe both.

Then silence.

Peter stepped back against the wall beside the doorway. "Go see what's going on."

Matt, his gun pointed in front of him, slunk out of the room.

We heard the faint squeak of the screen door to the cabin being opened and a squeak when it closed.

Peter looked around the doorway and then back over at us.

A moment later the screen door opened again and Peter crouched.

"It's us." We heard from the other room.

Peter rose up and lowered his firearm. "What happened out there? Could you be any louder?"

Matt came in, followed by a roughly bandaged Sig.

"A dog snuck up on Tom," Matt said. "He shot at it, but missed and it ran off."

So they have another guy outside named Tom. He must have had a silencer on his gun.

Morgan's mouth dropped. "You guys are fucking monsters. You tried to kill a curious dog?"

Sig raised his hand to his ear and winced. The bandage was soaked through with blood. "Shut up, sweetheart."

"You're just loser bastards." I shouldn't have provoked them, but I couldn't help it.

Sig slid forward and swung wide with the gun in the hand that wasn't holding his ear. The impact was in the exact same place he'd hit me the previous times. I felt a tear on my skin as the gun butt cut my right cheek. Warm blood immediately began to flow down the side of my face. I was dizzy, but he didn't hit me with enough force to knock me unconscious. More blood filled my mouth. The impact had re-opened the wound they'd inflicted earlier. I was bleeding inside and out.

"Shut it," Sig said.

"Fuck you." Spitting blood, the words didn't have the impact I'd wanted.

"Okay, enough screwing around," Peter snapped. "Let's get some answers."

I kept blinking to try see only one of Peter. Thoughts of getting to Oslo and publishing the book to protect the world from these horrific people were gone. There was only one thing to focus my vision and mind on – survival.

Peter repeated the question. "Where are Ivan Popov and Bill Clancy?"

"We don't know," Morgan said, in a last attempt of defiance.

Peter motioned toward Morgan. "Sig."

Sig walked around the bed and placed the barrel of his gun against her head.

Morgan flinched, "Please don't." All her anger and boldness disappeared in that instant.

A sound came from the corner. Sue had taken an audible breath. She moved her head, but was still unconscious.

Sig adjusted the gun to Morgan's temple. "You know if I angle this just right, I can send a bullet right through you and hit your boyfriend. That's what's going to happen if you don't answer the fucking question."

Morgan sat motionless, eyes closed, waiting for the impact of the bullet.

In that second I made my decision. My best friend was still alive, but needed help. The woman I was falling in love with was about to be killed. I had to say something to throw them off. And it had to be believable.

Peter motioned to Sig, "It doesn't look like they're going to tell us. You might as well get it over with."

"Wait," I blurted out. "You were right. Ivan and Bill are in London."

"How do I know you're not lying?" Peter leaned forward, his eyes boring right into mine. "Where exactly in London?"

"At an old colleague's of Bill's. They didn't give us the exact address." I had to give it my all, to convince him. "But it's too late for you. They've found a publisher who specializes in ecological issues and they're going to take the book on."

"Good to know." Peter looked unfazed. "But you're lying."

I opened my mouth and a name came out, "Glacier and Green Publishing. If you kill us, all the evidence will point to you and ultimately Dr. Schmidt." I pleaded. "Do you want to be responsible for that?"

Peter stared at me, most likely weighing his options.

Morgan opened her eyes, as the gun to her head was taken away.

I held my breath.

After a moment, Peter's look intensified. "Well, that's a chance I'm going to have to take." He nodded to Sig.

The gun went back against Morgan's head.

She gritted her teeth anticipating impact.

CHAPTER 50

A cell phone rang.

Peter raised his hand to Sig as he reached into his pant pocket with the other. He produced the phone and flipped it open. "Yes, sir, one moment." With a glance at Sig and Matt, he walked out to the bunk room.

Sig lowered his gun. "A moment's reprieve."

I turned my head to face Morgan, the rope tight around my neck. She looked back at me. She was shaking. The expectation of death was in her eyes. I wanted nothing more than to save her.

We could hear Peter talking, but couldn't make out the conversation.

Sue moaned. I turned and saw her twitch.

Peter strode back into the bedroom straight to me. He held the phone against my right ear.

Out of habit, I said, "Hello."

"Hello Mr. Nick Barnes, this is Dr. Hendrick Schmidt." His German accent was thick, enunciation articulate. "We have never been formally introduced. However, I'm sure you are familiar with who I am."

A rush of hatred welled up in me. This was the fucker responsible for everything.

"I must commend you, Mr. Barnes, on your ignorance and writing ability."

"What do you mean?"

"You've been able to concisely write your propaganda in such a way as to dupe both the Council for Ethical Farming and the World Health Organization. Yet you do not fully understand the inevitable consequence of your actions."

Dr. Schmidt knew more than Peter. He knew exactly what was happening. "I understand the consequences." It *really* sunk in that the manuscript was so true and authentic in its content that it compelled him to talk to me directly.

"And yet you continue your malicious attempt to taint the work of my organizations?" He spoke with authority and control. "You must understand, Mr. Barnes, I do not take these allegations lightly. You must be punished for your actions."

I had to fight with reason. "I believe in doing what's right and if there are consequences attached to that, then so be it." I wasn't going to beg for forgiveness.

"In your mind you may think that you're right. But I have the power to decide what's ultimately right or wrong. Therefore I have chosen your destiny for you."

I couldn't let him think that he could get away with his warped sense of ethics. "What I wrote is the truth. Otherwise we wouldn't be having this conversation. I did it so the world would know what you're really doing. You're purposely killing people and wrecking the environment to make a profit. That's the true wrong being committed here. You *will* ultimately be punished for your crimes against humanity."

There was a pause on the other end.

At least I'd had my say.

When he finally spoke, it was with controlled anger. "Mr. Barnes, you are tampering with generations of work of such enormity you could not fathom. I will not allow it to be halted by a meager mouse such as you." He paused again, as if for effect. "Do I make myself clear?"

I didn't have to think about my response, it just came out of my mouth, "Realize that killing me and my friends will just make our words truer."

"You underestimate my power. The minor damage you created is being taken care of as we speak. Our conversation and your meddling have come to an end. Good bye, Mr. Barnes."

"Then may I add, fuck you, Schmidt."

CHAPTER 51

Peter listened to Dr. Schmidt for a minute and ended the call.

I looked at Morgan. She gave me a bleak stare.

Peter pulled his gun from its holster. "Let's get this over with. Sig, Matt…"

There was a sudden thud outside. It sounded like something heavy falling onto the porch.

Everyone froze and listened.

Our captors hesitated for only a second. All eyes were on Peter. He jerked his head toward the doorway.

Sig slipped out, low to the ground.

It all happened so fast, yet in slow motion.

There was a muffled "bang." A tearing and cracking crash followed. It was like a sack of potatoes being thrown through the screen door.

At that exact moment a red dot appeared on Matt's forehead. A split second later, he was flung backward by the impact of a bullet.

A second shot followed, sending wood splinters flying from the wall where Peter was supposed to be. But he was gone.

Out of the corner of my eye I had seen flashes of light come from the open window on my side of the room.

Two quick bursts of automatic gunfire came from the bunk room. The whole building shook. There was a loud shattering of glass.

I looked to Morgan and then at what she was focused on. Matt was crumpled in a heap on the floor near Sue. His eyes were wide open staring into nothing. His face was expressionless. On the wall where he'd stood was a mess of blood, brain and skull fragments. A fine red mist settled in the air.

I felt nothing for him. Not even compassion.

More noise came from the main room. Someone was prying the screen door off its hinges. Wood cracked and gave way, followed by another thud onto the floor.

"Let's get this cleaned up," said a familiar voice.

Heavy boots came toward the bedroom.

Morgan exhaled and her eyes opened wide.

Jack Carter stood in the doorway. "Sorry it took so long." He was all in black. He wore a tight black long sleeved shirt, black pants and boots. Even the night vision goggles on his forehead, the automatic rifle slung over his shoulder and gun in his right hand were black. It made him look younger and virile.

Jack walked straight over to me. "You all alright?" He placed the handgun on the old nightstand and untied me.

I brought my freed hands to my neck, rubbing at the sting of the rope burns.

Jack went to Morgan and removed her restraints.

"Thanks," she said, in a melancholy tone. She looked dazed, in shock.

The sound of Sue taking a deep breath focused our attention.

In a few quick strides, Jack was over to free her.

Morgan and I tentatively slid off the bed on either side.

My whole body ached from tension. I touched my sore mouth to see if the bleeding had stopped. It had.

Sue lifted her head. "What's going on?" she asked in a weak, hoarse voice.

"You're conscious," I said. "What a relief."

Morgan had to step over Matt's remains to get to her. She knelt, quickly flicking a bloody fragment of Matt from Sue's hair. Her hand recoiled and she shuddered. "Are you in a lot of pain?"

Sue cupped her right hand under her chin. Her face had swollen, slurring her speech. "My mouth...neck...jaw are killing me. But I don't think anything's broken." She looked at the bloody heap on the floor. "What happened? Last thing I remember is the other asshole's freaked out face. Are they all dead?"

Jack stood, surveying the room. "One got away."

I looked at Jack, knowing it was Peter who'd escaped. Shit. Not good.

Morgan was looking at Jack too. She stared up as if trying to see something hidden on him. "Who are you?"

He gave a sympathetic smile. "Let's just say I'm someone with a great interest in you and your work."

"How long have you known what we were really doing?" I asked.

"Ever since you started writing the manuscript."

"How?" Morgan asked. "Why?"

"Let's get you over to the house and clean you up." Jack bent, wrapped Sue's arm around his neck and pulled her to her feet. "We can talk there."

Morgan stood up straight. "Let me grab a pair of shorts." She was just wearing a long t-shirt.

"Right." I looked down at my clothes from last night that I'd left on the floor. Parts of Matt were spattered on them. "Let me grab clean shorts and a shirt."

Jack and Sue waited while Morgan and I quickly dressed.

"Let me help." I grabbed Sue's free arm with one hand and placed the other around her waist.

She balanced her weight against Jack and me as we began to move.

In the bunk room bullet casings, glass shards and plywood splinters lay on the floor. Bullet holes marred the front and side walls. The one window only had jagged pieces of glass in its frame. The screen door lay twisted beyond repair.

There were two men in black from head to toe with automatic rifles slung over their backs. They were dragging Sig, the Lieutenant, off the porch. The scraping sound was eerie. A smear of blood followed the body.

There was relief in seeing his dead body. He wouldn't be coming after us anymore.

Morgan replaced Jack on the opposite side of Sue to help support her. "You probably have a concussion." She had four inches of height over Sue, so I could see the concern on her face.

Morgan glanced over at me. This time I was able to read her mind. "We all made it."

CHAPTER 52

Dawn approached. The air was still. All you could hear was the faint sound of breaking waves in the distance and our own footsteps.

Moose trotted out from the shadows and stopped in front of Sue. He looked up, opened his mouth and panted.

"Hi Moose." Sue tried to smile.

"He might just amount to something," Jack motioned to the dog. "He did a great job drawing the Naintosa guys attention, so we could get into position."

Moose moved to Jack's side.

As we crept up the dirt road, Jack kept his rifle ready.

His two men joined us at the rear. They were younger than him, but older than us. They looked comfortable carrying weapons and being on patrol.

With every slow step the events of the night sunk in deeper. I didn't feel guilty or bad. I was grateful for the deaths of the two men who had followed and tortured us for months. However, Peter, their leader, was still out there. We would be dead by now if Jack and his men hadn't saved us.

My whole body ached and my jaw was cramping up. I slipped on a loose rock veering all three of us to the right. "Oops, sorry." I tightened my grip under Sue's arm.

Morgan pulled on Sue's left arm to straighten us out.

That lingering question arose yet again in my mind: was this really worth it? The answer was clear as it could possibly be – you better believe it. The book would expose to the world what Naintosa and Pharmalin were really doing. I wanted to bring Schmidt down.

Morgan and Sue were quiet. Sue limped along.

We had to navigate steep stairs to get up to the porch. Jack swiveled the rifle around to his back and carried Sue. He was really strong for an older guy. Morgan and I hung onto the railing and took one step at a time.

One of the men with us stayed out front. The other went to check the perimeter.

The interior of the house was nothing like its rustic exterior. The entrance was into the living room. The hardwood floors were a dark mahogany. I recognized the furniture right away. It was from a store in Wailea that Morgan and I had browsed. It was all locally made and very expensive.

Jack led us to the open kitchen. "Grab a seat at the table, while I go get some medical supplies." He assisted Sue to a chair, then disappeared into a hallway.

It was obvious that the inside of the old house had been gutted and totally re-done. The kitchen had all stainless steel appliances. Rust colored veins ran through the cream granite counter tops. The off white tiled floor also had rust accents. In the corner we sat at a dark polished wood table on high backed brown chairs.

Morgan did a visual inspection of the room. "Very nice."

Moose had changed. He wasn't all over us. He just sat quietly near Sue and watched us.

Jack was back in moments with a white case bearing a thick red cross on the side. He set it on the table. "It's a field kit."

Morgan stood and examined the contents of medical supplies.

"Let's have a look at you." Jack pulled out various packages and cotton swabs, to attend to Sue.

Morgan looked at me. "The usual damage, huh?" She poured disinfectant from the brown bottle John had placed on the table onto a square pad. She pulled a chair closer and began wiping the dry blood from my face.

I cringed. "Ouch, that stings. I wish they'd hit me some place new."

"It's all part of the game," Jack said. "They intentionally kept hitting you in the same spot."

Sue winced as Jack curled back her puffed up lip to apply a salve on it with a cotton swab.

Morgan looked over at Jack. "So, are you going to tell us what's going on?"

"Maybe it's best I don't say too much...for your own safety."

"Oh please...safety?" Sue's words slurred, because Jack still had hold of her lip.

"Okay." He moved his attention to the cut and dark bruise on Sue's cheek. "My family has a lineage that allies closely with the Schmidt's and other such families. Let's just say we're part of the same club."

"We've suspected that there's such a *club*," I said.

"It's not a group you want to advertise. It's best that people don't know of its existence."

Morgan was frowning. "If you're a member of the same *club* as Dr. Schmidt, why are you helping us?"

Jack held his hand to Sue's cheek. "Well...I don't always agree with them. In your case I've been monitoring both sides."

Sue asked, "Why didn't you just speak up right from the beginning?"

Jack gave an inward smile. "It's not like we have weekly meetings, where we all get together over a beer and brainstorm. It's complicated. Most plans were started a long time ago."

Now it was my time to frown. "What if your cover's blown?"

"I'll deal with that when the time comes."

"They're not just going to kick you out of the club." Morgan sat forward. "They'll kill you."

Jack shrugged and gave her a cocky grin. "I'm fairly resourceful."

I sure was happy he was on our side. "Are you the same Jack Carter that until recently was in the oil and cattle business?"

"One and the same."

"Cool." Sue's eyes brightened.

"So how long exactly have you been following us?" Morgan asked.

"I learned about what you were doing just after Schmidt did. By the way, I'm sorry about your father's death, Morgan. He was a good man. I met him once. He did a great deal for the advancement of plant technology, just for the wrong company. With the right support, he would've achieved his goals of making food better and healthier."

Morgan sighed. "Yes, I know."

"I knew the Naintosa security force would show you no mercy. So, I wanted to help. I had a man tail Ivan Popov in Nelson, until he went to visit you in Christina Lake. My men have been shadowing you since then."

It was comforting to hear that Jack had been our guardian angel. His men proved better than the Naintosa thugs at tracking. Too bad they couldn't have prevented me from getting beat up so much.

Morgan's eyes brightened. "So, did one of your guys untie me in the warehouse, in Vancouver?"

Jack smiled. "Just loosened your binds, from what I heard. You did the rest."

Morgan nodded. "Thought so."

"I didn't want Naintosa finding out that you were getting help until it was absolutely necessary."

Sue looked thoughtful. "You mean today."

"Precisely. It was much easier to watch from a distance, stepping in only when needed. You all were doing a great job on your own. But, this morning we had no choice but to do what we did. They outsmarted us a bit."

"How so?" I asked.

"We didn't expect them until maybe tomorrow. They got through our defenses. The saving grace was that I managed to stay under their radar. Schmidt and Bail never knew I was helping you or that this place was mine."

No small feat. He really had to know his stuff to outwit them. One question still remained unanswered. "What about the camp in Bolivia and the atrocities being committed there? Are you the one who got us the information?"

"Yeah, my little team managed to infiltrate for a couple hours." Jack's face went grim. "One guy got caught. He didn't make it out. I really want to get back in there, but it's too difficult. I'm betting your book will blow it open."

Sue pulled back to look at Jack. "Did your man die?"

"Unfortunately."

Morgan clenched her fist, squeezing disinfectant out of the cotton ball she was holding. "These people don't care at all about human life?"

No one spoke for a minute.

It was insane. I wondered exactly how many people had died in all, trying to stop Naintosa from spreading their mutant food around the planet? Not to mention all the innocent people they and Pharmalin used as their guinea pigs.

Another question came to me. "How did you get the information into the locker in Vancouver?"

"Oh, simple." Jack gave a triumphant grin. "I did that one myself. Just followed Ivan at the airport, took the key from the back of the toilet after he left, placed the envelope in the locker, and put the key back."

I shook my head in admiration. "Yeah, you're right... simple."

"I've contacted Interpol," Jack said. "Let's finish getting cleaned up. It won't be long before someone arrives."

"Good," I said. "Finally the authorities are going to get involved."

Jack nodded. "After what happened here and if the W.H.O. investigates, they'll have to go after Schmidt. Even before your book comes out."

Morgan's eyes widened. "You mean there's even a possibility they won't?"

"Friends in high places, I'm afraid." Jack frowned. "The world works differently for guys like Schmidt."

"Seriously?" Even after everything, he might get away with it.

"Not to worry. Your book sounds plenty powerful. And I have some of my own friends in high places."

"Let's hope," Sue said.

Jack gave Sue's shoulder a gentle pat. "We'll make sure the police have a chat with your boss at the newspaper."

Sue tried to smile. "Oh, I hope they get that little bastard."

"Wouldn't that be nice." Even though he was a bit player, it'd be satisfying if he got some of what he gave out.

Jack pulled a small bandage from its wrapping and spread it across Sue's nose. "This holds your skin together like stitches."

Moose gave a low, guttural growl and rose up.

Out of the corner of my eye, I saw a glint of movement. A door was ajar that moments ago was closed. A gun barrel slid out of the opening.

Without hesitation I covered the twenty feet in a lunge and dove, grabbing the knob and reefed the door shut. The gun dislodged. It fired when it hit the floor. The table jolted sideways as splinters exploded from one of the thick legs. The impact sounded like a wooden bat hitting a baseball.

Recoil kicked the gun backward, bouncing it off the baseboard. I snatched it up, flung the door open and fired in the direction of movement. The table lamp on the nightstand exploded. Porcelain sprayed against the wall. Peter Bail's legs disappeared through the open window.

Jack raced past me. Sidearm drawn, he went to Peter's point of entry and exit.

Bursts of automatic fire sounded. One of the men outside sent a spray of bullets into the jungle.

Jack's eyes scanned for movement. "He's gone."

"But he may come back." My heart pounded, yet I felt numb.

"Not today. You have his gun."

I looked down at it. "I never fired one before."

Jack nodded as he reached out and took the gun from me. "Sorry for killing your lamp."

CHAPTER 53

We walked out just as the sun began to rise over the side of the mountain behind us. Birds chirped and sang all around.

Instant heat enveloped our skin when we arrived at the clearing.

Jack stayed at the house to wait for Interpol.

One of his men escorted us, just in case. He hung back about fifty yards, wary and watchful.

Morgan and I helped Sue to a lava rock outcropping at the edge of the beach. We sat down on a smooth, weathered part.

Morgan shielded her eyes from the reflection of the sun on the water. "I can't believe what you did back there, Nick. I've never seen anyone move so fast; especially after what you've been through." She placed her free hand on my lap. "Thank you."

"Yeah," Sue said. "You just went for him. I'm liking the new no fear Nick. You really saved us."

"I surprised myself." I looked back toward the cabins. "It was Jack who really saved us."

Morgan patted my lap. "It was the combination of both of you."

I said, "It was the result of all of us not giving up."

We each looked out at the water.

Sue placed her hand on my other thigh. "That's great that Jack offered to have his jet take us to Oslo."

"Yeah, that's going to make things easier," Morgan said.

My hands trembled. I put them behind me to lean on so the ladies wouldn't notice. I glanced at Sue, who winced with every breath and tiny movement. I turned my attention to Morgan and saw a few wrinkles on her forehead that hadn't been there until now. All of us were trying to be strong after the traumatic experience we'd lived through.

The only thing out in the ocean was a fishing boat in the distance. I thought about the snorkeler.

"I bet the snorkeler was the Lieutenant or Matt," Morgan said.

I couldn't help but smile at her sporadic ability to read my mind. "We'll never know, but my guess is that it was one of them."

Sue slowly got to her feet, trying to hide a grimace. She used my shoulder to push herself up. "My ass hurts. I'm going to start getting my stuff together."

I looked up. "You need help?"

"I'll be fine. You relax...hero."

"We'll be right there," Morgan said.

With noticeable effort Sue limped back through the stand of palms that separated the beach from the cabins.

I slid closer to Morgan and put my arm around her waist. She leaned against me. It felt comforting.

"Do you think we stand a chance?" she asked. "Dr. Schmidt and Peter are just going to re-group and come after us again."

"I remember Schmidt saying on the phone: 'you're tampering with generations of work of such enormity you couldn't fathom. I will not allow it to be halted by a meager mouse such as you.'"

"Wrecking his work only begins to avenge what he did to my parents."

"So we keep going with this. As far as we can," I said. "The finish line is in sight."

Morgan rested her head on my shoulder. Her warm hair brushed against my neck. She tilted her head to look at my face.

It mesmerized me every time I looked into those magnificent blue eyes.

I leaned in and our lips met.

It wasn't quite over, but we'd face the remaining challenges, danger, and truth together.

EPILOGUE

He stood, staring out at Lake Como from his study window, unconsciously tapping a cordless phone against his thigh. A blue with white trim Chris Craft Corsair idled past the front of his dock. But he wasn't admiring boats out on the water. He had other, more important things on his mind.

He'd faced adversaries all his life and crushed them all. Not even opponents as large as governments, countries he'd helped build, and competing multinationals could extinguish him.

How had those little *fickt* gotten so far?

He glanced down at the small end table. Next to a gold framed picture of him kneeling with his rifle beside a Siberian tiger he'd killed was a white bone china plate. On it was one of his simple pleasures – luscious unaltered bright red tomato slices sprinkled with coarse salt. They were grown from the seeds in his private seed bank. He sighed and left them there.

He had to restructure the security force at Naintosa and needed to sacrifice the Director of his personal team to oversee it. He was done trusting Peter Bail with that responsibility.

But right now he needed the help of one of his peers. One he didn't like to ask favors of, but who was the current chairman.

He brought the phone to eye level and adjusted his reading glasses. With a resigned breath that sighed on exhale he dialed the number.

"You've put yourself in a bind, Hendrick," said the polished voice on the other end of the line. It was distinctly American, but with a hint of British in its stiffness.

"You know I don't make social calls, Davis." Dr. Schmidt's

anxiety made his German accent more acute. "I need you to talk to Jacques."

"He may not be able to stop this, even in his position. It may be too far along. You know how Interpol works. We cannot jeopardize future favors."

Dr. Schmidt sat down in his overstuffed burgundy leather desk chair and swiveled it back toward the picture window. "Of course I know how it works. I was one of the people who created the system... or my grandfather and father were; as with your family. Jacques has to do what he can."

Davis Lovemark's voice was unemotional, "I will speak with him. But you should've taken care of your problem months ago, before it escalated."

Dr. Schmidt was doing all he could to keep his short temper in check. Davis was not a man he could raise his voice to. In fact, Davis was one of the few men in the world who intimidated him. The strain could be heard when he spoke, "If Jacques could at least slow the process, I will take care of the rest."

"Yes," Davis said. "What do you propose to do with Jack Carter? He really blindsided you."

That was a jab. "I haven't decided how devastating and painful the retribution will be yet."

"Think it through Hendrick. He's one of us. The Carters are a founding family." Davis paused for effect. "And what's happening with the W.H.O? You're suspended until the internal investigation is complete. Do you have a strategy?"

"Yes." Dr. Schmidt wanted to change the subject. "When will the group be meeting next? It's been several years."

"Very soon." Anxiety now surfaced in Davis' voice. "It's time for me to pass on my Chairman duties. As you know I have my own challenges that need my full attention."

Dr. Schmidt tried to sound sincere. "Yes, don't hesitate to ask if you need some assistance."

"Thank you, but you have enough to worry about. Times have changed...huh, Hendrick?"

"Yes they have."

"We'll speak soon," Davis said.

Dr. Schmidt swung the chair back around to his desk and placed the phone onto it. He looked over at the original Da Vinci *Holy Infants Embracing* hanging over the fireplace mantle. He saw the irony of his situation compared to the painting and scoffed at the foolish innocence of the chubby children.

Steering the direction of mankind and profiting in turn was increasingly becoming more difficult.

ACKNOWLEDGMENTS

I would like to thank the following people for their help:

Don McQuinn for his teaching of the craft. Without his detailed help I wouldn't have made it this far.

Authors Eve Gruschow, James Ullrich and Scotty Schrier for their input and sharing of work to help us each grow as writers. Mark Hood for his special comma and editing talents.

Marianne Verigin, Keelin McLeman, Steve Szentveri, Marky Thorsness and Jade Davidson for their opinions on how to fine tune the novel.

Fred Pinnock for his advice on how police would act.

Mary Rosenblum for the final editing.

Adrian Cunningham for designing the cover.

Elysse Gilbertson for the photography and Northlands Golf Course for providing the venue.

Ben Coles and Promontory Press for putting everything together.

Wife, Diana for her ongoing love and research skills.

Father, Paul who taught me to never give up and that actions speak louder than words.

Mother, Kathy for her love of reading and ongoing support.

The Maui Writers Conference and my instructors Nancy Holder and Dorothy Allison. They helped create my writing foundation.

The Centrum Arts Port Townsend Writers Conference and my instructors Bret Lott, Valerie Miner and Chris Abani. They helped further my writing education.

The Pacific Northwest Writers Conference and Surrey International Writers Conference. Great places to network and obtain current information on writing and publishing.

Thank you all.

ABOUT THE AUTHOR

Lawrence and his wife, Diana, live in Vancouver, Canada.

Lawrence's goal is to entertain readers while delving into socially relevant subjects.

Contact
Email: lawrenceverigin@gmail.com
Website: www.lawrenceverigin.com
facebook: Lawrence Verigin
twitter: @lawrenceverigin